PORTER'S MATE

THE SHIFTERS SERIES BOOK FOUR

ELIZABETH KELLY

EK PUBLISHING INC.

PORTER'S MATE

She'll make him an offer he doesn't want to refuse.

Wolf shifter, Porter Burke, isn't interested in finding his mate until the night the fragile and frightened human walks into his bar and asks for his help. She's a complication he doesn't need but resisting her plea for help, and the unexpected payment she offers for his protection proves much harder than he thought.

Maggie Wallace is in trouble. A hyena shifter wants her, and when his obsession with her turns dangerous, she's forced to make a drastic decision. Alone and desperate, she makes the wolf shifter she's just met an offer she hopes he can't refuse.

With the help of his brother's security company, Porter promises to keep Maggie safe. Pretending to be her mate is surprisingly easy. But with each passing day, their mutual attraction grows stronger, and soon Maggie's sweet kisses have his wolf howling to claim her as his mate for real.

CHAPTER 1

Porter took another drink of beer and stared moodily at the smooth top of the wooden bar as Arlo stopped in front of him.

"Hey, Porter. What's up?"

"Not much."

Arlo swiped the cloth in his hand across the already-gleaming surface of the bar. "You working later?"

Porter shook his head. "No, it's my night off."

"And yet, here you are. You know there are other bars out there where a guy can get laid."

"Shut up, Arlo."

Arlo laughed. "I'm just saying."

"Ask Mike to make me a house burger and fries, would you?"

"Sure."

There was a sharp whistle, and Arlo frowned irritably at the shifter waving at him. "Yeah, yeah, I'm coming. Keep your fur on."

He wandered away as Porter took another drink of beer. Tonight was Mal's and Willow's engagement party, and after it was over, feeling bored and a little lonely, he had stopped in at the bar on his way home. He was thrilled that Mal had found his mate, but he was also jealous for the first time in his life.

He groaned inwardly. What was happening to him? Since when did he want to settle down with one woman? Sure, he was thirty, and his mother had been bugging him for years to find a good woman and give her grandpups, but that had stopped the moment Mal brought Willow home to meet them. He didn't think she had given up on her quest for him to find a mate, but the upcoming wedding had taken away some of the pressure.

He laughed a little bitterly. It was ironic that his mother had stopped voicing her desire for him to be mated, and now it was something never far from the back of his mind. He shook his head. He was being ridiculous. His brother's happiness with his mate was just making him a little jealous. Nothing more. He might enjoy taking as many different women to his bed as possible, but it didn't mean he didn't occasionally wish for something more. Who didn't come home from work and occasionally wish there was a warm and willing woman waiting in his bed? Someone to ask him how his day was, someone to listen when he'd had a bad day, someone to curl up against when the nights were cold and –

He snorted loudly. He was acting like a love-struck school girl. These ridiculous feelings of – he could think of no other word than nesting – would fade, and he would find himself perfectly content with bedding a different woman every night. His mother might act like he was on the verge of dying old and alone, but he was only thirty, for God's sake. He had plenty of time to find a mate.

There was a startled yell from behind him, and he turned to see a boar shifter glaring impudently at the bouncer. A tall and imposing bear shifter, Judd returned his look with an amused grin.

"I am not too drunk to enter your establishment!" The boar shifter raised himself to his full height, looking ridiculously puny next to Judd, and puffed out his chest. He snorted loudly, his round cheeks bright red, and Porter rolled his eyes when he poked Judd in the chest.

"Do you know who I am?" He poked Judd in the chest again.

"You're about to become a side of bacon," Porter muttered. His eyes widened when the man suddenly launched himself at Judd. Taken by surprise, Judd staggered backward into a table and roared in anger.

As the two of them began to scuffle - the boar was shockingly strong and giving Judd a run for his money – a flash of pink caught Porter's eye. He watched as a woman wearing a stained and dirty pink dress slipped into the bar past the angry Judd and the indignant boar.

Porter frowned. It was cold out, but the woman wasn't wearing a jacket, and her dress was thin and short sleeved. He studied her pale legs. They were bare and streaked with dirt, and the heels on her shoes had been broken off.

She hovered in the corner for a moment. She was too far away for him to see her face clearly, but she was obviously nervous. She was short like Willow and, although not as slender as Mal's mate, it still looked like a strong wind would blow her over. Her light brown hair was shoulder length, and it hadn't seen a brush in a few days.

He watched as she took a deep breath, straightened her spine, and looked around the bar. Her gaze landed on him, and she twitched all over as he stared silently at her before nodding slightly and turning back around. He studied the bottle of beer in front of him and wasn't at all surprised when he felt a light tap on his shoulder.

"Excuse me?"

The woman's voice was low and raspy, and a weird little shiver went down his spine at the sound of it. He turned his head and gave her a once over. She was even dirtier up close. He could smell her fear pulsing through her like a living, breathing thing and underneath that the sour odour of her sweat. Her pale face had streaks of dirt, and he frowned at the scratches that ran across her forehead and down her right cheek. Her eyes were a lovely shade of blue, and they were staring at him with a hint of desperation mixed with fear.

"This is a paranormal only bar, and you," he inhaled deeply, "are definitely not a paranormal."

She flushed and pulled nervously at a rip in her dress. "I'm sure there are other humans here."

He shook his head. "Nope. You're the only one."

She looked around the bar, noticing for the first time that all of the patrons close to them were staring at her with suspicion and hostility. Her eyes widened, and she stepped a little closer to Porter.

"The only human?" she whispered.

"Yes. You should leave," he advised before taking another drink of beer.

Arlo approached them and smiled easily at the woman. "Can I get you a drink?"

"She's human, Arlo."

"So? Humans aren't forbidden." Arlo shrugged. "What will you have, pretty lady?"

"Oh, um," she touched her rat nest of hair self-consciously before clearing her throat, "could I trouble you for a glass of water?"

"Sure."

She cleared her throat again and gave Porter a weak smile. "So, um, what's your name?"

"Porter."

"I'm Maggie. It's nice to meet you." She held her hand out, realized it was covered in dirt and dried blood, and snatched it back. She wiped it hurriedly on her equally dirty dress before giving him an apologetic look.

"Forgive me, Maggie, but you don't look like you're having a very good day." He studied her face and body again, and she flushed to the roots of her hair.

"It's been a rough few days," she mumbled.

"So, you decided to make it better by waltzing into a paranormals-only bar?"

"Humans aren't forbidden," she echoed Arlo's words desperately.

"True. But shifters in this place aren't always appreciative of humans who wander in off the street without an invitation."

"Are they dangerous?"

"Yes."

"Good."

He frowned at her. "Excuse me?"

Arlo set down the glass of water in front of her, and she smiled in thanks before snatching the glass and drinking all of it in four large gulps. She wiped her hand across her mouth as Arlo raised his eyebrow at her. "Do you want another water or something stronger?"

"Another water would be great."

She studied the paranormals in the bar as Arlo left. "Which one is the most dangerous?"

"What?" Porter said. What was going on with this human?

"Which one of these shifters would you say is the most

5

dangerous?"

"Why?"

"Because I want to speak to them." There was a touch of impatience in her voice, but she cringed back when he touched her arm.

"You really should leave, Maggie."

"I – I can't." The desperation was back in her voice. "Please, can you just tell me which one of these shifters is the most dangerous?"

"Tell me why you want to know first," he said.

Frustration crossed her face, and she leaned against the bar. "I'm in trouble, and I need some protection. I want to hire a paranormal."

"Why not just go to the police?"

"They can't help me," she said with a new thread of fear in her voice.

"What kind of trouble?"

She picked at the rip in her dress again. "I don't want to talk about it when there are so many people around."

Oddly fascinated by the woman, Porter slid from the barstool and took her arm. "Come with me."

"Wh-where are we going?" she squeaked out.

"Just to one of the booths. It's more private, and you can tell me what's going on."

She followed him willingly enough to the booth and slid in across from him before giving him a careful look. "Are you dangerous, Porter?"

"As dangerous as they come, darlin'." He winked at her.

"What kind of shifter are you?" she asked.

"I'm a wolf shifter."

Her eyes widened, and she blew out her breath in a shuddering rush. "Wolf. Good, that's good. You're big and strong, right?"

He nodded. "I am."

"Okay, good."

One of the servers, Tori, stopped in front of them and set down the plate of burger and fries in front of Porter and the glass of water in front of Maggie. "You want something to eat, hon?"

"Oh, um, no, thank you. The water is enough." Maggie smiled faintly at her.

Tori nodded and grinned at Porter, running her fingers affectionately through his dark hair before sauntering away. Porter watched the sway of her hips for a moment. Two years ago, he had slept with the pretty brunette shifter, and she had made it clear she was willing to have another go at him. He hadn't taken her up on the offer.

She'd been a firecracker in bed, full of unlimited energy, but rabbit shifters were notorious for accidentally getting pregnant. They loved nothing more than having babies, and with three kits already, Tori was no exception.

He turned back to the human. She stared at his plate of food with a look of feral hunger, and he clearly heard her stomach when it growled.

"Would you like some?" He pushed the plate toward her, and she shook her head.

"Oh no, I don't want to eat your food. I'm fine."

"Take some, I insist." He was reasonably certain she was going to start drooling any moment.

"I'll just have one fry. Thank you." She reached out, her hand trembling badly, and plucked a French fry from his plate. She popped it into her mouth and chewed slowly, her eyes closed in utter bliss. He used his knife to cut the burger in half before pushing the plate a little closer.

"Take half the burger and the fries," he said.

7

Her eyes popped open, and she stared at the burger, swallowing thickly as she shook her head. "Oh no, I can't."

"Yes, you can. It's a lot of food. I'll never be able to eat it all."

There was a stack of four appetizer plates on the table, and he grabbed one and transferred half the burger and half the fries to the small plate. "Eat."

"Well, if you're sure?" she said tentatively. He could see the shame in her eyes, and his stomach twisted a little.

"I'm more than sure. Eat, Maggie."

"Thank you," she said.

He blinked in surprise, a small smile crossing his face when she nearly inhaled the burger. She ate quickly and enthusiastically, shoving the fries into her mouth and chewing loudly. When her plate was clean, she sat back and gave him an embarrassed look.

"I'm sorry."

"Don't be. I like a woman with an appetite." He grinned at her, and she blushed again.

"When was the last time you ate?" he asked.

She shrugged. "It's been a few days."

He cursed under his breath before leaning forward. "So, tell me about this problem."

She took a deep breath. "There's a man – a shifter – stalking me, and I need someone to make him stop."

"Why aren't you going to the police?"

"They can't help me," she repeated.

"Of course, they can. It's their job to -"

"They can't!" There was a slight note of hysteria in her voice, and he made a soft, soothing noise as she stared nervously around the bar.

"Please, just believe me when I say they can't help me,

okay? I'm not stupid! I would have gone to them if I thought it would help."

"Okay, okay. I know you're not stupid, Maggie," he said quietly. "What kind of shifter is after you?"

"A hyena shifter," she said.

He grimaced. He hated hyena shifters. They were sneaky and cruel bastards and were often looked upon as the scum of the shifter world. They had earned their reputations honestly, and he wasn't surprised that one was harassing Maggie. When they wanted something, they stopped at nothing to get it.

"How did you meet him?"

"At a party," she said. "At first, he was nice and sweet, but then he started to act differently. He kept showing up at my apartment or job, then at random places when I was out. I told him I wasn't interested and broke it off with him, but he – he got a lot worse after that."

She grimaced and clutched at her stomach for a moment.

"Are you okay?"

She nodded. "Yes. I think I, uh, ate too fast."

"So, you broke it off with him, and things got worse?" he prompted.

"Yes. At first, it was just him showing up but then more and more of his friends started appearing too."

"Hyenas are most comfortable in packs."

"Right," she said before rubbing gingerly at her stomach. "Anyway, he showed up at my apartment a few nights ago, and he – he broke the door down when I wouldn't let him in. He was so mean and rough, and he said that I – I was his now and that there was no point in fighting it. I was going to be his mate, and that was that."

Her trembling grew worse, and tears slid down her face.

He reached out and touched the top of her hand gingerly. "It's okay, Maggie."

"It isn't," she said. She swiped at the tears on her face before taking a deep breath. "I played along and offered to make us something to eat. He agreed, and I went into the kitchen and got the biggest butcher knife I could find and then I – I tried to stab him with it."

"Did you?"

She nodded. "I stabbed him in the thigh. It made him so angry, and he pulled the knife out, and there was blood every-where, and then I just ran."

She suddenly latched onto his hand and held it tightly. "I waited a few hours, and then I went back to my apartment, but I was careful, you know? I hid in the park across the street, and I watched my apartment building. I was pretty sure he would still be there, but I was wrong. Vaughn had left, but his pack was there. All ten of them were just, like, prowling around my apartment building. They were trying to blend in, but I saw them. So, I ran again. I work at a coffee shop, and I went there the next morning. They were waiting there too. They – they went to my job and my apartment, and I didn't know what else to do."

"So, you've been running since then?"

She nodded and sniffed loudly before staring at their clasped hands. "Oh, I'm sorry." She yanked her hand free and slid it into her lap, where it twisted and turned against her other.

"Do you not have any family? Friends who can help?"

"I don't have any family. My parents died when I was young, and I went into foster care. I have a few friends, but I can't involve them in this. Vaughn is dangerous, very danger-ous, and my friends are only humans. It's why I came here. I thought maybe what I needed was a shifter. A bigger, stronger shifter than Vaughn."

He studied the dark circles under her eyes. "When did you sleep last?"

"Wh-what?" she said.

"When did you sleep last?"

"I don't know. What does it matter?" she asked a bit impatiently. "I'm sorry, I don't mean to be rude, but can you help me? I can pay you for your protection."

He doubted that statement was true. The woman had no purse and was obviously starving. "What exactly do you think a shifter can do for you?"

"Well," she leaned forward eagerly, "I thought maybe they could talk to Vaughn and tell them that I was their mate, not his. I know a little about shifters, and I know most are very protective of their mates. If a bigger, stronger shifter – a wolf shifter like you – told Vaughn that I was dating them and that I was their mate, he would back off. Right?"

"Maybe," he said.

"Once Vaughn gave up, we could go our separate ways. And if pretending we were dating didn't work – I thought maybe the shifter could, I don't know, beat him up?"

He pressed his lips together. The woman was almost ridiculously naïve when it came to shifters, but then again, most humans were.

"Not that I condone violence," she said hastily, "and I would only ask for that if we had no other choice."

He didn't reply, and she rubbed at her stomach again before giving him a tentative smile. "Do you think you could help me, Porter?"

"You said you would pay for protection. Forgive me, Maggie, but you don't look like you have money."

She took a deep breath. "You're right – I don't. I didn't think to grab my purse when I ran, and honestly, I don't have much, uh, cash anyway. Working at a coffee shop doesn't pay very much."

She leaned forward and gave him a hesitant smile. "But I have something better than money. Something I know will appeal to you even more."

"What's that?" he asked.

"My virginity."

CHAPTER 2

P orter's mouth gaped open, and he stared at Maggie. His surprise was so great he couldn't think of a single thing to say. She turned a fiery red as she spoke again.

"A virgin is a big thing to shifters, right? I know you – your type likes it when a woman is a virgin. If you help me and agree to protect me from Vaughn, I'll give it to you. I'll spend one night with you, and I'll have sex with you as, um, many times as you want. I promise."

He continued to stare at her. She gave him a miserable look before patting her hair self-consciously. "I know I don't look like much right now, but I'm pretty once I shower and clean up. I swear it."

She suddenly bent over, grabbing at her stomach and making a small moan of pain.

"Maggie? Are you all right?" he asked worriedly.

"I'm fine. I just ate too much." Her eyes suddenly widened. "I think I'm going to throw up. Excuse me."

She slid out of the booth and ran across the bar toward the ladies' room. His mind whirling, Porter sat back in the seat and stared dumbfounded at his uneaten burger and fries. The woman had just offered her virginity to him as payment to protect her from a hyena shifter. For a moment, he wondered if she was playing some kind of scam on him, but he dismissed it almost immediately. The woman's fear was genuine, and he felt another strange twisting in his stomach at the level of her desperation.

When she still hadn't appeared after ten minutes, he slid out of the booth and started toward the ladies' room. He walked down the narrow hallway and was just about to knock on the door when it opened, and she stepped into the hallway. Her face was pale, but she had washed most of the dirt from her face and hands. She gave him a wan smile.

"Are you all right?" he asked.

"Yes, I think so." She swayed a little on her feet, and he took her arm gently.

"You should sit down, Maggie."

"I'll be fine. Can you help me?"

He hesitated before shaking his head. "You need to go to the police."

She pulled free of his grip. "Thank you for sharing your food with me."

She started down the hallway, weaving unsteadily. He chased after her. "Where are you going?"

"To talk to another shifter. There has to be someone in this bar willing to help me," she said.

"That's not a good idea."

"Are you saying there isn't a single shifter in here who wants my virginity?" she snapped at him. "Am I that repulsive?"

"No, of course not," he said. "But what you're offering to do isn't a good idea. The shifters in this bar, they aren't – well, not all of them are good people, and they're not going to be gentle or -"

"I don't care!" she said. "I don't care if he's a good person or if it hurts when I have sex with him. If he can convince Vaughn to leave me alone, then it'll be worth it, okay?"

He retook her arm, and she wrenched it free, staggering backward into the wall with a hard thud. "You don't want to help me, and that's fine. I get it – I look terrible. But there has to be someone here who...."

She trailed off. The scratches on her face were bright red against the paleness of her skin. She slid down the wall, and he grabbed her by the arms.

"Maggie!"

"I think I'm going to faint." Her voice was full of mild bewilderment.

With a muttered curse, he scooped her up. Her head fell against his shoulder with a weak thud. Crying softly, she said, "Put me down," before her eyes rolled up in her head, and she slumped against him.

———

MAGGIE OPENED HER EYES AND STARED AT THE UNFAMILIAR ceiling. She was lying in a bed - not her bed - and confusion swept through her. Why was she not in her apartment? She sat up and studied the small bedroom. She had no idea where she was.

She remembered being at the bar and talking to the wolf shifter, and she remembered throwing up. Everything after that was a blur. She slid from the bed as panic set in. Maybe the wolf shifter had delivered her to Vaughn. Maybe she was in Vaughn's house right now, and he was going to hurt her.

There were footsteps outside the room, and she moaned in fear before snatching up the alarm clock. She wouldn't let him take her without a fight. She stood in the middle of the room and raised the alarm clock over her head as the door-knob turned.

"Maggie? Are you awake?"

The wolf shifter from the bar ducked as his alarm clock came flying at him. It smashed into the wall behind him, and he gave her a cautious look. "Maggie?"

"Oh my God!" She clapped her hands over her mouth. "I – I'm so sorry. I thought maybe Vaughn had found me, and I… I'm so sorry, Porter."

"That's fine." He stood in the doorway. "You're at my apartment. I brought you here after you passed out last night."

"Right. Thank you." She swallowed nervously. "I should probably get going."

"It's almost dark. You've been asleep for nearly twenty-four hours," he said.

"What?" she said as shock rolled through her.

"It's true," he said. "Listen, why don't you have a shower? I'll make us a bite to eat, and we can talk, okay?"

She didn't want to talk. What she wanted to do was find a shifter who would help her get rid of Vaughn, but the tempta-tion of a hot shower and food in her belly was too great for her to ignore. "Okay."

"Great!" He gave her a wide grin, and the area between her thighs tingled pleasantly. She squeezed her legs together. The wolf shifter was very handsome with his dark hair and bright green eyes, and he certainly looked strong. He wore faded jeans and a tight grey t-shirt, and she studied the faint outline of his abs as he cleared his throat.

"So, let me show you the bathroom."

"Okay, thanks." She tore her gaze away from his flat stomach and followed him gingerly out of the bedroom and down the hall.

"Clean towels are on that shelf, and there's a new, unwrapped toothbrush in the medicine cabinet. Okay?"

"Yes, thank you." She was itching to shed her filthy dress and ease away the aches in her body.

"There's a shirt hanging behind the door. Go ahead and wear that," he said.

She nodded, and he shut the door. She locked it before she quickly brushed her teeth and then stripped out of her dirty clothes, shoving them into the garbage can under the sink. She turned the shower on, leaving the water as hot as she could stand, and stood for long minutes under the hot spray. Her body was peppered with scratches and bruises, and after washing her hair, she washed her body gingerly, wincing a little at the pain. She would swallow her pride and ask Porter if she could borrow some cash to buy new clothes.

She didn't leave the shower until the water started to cool. She dried herself quickly and ran a comb through her hair. She swiped the steam from the bathroom mirror before studying her face carefully. It was pale, there were still dark circles under her eyes, and it was covered in scratches from the bushes in the park.

"Ugh," she whispered. No wonder the wolf shifter didn't want her virginity.

She slipped into his shirt. It fell to her thighs and billowed around her small frame, and she felt a little less self-conscious about her nakedness underneath it.

She followed the smell of toast to the kitchen and stood nervously in the doorway. Porter stood at the stove, stirring something in a pot. He gave her another cheerful smile. "Feeling better?"

"Yes, thank you very much."

"You're welcome."

"Can I help you with dinner?"

"Nope. Have a seat," he said.

She sat down gingerly in the chair, smoothing his shirt down over her knees as he placed a stack of toast on the table before ladling soup into two bowls. He set the steaming bowl down in front of her before sitting down.

"It's only soup and toast, but I think you need to eat a bit light," he said. "You don't want to throw up again."

She blushed a little. "Right."

The soup smelled delicious, and her stomach growled loudly.

"Eat slowly," he cautioned.

"Okay." She forced herself to take small bites of the toast and small sips of the soup. It was a beef vegetable, swimming with tender bites of carrot and potatoes and well-seasoned beef.

"This is really good." She smiled tentatively at him.

"Thanks. I'm not half-bad as far as cooking goes."

When they were finished eating, Maggie stared longingly at the pot on the stove, and Porter gave her a crooked grin. "You can have more later. It's probably best to see if the first bowl is going to upset your stomach."

He waved her off when she tried to help clear the dishes. "Go and relax on the couch. I'll clean up."

She wandered into the living room. It was small but tidy, and she glanced out the window at the traffic below before sitting down on the couch. After a few moments, Porter joined her and sat down in the large armchair across from her.

She gave him an uncomfortable smile. "Thank you again for the shower and the food."

"You're welcome. Are you feeling better?" He studied the scratches on her face and legs.

"Yes. Thank you."

There was an awkward silence, and she started to stand. "I should go."

"Where are you going to go?" He raised one eyebrow at her.

"I don't know. I'll think of something."

He glanced at her body. "You don't have any clothes to wear."

"Do you – could I, um, borrow some cash for some clothes? I'll pay you back, I swear."

He nodded. "Yes, but on one condition. You stay the night. It'll be getting dark soon, and you shouldn't be out wandering the streets."

"I'm sorry, but I can't take advantage of your generosity any further." She smiled faintly at him. "I really do need to find someone to help me take care of my, uh, problem, and I can't afford to waste any more -"

"I'll help you," he said.

She stared wide-eyed at him. "You will?"

"Yes."

"I – that's great. Thank you so much!" Relief flooded through her, and she sank back against the couch as Porter shifted in his chair.

"Tomorrow morning, I'll go to your apartment and check things out – see if the hyenas are still hanging around."

"I can go with you."

He shook his head. "Not a good idea. If they're still there, I don't want them catching your scent."

"What if they're gone?"

"I'll come back and get you and bring you to your apartment. You can grab your purse and some extra clothes, and we'll go from there. Okay?"

"Sure, okay. Thank you, Porter. I can't tell you how grateful I am," she said.

"You're welcome, Maggie."

There was more awkward silence, and Maggie took a deep breath. It was apparent what he was waiting for, and, steeling herself, she stood and walked toward him. The wolf shifter was handsome enough, and he seemed nice. She hoped he would be gentle with her, but she would just close her eyes and wait for it to be over if he wasn't.

Her idea of her virginity being a gift, of waiting and giving it to someone she loved, was ridiculously old-fashioned anyway. The wolf shifter was big and strong. If anyone could get Vaughn to leave her alone, it would be him. Giving him her virginity would be worth it to have Vaughn out of her life.

Vaughn might not want you once he knows you're not a virgin anymore. Have you thought of that?

Of course, she had. It was part of the reason she had come up with the idea of her virginity as payment. Her virginity was what appealed most to Vaughn. He had told her that himself. Shifters only wanted pure women, he had explained as he held her captive in her apartment. It was rare for women to be untainted, he'd said, and he wanted her and her unclaimed innocence.

Her legs shaking with nerves, she quickly straddled Porter in the chair. His shirt rose to mid-thigh, and she yanked on the hem nervously when his eyes dropped to her pale legs.

"What are you doing, Maggie?" His voice was hoarse, and she made herself smile at him.

"Paying you for your protection, Porter." She aimed for sexy and confident and succeeded in sounding weak and terrified.

She cleared her throat and tried again. "I want you. I – I want you inside of me."

Even to her, it sounded like a lie. She cursed inwardly and

gave up on the sex talk. She wasn't completely naïve. She might be a virgin, but she'd dated and had her fair share of grope sessions. But talking sexy to a man was a completely foreign concept to her. She bent her head to his thick neck and pressed her mouth against his flesh instead. He didn't move, and she licked up his neck to his earlobe. He inhaled sharply, and she sucked on his ear as her hands slipped under his shirt and stroked his abdomen.

His hand gripped the back of her neck, and she lifted her head and kissed him on the mouth. He grunted in surprise, and she twitched when he pulled his mouth away.

"What's wrong?" she breathed against his lips.

He studied her quietly for a moment before growling, "Open your mouth."

Her stomach twisting and her heart pounding with fear, she parted her lips. His mouth moved toward hers, and she reminded herself not to pull away.

You can do this, Maggie.

She jerked when instead of thrusting his tongue into her mouth as she expected, he sucked gently on her bottom lip. She closed her eyes as he switched to her upper lip, curving his tongue along the inside of it and sucking a little more roughly.

She was surprised to feel a soft bite of lust in her belly and even more surprised to hear the soft moan she made when he threaded his fingers into her hair. He held her firmly as his mouth moved over hers. She found herself wanting his tongue, wanting to taste it and suck on it. She made a low whimper of need before licking at his lips. He captured the tip of her tongue between them and sucked roughly before releasing it. She moaned again and opened her mouth wide, hoping he would take the hint.

He didn't disappoint. She shivered when he pushed his

tongue between her lips and explored her entire mouth. Her heart was pounding again, this time with lust. Without thinking, she pressed her body against his. The shifter tasted wonderful, and he was delightfully warm.

Her earlier hope that he would be gentle had disappeared under a crush of overwhelming desire. She urged him to kiss her harder and more deeply. He groaned, and one arm slipped around her waist, holding her tightly against his hard chest as he explored her mouth with a barely restrained hunger.

When his hand cupped her breast, her nerves shifted into high gear and pushed her lust away. She stiffened before forcing herself to relax. She had to do this. She had made a promise to him. She blinked in surprise when he suddenly pushed her back. Breathing heavily, he stared at her. His light green eyes were glowing, and she stared at them in fascination as he took a deep breath.

"You should get some rest, darlin'," he muttered.

"I – what?" she said.

"Go to my room and get some rest. I'll sleep on the couch tonight."

"Porter?" She touched his chest tentatively. "Did I do something wrong?"

"No," he gritted out.

"Then why did you stop? I told you, I – I want this."

"I don't," he said.

"I'm sorry. I thought you had agreed to - I'll go now." Her face flamed, and she stumbled off of his lap before staring at the floor.

He stood and caught her arm. "No, don't go, Maggie. I just mean that I don't want this tonight. You're still tired and in pain. You need more rest."

"I am so embarrassed right now."

"Don't be," he insisted. "You're a beautiful woman, and I want you very much. Really."

She didn't reply, and he tried again. "Maggie, you're gorgeous. Any man would be a fool not to want you. I just think you should get more rest and then we'll talk about this later, okay? I'm worried that you're not thinking straight, and I don't want you to regret anything you do with me."

"I won't," she said. "Please, Porter. I can't live like this any longer, and I don't care what or who I have to do to get Vaughn away from me."

He winced, and she made a soft moan. "I'm sorry, that didn't come out right. I just mean that I -"

"I know what you mean. Just go and get some rest, please? We'll talk more later about your… your payment to me, okay?"

"Are you sure?" she asked hesitantly. "I'm not that tired, and I'd rather just get it over with."

He winced again, and she could have smacked herself in the head. "God! I'm sorry. I'm such an idiot. I didn't mean it like that."

"Please, Maggie. Go to bed," he said through gritted teeth.

She backed away. "Um, okay. I'll see you in the morning?"

He nodded, and she hurried out of the living room, her face burning.

HOLY FUCK, HE WAS IN TROUBLE.

Porter dropped back into the chair as Maggie turned and nearly ran from the living room. He rubbed a hand over his face. When Maggie sat on his lap, he was surprised, but his wolf had positively howled with delight. He wanted to mate with the soft, delicious-smelling female and didn't care about her reasons. It was his wolf who had surged forward and growled for her to open her mouth.

When she obeyed, Porter couldn't resist tasting the sweetness of her mouth. But when he cupped her breast, and fear replaced the smell of her desire, his own need disappeared quickly. He liked his woman willing, and he wasn't going to take her when she was only doing it as some sort of payment for his protection.

He sighed and moved to the couch, stretching out with his feet hanging over the end and staring blankly up at the ceiling. What had he gotten himself into?

CHAPTER 3

Maggie took a deep breath and stared around the tidy kitchen. When she woke this morning, Porter had cooked her pancakes. Embarrassed but unable to stop herself, she had eaten four of them. He hadn't seemed to mind, and she had insisted on helping him clean up afterward.

Before things could get awkward, Porter got the address of her apartment from her and left. He had smiled reassuringly at her before promising he wouldn't be long. That was an hour ago, and she was feeling restless and worried. What if Vaughn and his hyena pack were there? What if they smelled Porter and somehow knew that he was helping her? If they hurt him, she would never forgive herself.

There was a loud knock on the apartment door, and she shrieked softly, whirling around to stare out the doorway of the kitchen. She couldn't see the front door from the kitchen, and she paced back and forth as her heart pounded. What now? Should she creep to the door and check the peephole? It wouldn't be Vaughn, there was no way it could be, but what if it was?

She bit nervously at her bottom lip as there was another

knock. She had to do something. She couldn't just stand in the kitchen like a frightened rabbit. Her eyes widened when she heard a key in the lock, and she looked around frantically for a weapon. Her gaze fell on the knife block, and she pulled the largest knife from it, holding it in front of her as heavy footsteps thudded down the hallway.

"Porter? Are you in here?" A large, dark-haired man stuck his head into the kitchen. "You were supposed to meet us at the tux place an hour ago."

She swallowed thickly before raising the knife. "Stay away from me. I'm warning you."

"Who are you? Where's Porter?" The man scowled at her, and she took a step back as he stepped into the kitchen. She moaned in fear when an even bigger man stepped in behind him. This one was dark-haired as well with a neatly trimmed beard, and he was so large he had to duck to get through the doorway. Their wide bodies filled the small kitchen, and her hand shook as the giant of a man stared curiously at her.

"Who's this, Mal?"

"I have no idea, Bishop. I was just about to find out." The man named Mal gave Maggie a stern look. "Put the knife down."

"No." She took another step back until her butt hit the counter. "You'll stay away from me if you know what's good for you."

The one named Bishop chuckled out loud, and she flushed before glaring at him. "I'm tougher than I look."

Mal took another step forward, and she waved the knife in his direction. "This is your last chance. You'd better leave before –"

She blinked in surprise when a short, slender woman with dark hair in a bun high on her head popped into the kitchen. She squeezed around Bishop and rolled her eyes when Mal put his arm around her and pulled her protectively into his embrace. A second woman appeared. She had long, red hair and was pregnant, and she stared at Maggie as Bishop took her hand.

"Hello!" The dark-haired woman said brightly as she stuck out her hand. "I'm Willow." She eyed the knife in Maggie's trembling hand. "That's a pretty big knife you have there. What's your name, honey?"

PORTER OPENED THE DOOR TO HIS APARTMENT AND CLOSED and locked it before kicking off his boots. He hung his jacket on the hook, pausing when he heard the soft murmur of voices in the living room. Adrenaline racing through his veins, he ran down the hallway and skidded into the living room.

"Maggie! What –"

"Hey, little brother." Mal sat on a kitchen chair in the living room. Bishop, Mal's best friend, business partner, and a massive grizzly shifter had crammed his large body into the armchair. Willow sat next to Maggie on the couch. She stroked her hair gently as Bishop's human mate, Ava, applied clear salve to the scratches on Maggie's lower legs.

"Go on, honey. What happened then?" Willow said to Maggie.

"Well, then I had the idea that maybe another shifter could help me, and I knew about Bud's being a paranormal-only bar, so I figured that would be my best chance, you know?"

Bishop stared at her. "You went into Bud's on your own?"

Maggie nodded, and Bishop rolled his eyes. "Not a smart idea."

"Bishop," Ava said gently, and he flushed slightly before mumbling an apology.

"I met Porter, and I hired him, and now he's, uh, helping me." Maggie gave Porter a hesitant smile as he sat down on the other end of the couch.

"Of course, he is," Willow said. "He's a sweetheart."

Mal snorted, and Willow scowled at him. "Cork it, Mal."

"Porter is not a sweetheart," Mal said.

"I am, too," Porter said.

"Whatever," Mal said with a grin.

Ava patted Maggie's knee. "None of the scratches look infected, but you might want to keep using the medicated cream on them for the next few days, okay?"

"Okay. Thank you, Ava."

"You're welcome, Maggie." Ava was sitting on the floor in front of Maggie, and as she struggled to stand, Bishop stood and hooked his hands under her arms. He lifted her easily to her feet and rubbed her belly before smiling at her.

"Take my seat, honey."

"Thank you, love." Ava stood on her tiptoes and kissed him on the mouth before settling into the chair. Bishop sat on the floor at her feet, and she stroked his hair as he rested his arm across her lap.

"Are all hyenas this overzealous about their dates?" Willow asked Mal.

He shrugged. "They're all assholes, if that's what you mean."

"Really? There must be one nice hyena," Willow said.

Porter shook his head. "There isn't. Trust us, Willow. They're assholes."

"Were they still at Maggie's apartment?" Mal asked.

Porter hesitated. "Yeah, they were there."

Maggie made a soft moan of dismay, and Willow put her arm around her. "It's all right, honey."

"How many of them?" Bishop asked.

"Two," Porter said grimly. "After I left Maggie's apartment building, I acted on a hunch and drove to the coffee shop that she works at."

"And?" Mal said.

"There were another three. One of them was hanging outside, and the other two were in the shop, drinking coffee and, no doubt, waiting for her."

"Shit," Maggie said.

"Don't worry, Maggie." Willow gave her a reassuring smile. "Everything will be fine, you'll see."

She stared thoughtfully at Mal. "We could have Davis keep an eye on her when Porter is at work. She might as well just stay with Porter for now, especially if they're pretending to date, while we look into this Vaughn jerk."

Maggie frowned at her. "What? Who's Davis?"

"He's one of Mal and Bishop's employees. They own a security firm and provide personal protection for shifters."

"I'm not a shifter."

"They protect humans as well. Anyway," Willow turned back to Mal, "Porter can keep an eye on her when he's not working, and Davis can camp out in the apartment with her when he is. Once we -"

"No," Maggie said.

The others turned to stare at her as she clasped her hands nervously across her torso. "I'm sorry, but I – I don't have any money to pay you for a personal security guard."

"If you don't have any money, how are you going to pay Porter?" Mal asked.

Maggie turned bright red, and she stared down at her knees as Porter flushed as well.

"What?" Mal asked. "What did I say?"

Willow stared at Maggie and Porter for a long moment before saying, "It's fine, Maggie. Mal and Bishop were talking about taking on some pro bono work, and they'd be happy to provide you with some security for free. Isn't that right?"

She stared at the two shifters, who both nodded.

"Sure. No problem," Mal said.

"I can't let you do that," Maggie said.

"It's already decided," Willow said happily. "Besides, we'll only need to use Davis when Porter is working."

"Vaughn is obviously a bad guy. Shouldn't we be taking Maggie to the police?" Ava asked. "She could get a restraining order against him."

"No," Maggie said. "I can't go to the police."

"Why not?" Willow asked.

"Vaughn is – well – he's a cop."

"Shit," Porter replied. "Is his pack all cops too?"

"I'm not sure. I think some of them are," she said hesitantly. "I can't go to the police station. Vaughn will be there, and even if he isn't, what do you think they'll say if I ask to have a restraining order put against one of their own?"

"It shouldn't matter if he's a cop or not," Porter said. "Just because he's a cop doesn't mean he isn't an asshole who's stalking an innocent woman. I think we should still go to them."

"No." Maggie shook her head. "They won't believe me. Besides, he's a bit of a celebrity. He was the cop who stopped the assassination against that senator last year."

Bishop whistled. "I remember that. It was all over the news. Hero cop saves the senator. Didn't they give him the key to the city?"

"Yes," Maggie replied dully. "He told me all about it on

one of our dates. He was pretty scornful and bitter about it, actually. Said that if he had known it was the senator they were attempting to kill, he would have just let them go ahead and do it. I don't know why he said that."

"The senator he saved is a well-known paranormal racist," Mal said. "He's tried a few times over the years to put legislation in place requiring us to register as paranormals. He also tried to ban us from having any sort of contact with humans."

"Ridiculous," Ava snorted. "I read somewhere that there are more paranormals than humans in the world. He's fighting a losing battle."

"Well, there are definitely more paranormals than humans in our city," Willow piped up. "It's because the paranormal fault line runs right through the city."

"Willow, you know that's a myth," Mal said.

"Says you." Willow winked at him before turning back to Maggie. "So, it's decided. For now, we're going to go with Maggie's idea of convincing Vaughn that she belongs to Porter. Do you think it's safe for her to go back to work?"

"I'm pretty sure I don't have a job anymore. My boss would have fired me when I missed two shifts in a row without any explanation," Maggie said. "I wanted to call, but I didn't have my cell phone, and I was too afraid to go in."

"It's probably best if she stays in Porter's apartment for now," Bishop said. "She can't hide away forever, but we'll give it a week or two for Vaughn to cool off, and then Porter and Maggie can start going out together to some of her regular spots. If this asshole hyena is still looking for her, it won't take long for him to find her and Porter."

"What if he attacks Porter?" Mal asked. "Then what?"

"I can handle the hyena," Porter said.

"Vaughn by himself, yes. But what if he has his pack with him?"

"It won't come to that," Porter said confidently. "Hyenas are cowards at heart. They won't attack a wolf shifter in public. Once he realizes that Maggie belongs to me, he'll slink back to the hole he crawled out of."

"Good!" Willow said. "Mal, you'll talk to Davis about keeping an eye on Maggie when Porter's at work, right?"

"I will," Mal said.

Willow wiped at the tears that were sliding down Maggie's face. "Don't cry, honey. You don't need to be scared, okay? We'll keep you safe."

Maggie sniffed loudly. "I don't know how even to begin to thank you. I've never had anyone be so nice to me before or…."

Willow hugged her impulsively. "We're happy to help. Now, you're going to need some clothes. As cute as you look in Porter's shirt, you can't go out like that in public. Ava and I will go to your apartment and get some of your things, okay? You can make us a list."

"Ava's not going to that apartment," Bishop growled as his hand tightened on Ava's knee. "Not with those hyenas hanging around."

"We'll be fine," Willow replied. "Mal, tell him."

"Definitely not, Willow," Mal said. "Bishop's right. Maggie will have to make do with what she has at the moment. There's no point in any of us going to her apartment while the hyenas are still watching it. We don't want them following us back to Porter's place and finding Maggie before Vaughn has a chance to cool down. Who knows, Maggie and Porter may not even have to confront him. He might just lose interest."

"He's not going to," Maggie said miserably. "He already told me he'd never stop hunting for me."

Her face crumpled, and she buried her face in her hands. "Why won't he just leave me alone? I can't be the only damn virgin in this entire city, can I?"

Willow hugged her tightly and gave Ava a look of confusion. The redhead shrugged as Bishop's face reddened. "Uh, I think it's time we headed back to the office. Kat's going to wonder where the hell we are. We were only supposed to be gone for an hour or so."

"You missed the tux fitting, Porter," Mal said.

"Shit! I'm sorry, I completely forgot with everything that happened," Porter said.

"It's fine," Willow said. "This is more important. I'll just reschedule the fitting."

She hugged Maggie again and kissed her forehead. "I'll come by later this evening with some of my clothes. They should fit, and you can use them until we can go to your apartment, all right?"

Maggie nodded and smiled faintly at the others as they filed out of the living room.

MAGGIE TOOK A DEEP BREATH AND PEEKED INTO THE kitchen. Porter stood at the sink staring blankly out the window, and she crept toward him. It was later that afternoon, and she didn't think she imagined that he was avoiding her as best he could in the tiny apartment.

Her steps toward him faltered for a moment. She was pretty sure he wanted her - he had kissed her last night like he did - but what if he didn't? She was making a fool of herself if he didn't.

Stop it, Maggie. Porter agreed to help you, and you've promised to give him your virginity. Obviously, he wants you, or he wouldn't have agreed to it. Shifters want virgins, remember? So, stop being such a big baby and give him what you said you would. It's better to get it over with sooner than later.

She marched toward him and wrapped her arms around his waist, ignoring the way he stiffened at her touch.

"I'm feeling better, Porter. Why don't we go to your room?" Ignoring her racing heart, she reached down and rubbed at his crotch. His cock hardened against her palm, and she pressed herself against his back and ass.

"So you can get it over with?" he asked.

She winced. "No. That's not it. I want you."

"You don't even know me."

She hesitated, and he turned before gently pushing her away.

She flushed at the look on his face and crossed her arms over her torso. "What do you want me to say? You said you would help me, which means you accept my... my payment terms. But every time I try, you reject me."

"Maybe it's because I prefer the women in my bed to be there because they want to be, not because they're paying a debt," he snapped.

She scowled at him. "I said I would do it. That means I want to be in your bed."

"Bullshit," he muttered. "You went into that bar looking for any shifter - you didn't care who - to help you. You would have offered up your virginity to any of them."

Tears welled up in her eyes, and she swiped at them defiantly. "So what? Are you saying that I'm a whore now?"

"No! Maggie that isn't what I mean."

She sighed. "I don't want to argue. I'm trying to pay my debt to you. Do you want my virginity or not?"

He hesitated, and she took a step backward in surprise when he shook his head. "I don't."

Shame, anger, and – oddly enough – disappointment flooded through her. "Fine. I'll go now. Tell your brother thank you for offering to help. I really appreciate it."

She marched out of the kitchen toward the front door. Porter chased after her and pulled her to a stop. "You're not leaving, Maggie. You have no place else to go."

"I'll find something," she said.

He rolled his eyes. "No, you won't. Vaughn will find you first."

"I can't stay here."

"Yes, you can. I didn't say I wouldn't help you. I just said that I wouldn't take your virginity as some damn payment for my help."

"I don't have any money, remember?"

"I remember. Can't I just help you because I'm a nice guy?" he said.

"I have no idea if you're a nice guy or not," she said. "I just met you."

"That's my point!" He glared at her. "You've just met me, but you've tried twice now to get me to take your virginity. You're twenty-five years old and -"

"How do you know that?" she said.

"I can smell how old you are," he said impatiently.

"Really?"

He ignored her look of surprise. "You're twenty-five years old, and you haven't had sex. Obviously, you were waiting for a reason."

"What does it matter? I'm willing to give it to you. What do you care?"

"I care because I'm a nice guy!" he shouted.

"Fine! You're a nice guy!" she shouted back.

He raked his hand through his hair. "Look, Maggie, I'm not going to take you to my bed. I'll help you, and my brother will help you, and you don't have to pay us back for it with money or your damn virginity, okay?"

"Porter, I -"

"Just agree with me, Maggie," he said wearily.

She bit at her lip and rubbed her elbows with her cold hands before nodding. "Okay."

"Good. I have to leave for work in a few hours. I didn't sleep well last night, so I'm going to take a nap."

She watched as he walked down the hall and disappeared into his bedroom, shutting the door behind him. She sighed and wandered into the living room, collapsing on the couch and staring up at the ceiling. Porter wasn't going to make her sleep with him, and she was happy about that.

Wasn't she?

CHAPTER 4

"Well, the shirt is a little tight in the chest, but it'll do," Willow said critically as she stared at Maggie. She stared down at her chest. "Man, I have the smallest boobs in the world."

Ava laughed as she poured the boiling water over the teabags. "I keep telling you, Willow, big boobs aren't that great."

Willow snorted. "Maybe we should ask Bishop what he thinks."

Ava placed the mugs of tea in front of Willow and Maggie. "Don't you be asking Bishop anything about our sex life. He'll probably burst into flames from embarrassment."

"Is Bishop a wolf shifter?" Maggie asked as she sipped at the tea.

Willow and Ava and a powerful looking lynx shifter named Davis had shown up just as Porter was leaving for work. Davis had introduced himself and shook her hand before retreating to his car parked in the street outside the apartment building. After Porter had left, Willow had urged her to try on the clothes she brought while Ava made tea.

"No. He's a grizzly shifter," Ava said.

"He's, um, the biggest man I've ever seen."

Ava nodded. "He certainly is."

Willow snickered. "He's also the biggest softie you'll ever meet. Well, most of the time. You don't want to threaten Ava. That brings out his angry side."

Ava flushed prettily. "He's not that bad, Willow."

"Remind me to tell you about the time a lion shifter hit on Ava. There was nothing left but blood and pulp when Bishop finished with him," Willow said.

Maggie's eyes widened, and Ava patted her hand. "She's exaggerating."

"I'm totally not," Willow said. "So, how did you meet this Vaughn, anyway?"

"At a party. I didn't know he was a cop or a shifter, and he was very, um, charming at first. He told me he was a shifter on our second date. But then, after our fourth date, he started to get – well – weird. He would just show up at the coffee shop or my apartment without invitation, and he started talking about what would happen when we got married. I told him he needed to slow down and tried to kind of joke with him, you know? But he just became more and more persistent. It started to scare me, so I broke it off with him, and that's when he started stalking me."

"Asshole," Willow muttered.

"I knew I couldn't go to the cops. That's why I decided to try another shifter. One who was more powerful than Vaughn and would maybe scare him off once he thought I was dating him. I went to Bud's, and then I met Porter, and he agreed to help me."

Willow cleared her throat before giving Ava a quick look. "Maggie, can I ask you something?"

"Sure."

"Earlier this morning, you said something about there being other virgins in the city. What did you mean by that?"

"Well, I – I just meant that I didn't know why Vaughn wants mine so much. There are other girls who haven't slept with anyone. Not that I would wish Vaughn on them, but why did he have to choose me, you know?"

"So, you think Vaughn wants you because you're a virgin?" Willow frowned at her.

"Yes?" Maggie said tentatively. "All shifters want virgins."

Willow stared at her, and Maggie said, "What?"

"I'm sure that there are some shifters out there who prefer virgins, but not all of them do," Willow said.

Maggie frowned at her. "That's not right."

She glanced over at Ava. The redhead was staring at her in confusion, and Maggie bit at her lip. "Were you not a virgin before you started dating Bishop?"

"No," Ava said. "I didn't have a lot of experience, but I wasn't a virgin."

Maggie blinked in confusion as Willow touched her hand. "Maggie?"

"You were a virgin, though, right?" Maggie asked her.

Ava snorted loud laughter. "Oh hell no."

Willow scowled at her. "Be quiet, you!"

"I don't understand," Maggie said. "Mal started dating you even though you had slept with another person first?"

"Person? Oh, honey, it was more than one person. Trust me." Ava giggled.

"Hey! You make it sound like it's whoreville - population Willow." Willow laughed. "Besides, Mal has no complaints about my bedroom abilities."

She turned back to Maggie. "Honey, why do you think shifters only want virgins? Did Vaughn tell you that?"

She nodded. "He said shifters liked their women pure, and it was rare to find one. He said I was destined to be his mate and that my virginity belonged to him. It's why I told Porter I would pay him for his protection by giving him my -"

She stopped abruptly. "Never mind."

Willow leaned forward. "Did you tell Porter he could have your virginity in exchange for helping you?"

Maggie stared at the table as a hot blush rose in her cheeks. "Yes. I don't have any money, and I thought that maybe it would help with the Vaughn situation. If I'm not a virgin, maybe he won't want me anymore, you know?"

"Oh, honey," Willow sighed and squeezed her hand.

"Only," Maggie swallowed thickly, "Porter won't take it. I've offered it twice since he brought me back to his apartment, and he keeps rejecting me. He said it's because he doesn't take women to his bed who, uh, don't want to be there, but I think it's because he's not attracted to me. I feel awful about it. I would have found another shifter - one who did find me attractive - if I had known Porter didn't want to have sex with me. But in the bar that night, he said yes after I told him I would sleep with him in exchange for his help, so I thought…."

She picked at a chip in her mug as Willow sighed again. "Well, Porter is a lucky man."

"What do you mean?" Maggie said.

"I mean, if I had found out he took your virginity as some sort of damn payment, I would have beat the crap out of him. And if I hadn't, his brother most certainly would have," Willow said cheerfully.

Maggie flushed. "I offered it to him."

"I know, but that doesn't mean he should take it. Maggie, you shouldn't have to auction off your virginity to get help. I understand why you did, and I'm not judging you, but you're fortunate that you ran into Porter at the bar. Do you realize that?"

"I'm starting to," she said.

"Your virginity should be shared with a person who you care about and who cares about you. Your first time is supposed to be special, and I think you know that. Otherwise, you wouldn't still be waiting for the right person."

"Damn, Willow, I had no idea you were so romantic," Ava said.

"I'm incredibly romantic," Willow said. "Hey, are you going to Mara and Roland's tomorrow night for dinner?"

"We are," Ava said.

"Oh, good." Willow smiled at Maggie. "You're going to love Mara."

"Who's Mara?" Maggie asked.

"Mal and Porter's mom. She's also sort of Bishop's adopted mom. It's a long story."

"Why would I meet Mara?" Maggie said.

"Because it's a family dinner. Porter will be there, and I'm sure he'll bring you."

"Why would he?" Maggie said.

"Why wouldn't he?" Willow said.

"I'm not family," Maggie said. "I can't intrude on the dinner."

"Nonsense," Willow said. "Porter will bring you with him. Mara will have his head if she finds out he left you here alone. She's got the protective mama wolf thing down to a science."

"But she doesn't even know I exist," Maggie said.

Willow hesitated, and Ava laughed. "Already, Willow?"

"Already what?" Maggie said.

"I might have told Mara about you," Willow said sweetly. "I stopped by the house after work to show her some wedding cake ideas, and you might have come up in conversation."

Maggie gave her a look of disbelief, and Willow said, "What? It was totally a natural progression in conversation from 'hey, here's what I'm thinking for wedding cakes' to 'Porter has a human living with him who a hyena is stalking'."

Ava laughed again. "Totally natural." She glanced at her watch. "I'd better run. I have an early shift at the hospital tomorrow, and I need all the sleep I can get. This baby is sucking up my energy like you wouldn't believe."

"Do you know if you're having a boy or a girl?" Maggie asked.

"We're keeping it a surprise," Ava said. "We almost caved at the last ultrasound, but it's only a couple of months until the baby's due, so we managed to resist."

"Congratulations," Maggie said.

"Thanks," Ava said. "I'm not looking forward to waddling down the aisle at Willow's wedding, but she refused to wait until I gave birth to get married. Some best friend."

She gave Willow an affectionate look as Willow grinned at her. "Hey, I was willing to wait, but Mal refused. I'm lucky he even gave me five months to plan the wedding. He wanted to elope the day after he asked me to marry him."

"How did you meet Mal?" Maggie asked.

"I started working for his company. He, Bishop, and a jaguar shifter named Kat own the security company. I got a job as their receptionist, and a few months later, Mal and I started dating. Ava met Bishop through us, and they hooked up almost right away."

"Not true," Ava said.

"Mostly true," Willow said. "Anyway, she moved in with

him and got knocked up with his grizzly baby after a bout of angry make-up sex."

"Willow!" Ava said.

"Sorry!" Willow gave her a chastised look as Maggie grinned.

Ava leaned down and kissed Willow on the forehead. "You're the worst."

"The best, you mean." Willow stood and slipped into her jacket. "I should get going too. Maggie, we'll see you tomorrow night, okay?"

"Um, sure, okay." She was pretty confident that Willow was wrong. Porter wouldn't bring her to a family dinner, but she didn't feel like arguing about it anymore.

She walked Willow and Ava to the door. Willow smiled at her. "So, Davis is just downstairs. Lock the door and don't answer it. If you're afraid, you have Davis' cell number. Just call him, and he'll be upstairs in a flash. Okay?"

"Okay," Maggie said. "Thank you so much for everything. I don't know what I would have done if I hadn't met you guys."

"You definitely stumbled onto the right wolf shifter," Willow said. "Porter's a great guy, Maggie. Don't worry about a thing. We'll get this hyena mess sorted out in no time."

She and Ava left, and Maggie locked the door before leaning against it. She was used to living alone, but the apartment suddenly felt too quiet. Being alone gave her too much time to think about Vaughn. To remember the look of rage and disbelief on his face when she'd stabbed the knife into his leg. She shuddered all over and hurried to the small couch. She wrapped herself up in the blankets and stared blankly at the dark TV.

Everything would be fine. She had Porter and his friends

to help her, and they seemed nice. She wasn't alone anymore. Everything would be fine.

PORTER QUIETLY CLOSED THE APARTMENT DOOR AND LOCKED it. It was just after two in the morning, and he didn't want to wake Maggie. He had spoken briefly with Davis, who sat in his car outside the apartment. It'd been quiet all night with no sign of any hyena shifters. Not that he expected there to be. The hyena had no idea where Maggie was, but he'd still felt better knowing that Davis was there while he was at work.

He took off his jacket and boots and moved silently to the kitchen. He didn't look into the living room as he passed. Maggie would be sleeping on the couch, and already his wolf was making soft demands for him to go to her.

He cursed at his wolf in his head. One kiss from Maggie and the damn thing had lost his mind.

There's nothing special about her, he snapped at his wolf. *We're not mating with her.*

I want to mate, his wolf growled.

If you want to mate so much, then I'll take Tori up on her offer to –

No! His wolf growled fiercely at him, and Porter sighed inwardly.

Not that he would have mated with the rabbit shifter. He wasn't about to admit it, but he wanted Maggie nearly as much as his wolf did. Stupid, considering he had just met her and hardly knew anything about her, but when had that stopped him before? He'd seduced plenty of women into his bed without knowing a thing about them. So, why was he balking at seducing Maggie? If that one smoking hot kiss in the living room was any indication, she wanted him as much as he wanted her.

She's different, his wolf growled. *She's sweet and innocent and mine. Give her to me.*

He jerked wildly before taking a few deep breaths to calm his suddenly racing pulse. His wolf was not trying to claim Maggie. It was just oddly obsessed with mating with her. He flicked on the light over the stove. He would have a quick bite to eat and go to bed. He wasn't the least bit tired but –

"Porter?"

Her soft voice scared the hell out of him, and his fangs dropped. He growled and whipped around. She stood in the doorway, and she took a step back when she saw his fangs.

"I'm sorry," she said as she backed away.

He retracted his fangs with a soft pop. "Maggie, wait. You just scared me. I'm sorry, I didn't mean to wake you."

"You didn't," she said. She walked into the kitchen and gave him a tentative smile. She wore his shirt, and his wolf growled in approval. "I wasn't sleeping."

"It's late," he said.

"I know."

He cleared his throat. "I was going to have a bite to eat. Did you have dinner?"

She nodded. "I made myself some chicken. There are leftovers in the fridge."

"Thanks," he said.

"Would you – why don't you let me make you a sandwich," she said.

"That's okay. You don't have to do that."

"I'd like to," she said. "I'm not sleepy at all. Sit down, and I'll make it."

"Uh, sure, okay," he said.

He sat at the table and tried not to stare at Maggie's pale

legs as she opened the fridge door. "Do you want mayo or mustard?"

"Both," he said.

She poured him a glass of water and set it on the table in front of him before grabbing leftover chicken and the other ingredients for the sandwich. "How was work?"

"Good. Not that busy, but Tuesday nights rarely are."

"I suppose not," she said.

"Tomorrow night will be busy," he said. "Wednesdays are karaoke night."

She grinned at him as she spread mayo on a slice of bread. "Shifters like karaoke?"

"A shockingly large number of them like it," he said. "It's unfortunate that not many of them can sing."

Her laugh sent a rush of warmth to his belly. She spread mustard on the second slice of bread before cutting the left-over chicken into thin slices.

"How long have you worked at Bud's?" she asked.

"Over five years," he said. "Bud is thinking of selling the bar."

"Oh yeah?" She layered the chicken on the sandwich and added some lettuce before cutting it in half and placing it on a plate. She set it in front of him and sat in the chair across from him.

"Yes. I'm thinking about buying it."

He hadn't told anyone, not even his family, about his idea of buying the bar. He gave her an anxious look, wondering what she thought of it.

"Good for you," Maggie said. "Owning your own business is a lot of work, but I bet it's a rewarding experience."

"I've already talked to the bank about a business loan, and I've been approved," he said. "The bar is a solid investment. It needs some cosmetic upgrading and repairs, but I'm good with my hands. I could do most of them myself and save some money that way."

"That's exciting," she said. "Have you made an offer yet?"

"Not yet," he said, "but I think I will."

"Well, congratulations," Maggie said.

"Thanks. I haven't, uh, told my family yet."

"I'll keep it quiet," she said.

He ate half his sandwich as she sat silently. He smiled at her. "This is delicious. You're a great cook."

"It's just a sandwich," she said.

"It's really good."

"Would you like another one?"

He nodded. "Yes, but I can make it."

She had already jumped up. "Nope, let me. You've been working all night, and I've just been sitting around doing nothing."

He finished the first sandwich as she made the second. "What about you? Do you like working at the coffee shop?"

She shrugged. "It pays the bills. I've been saving up to go back to school."

"What do you want to take?"

She grinned at him. "Accounting. I know – I'm a nerd."

He laughed. "Nothing wrong with nerds."

"Thanks." She handed him the second sandwich, and he devoured it down.

"Good?" she asked when he finished. "Or do you want a third one?"

He shook his head and patted his flat abdomen. "Better not. I'll have to work out twice as long tomorrow if I do."

She studied his lean body as colour rose in her cheeks. He cleared his throat. "So, uh, my mom texted me earlier tonight. She, well, she knows about you and -"

"I know," she said. "Willow said that she told her. She also said that I was invited to dinner, but I said I would stay here."

"No, you should come with me," he said.

"I don't have to," she said. "I don't want to intrude on your family dinner."

"I want you to go," he said.

Another flush of colour to her cheeks, and she stared at the table. "Okay. If you're sure?"

"I'm sure," he said. "I should warn you about my grand-father, though. He's not great with humans. He's better now that Willow and Ava are around, but he might say something rude to you. Don't take it personally, okay?"

"Maybe I shouldn't go," she said tentatively. "I don't want to upset your grandfather."

"You won't. I'm more worried that he'll upset you. He speaks without thinking a lot. Besides, if we're going to be pretend dating for a while, it makes sense that you meet my family, right? It makes it more believable."

"Right," she said. She glanced at the clock on the microwave. "It's pretty late. I guess I'd better try to get some sleep. Good night, Porter."

"Maggie, wait," he said as she headed out of the kitchen. "Do you want to sleep in my bed?"

Her eyes widened, and for a moment, he thought he saw a flash of desire before anxiety replaced it. "Um, I thought you said that you didn't want – I mean, it's fine that you do. I just – could I have a few minutes to prepare for…."

He stared blankly at her before suddenly shaking his head. "Fuck, no! That isn't what I meant. Jesus, I'm sorry. I just meant that you could have my bed, and I would sleep on the couch. I know it's not very comfortable."

"No," she said. Now the flush in her cheeks spread down

her neck and chest. "Definitely not. The couch is just fine. I'm not kicking you out of your bed."

She crossed her arms nervously over her torso, and his wolf made a low howl of delight. Maggie's nipples were visible against the fabric of her shirt, and he was very grateful that he still sat. The table hid his sudden and obvious erection.

Maggie glanced at her chest and made a soft "eep" of dismay before abruptly turning away. "Good night, Porter," she called as she nearly ran out of the kitchen.

"Good night, Maggie." He dropped his head into his hands and grimly ignored his wolf's insistence to grab Maggie and take her to his bed.

CHAPTER 5

M aggie was barely on the porch of Porter's parents' home when the front door was flung open. A tall and slender woman with dark hair and green eyes like Porter's said, "You must be Maggie!"

She pulled Maggie into her embrace and hugged her. "What a pretty little thing you are. I'm so sorry those horrible hyenas are giving you a hard time."

"Oh, um, thank you," Maggie said.

"Mom," Porter said as Mara stroked Maggie's hair and smiled at her, "you're suffocating her."

Mara released Maggie but took her hand. "Sorry, dear. I do tend to be overexuberant in my greetings."

"I don't mind," Maggie said. She didn't. She was immediately drawn to Mara's warmth and the way she practically exuded the mother vibe. None of her foster mothers were particularly motherly, and embarrassingly enough, she almost wished that Mara would hug her again.

As if she'd read her mind, Mara put her arm around her shoulders and drew her closer as she led her into the house.

"Peanut, your father and brothers are outside. Why don't you join them while I take Maggie to the kitchen?"

"Maggie, is that okay?" Porter asked as he followed them down the hall.

"Yes." Maggie smiled up at Mara as she led her into the kitchen. "Thank you for letting me crash your family dinner."

"Of course. You're welcome here anytime," Mara said.

"Hi, Maggie!" Willow stood at the counter slicing tomatoes, and she waved the seed-splattered knife at her. "How are you?"

"I'm good, thanks. How are you?"

"Good."

"Maggie, this is my daughter Jessa. Jessa, this is Porter's friend Maggie," Mara said.

"Hi, Maggie." Jessa was tall like her mother but with the toned body of an athlete. Her eyes were blue instead of green, but she had the same warm smile as her mother.

"Hi, Jessa. It's nice to meet you."

"You'll meet Porter's brothers in a little bit, but I'm afraid you won't get to meet Becky this time," Mara said. "Sit down. I'll get you a glass of iced tea."

"Where is Becky?" Willow asked as she popped a slice of tomato into her mouth.

"Oh, she's out with friends. You know how it is with teenagers," Mara said with a laugh. "They'd rather be anywhere but with family."

"How many children do you have?" Maggie asked as Mara set a glass of iced tea in front of her.

"JJ, I think the potatoes are done. Would you drain them for me, please?" Mara asked. "I want to let them cool a bit before we make the salad."

"Sure," Jessa said as Mara sat beside Maggie.

"Roland and I have six children. Mal is the oldest, then Porter, Heath, Ellet, Jessa, and Becky."

"Wow," Maggie said.

"Do you have any siblings, dear?" Mara asked.

"No. My parents died when I was young, and I went into foster care."

"How dreadful for you," Mara said. "Family is so important. I couldn't imagine how awful your childhood must have been."

"Mom," Jessa said, "not everyone is like wolf shifters. Humans don't crave a pack like we do."

"I suppose not." Mara smiled at Maggie. "What do you do for a living, Maggie?"

"Well, I worked at a coffee shop while I was saving up to go back to school," Maggie said. "But I lost my job because of the whole hyena thing."

Mara squeezed her hand. "Hyenas are the worst. I'm so happy my Peanut is helping you."

Maggie tried not to grin. Mara's nickname for Porter was somehow both adorable and ridiculously unsuited for him.

Ava walked into the kitchen, and Mara bounced to her feet. "Ava! Look at how gorgeous you are."

Ava laughed as Mara hugged her. "Yes, my giant belly and swollen feet are simply stunning."

"Sit down, honey," Mara said.

"I can help with dinner," Ava said.

"Don't be silly. You just relax. Willow, Jessa, and I can handle dinner preparations."

Ava lowered herself into the chair next to Maggie. "Hi, Maggie."

"Hi, Ava."

"Where's Bishop?" Mara asked.

"Right here." Bishop stepped into the kitchen, and

Maggie watched as he lifted Mara off her feet and hugged her tightly.

Mara kissed his bearded cheek. "Hi, Button. The boys are out back. Why don't you join them?"

Bishop pressed a kiss on the top of Ava's head before leaving the kitchen.

"How was your day, Maggie?" Ava asked.

"Good. Porter went to my apartment building again and said he didn't see or smell any hyenas. I'm hoping maybe Vaughn has finally given up and that I'll be able to return to my apartment."

"You might want to give it a couple more days," Willow said. "Just because they weren't there today doesn't mean they won't try again."

"I guess. I just hate imposing on Porter the way I am."

"Nonsense. He doesn't mind," Mara said as an old man wandered into the kitchen.

He stopped and sniffed the air before growling, "Great, another human."

He glared at Maggie as Jessa said, "Grandpa, behave."

"More humans than shifters in this house now," he grumbled.

"You know that it isn't true," Mara said. "Maggie, this is Porter's grandfather, Amos."

"Hello," Maggie said timidly.

Amos just grunted at her, but his expression softened when he glanced at Ava. "Hello, Red."

"Hello, Amos," Ava said. "How are you?"

"Surrounded by humans," he said as he sat down next to her. He watched with interest as she flinched and pressed her hand against her belly. "The baby bear kicking you?"

Amos had a look of yearning on his face, and Ava reached out and took his hand. She placed it on her belly, and

Maggie watched as a grin of pure delight lit up his wrinkled face.

"You felt that?" Ava said with a smile.

Amos nodded and patted her belly gingerly. "He's strong like his daddy."

"Did you and Button find out it was a boy?" Mara said in surprise. "I thought you weren't going to find out."

"We haven't," Ava said.

"It's a boy," Amos grunted. "I know it is."

"I think it's a girl," Willow said. She leaned down and kissed Amos's cheek. "Hi, Amos."

He didn't give her the same look of affection he'd given Ava, but he didn't flinch away either. "It's a boy. I'm never wrong about these things."

"You said Jessa was a boy," Mara said.

Amos rolled his eyes and stood up slowly. "I was wrong once. Meat's just about ready."

"All right. Tell Roland we'll be right out," Mara said.

Amos grunted and left the kitchen. Willow grinned at Ava and Jessa. "The two of you owe me five bucks each. Pay up."

At Maggie's look of confusion, Willow said, "I bet them I could kiss Amos's cheek without him wolfing out on me. He's not that fond of me."

"He likes you just fine," Mara said.

"Eh, I'm growing on him," Willow said. "But he doesn't think I'm the bee's knees like he thinks Ava is. You need to tell me your secret, Ava."

Ava laughed and hauled herself up out of the chair. "As soon as I figure it out, I'll let you know."

"WHAT'S WRONG WITH YOU?"

Porter frowned at Ellet. "Nothing. Why?"

"Because you're growling under your breath." Ellet took a swig of beer. "Does it have something to do with Heath hitting on your friend?"

"No," Porter snapped.

Ellet nudged Mal. "He's lying."

"Shut up, Ellet," Porter said. "One, Heath is not hitting on Maggie and two, I wouldn't care even if he was."

"Then what's with the growling?" Ellet asked.

"You're pissing me off," Porter retorted.

Ellet just shrugged before grinning at Mal. "You ever seen Porter worked up like this over a woman?"

Mal shook his head. "No. He's not usually the 'stay away from my woman' type."

"I am standing right here," Porter said through gritted teeth. "Stop talking about me like I'm not. Maggie isn't my woman. We're just friends and I -"

Another loud growl rumbled up from his chest. Across the yard, Heath had draped his arm across Maggie's shoulders and was smiling down at her. He said something that made her laugh, and Porter could feel the thick, dark beard growing on his face as jealousy ripped through him.

"Porter, go inside and cool off," Mal said.

Porter ignored him as his wolf howled angrily.

He's touching what belongs to us! Are you going to allow that?

No, Porter decided, he wasn't. Maggie was his, and if his bratty little brother thought he could take Maggie from him, he was about to learn a very hard lesson.

He started forward, snarling when Mal caught his arm. "Let go of me, Mal."

"No," Mal said. "Go inside before you do something stupid."

"He's touching her!" Porter growled.

"Heath doesn't know you like her," Mal said.

"I don't!"

"Then Heath isn't doing anything wrong," Mal said. "Go inside."

Porter growled loudly but turned abruptly and stomped toward the back door. As he yanked open the screen door, he heard Ellet say, "Doesn't like her, my ass. You can smell it all over him."

He stalked down the hallway to the empty kitchen. Restless and angry, he yanked open the dishwasher and loaded it with the dishes from dinner. He took deep breaths and tried to calm his angry wolf.

She's not ours, she's not ours, he repeated in a litany in his head. *We have no right to tell her who she can touch. Just calm down.*

"Porter?"

Maggie's soft voice made him whip around. He stared at her as she smiled hesitantly. "Do you need some help?"

Growling low in his throat, he crossed the kitchen and pushed her up against the wall. His brother's scent covered her, and his wolf snarled with anger.

"What's wrong?" Maggie asked.

He curled his hand into her soft hair and tugged her head back before sniffing at her neck. "You smell like him."

"Who?" she said.

"My brother." He winced inwardly at the sulkiness of his tone but couldn't seem to shut his mouth. "He was touching you. Do you like him?"

She frowned at him. "Are you talking about Heath?"

"Yes. Do you like him?"

"He's nice," she said. "Porter, what's wrong?"

He didn't reply. Instead, he licked her throat before

nipping it. She gasped, and he made a hard grin of satisfaction when the sweet scent of her lust immediately drifted over him. He licked her again before pressing his body against her slender one.

"Do you want to mate with him?" he whispered into her ear.

She jerked against him as her hands clutched at his waist. "Wh-what?"

"Do you want to mate with my brother?" he repeated.

"No, of course not," she said. "Why would you think that?"

"Don't let him touch you again," he said. "I'm the only one who's allowed to touch you."

He licked the curve of her ear before sucking on her earlobe. She made a soft moan that set his nerves on fire. He tasted the soft skin just below her ear as her fingers dug into his waist.

"No one touches you but me. Say it, Maggie."

"Porter, what is going on with you?"

"Say it," he demanded again.

"No one touches me but you," she whispered.

Mark her, his wolf commanded. *Mark her now, and your brother won't go near her.*

Excellent idea. He pulled her head back further and rubbed his stubble across her throat. She squeezed his waist, and he marked her again before nuzzling her reddened skin. "You're mine, Maggie. Say it."

"Porter, I -"

"Maggie? Are you in here?"

His brother's voice sent a surge of anger through him, and he stepped away from Maggie. He glared at Heath as his brother gave them a curious look before sniffing the air. His eyes widened, and he returned Porter's glare.

"You ass! What the hell, Porter? If she was -"

Growling, Porter grabbed Heath's arm and yanked him down the hall and out the back door. Heath tore out of his grip and rubbed his arm before glaring at him. "Jesus, Porter! You marked her?"

"Stay away from her, Heath!" Porter snapped.

"You were the one who said you were just friends," Heath said. "It's not my fault that you can't control your goddamn wolf."

"Don't touch her again," Porter snarled.

"Does she even like you?" Heath said. "Does she even know that you marked her like some randy teenage wolf who can't -"

His body swelling and dark hair sprouting on his face, Porter growled in outrage and leaped on his brother.

As Porter dragged Heath out of the room, Maggie stood stunned in the kitchen. She touched her throat before hurrying toward the back door. She could hear the faint sounds of growling and snarling, and she yanked open the door. She stared wide-eyed at Porter and Heath rolling around in the dirt. They were snapping and snarling at each other, and she twitched wildly when Mara put her arm around her shoulders.

"It's all right, Maggie."

"They're going to hurt each other!" Maggie said.

She couldn't believe how nonchalantly the rest of Porter's family acted. Jessa texted on her phone and didn't even look up when the brothers rolled past her with fists flying. Ellet grinned at Mal, and Maggie made a small moan of dismay when he said, "Fifty bucks on Porter."

Mal shook his hand. "You're about to lose fifty bucks. Heath joined a boxing gym."

"Shit, now you tell me," Ellet groaned.

"Mara," Maggie said. "Please make them stop."

"It's fine, honey," Mara said soothingly. "They've been doing this since they were teenagers. I have no idea what they're fighting about this time, but I'm sure they'll work it out. Honestly, it's better for them to get it out of their systems. Would you like another glass of iced tea?"

Maggie shook her head. She cried out when Heath and Porter climbed to their feet, and Heath immediately punched Porter twice in the face. Blood poured from his nose as Mal grinned triumphantly at Ellet.

"Dammit, Porter! Duck, you idiot!" Ellet shouted. "Move to the left! No, your other left!"

Mara suddenly sniffed at Maggie before giving her a curious look. Before she could say anything, Heath made a howl of pain when Porter punched him hard in the stomach. He doubled over, holding his abdomen. He growled loudly when Porter threw him to the ground. They wrestled and twisted as their growling grew louder.

"Please," Maggie said. "Please make them stop."

Mara squeezed her again. "Of course, honey. Roland, my love – break them up, would you?"

Roland gave her a look of surprise, and Mara nodded. He started toward his sons. "Bishop, a hand?"

The grizzly shifter crossed the yard, and he and Roland pulled the two brothers apart. Both brothers had grown dark beards, and Heath's body had swelled so much that his t-shirt had torn and hung in strips around his lean torso. He bared his fangs at Porter as Porter snarled again.

"Cool it, buddy," Bishop said. He held the back of

Heath's neck with one hand and grabbed his arm with the other. "Come over here and have a beer with me."

He dragged him to the far end of the yard as Roland pulled Porter toward the house. "Ava? Can you look at Porter's nose?"

Ava nodded and followed them into the house.

MAGGIE PACED RESTLESSLY IN PORTER'S LIVING ROOM. AVA had patched Porter up after his fight with Heath. Not that he needed it very much – even Maggie could tell that his nose and the swelling under his eye were already starting to heal. Despite Mara urging them to stay, she and Porter had left as soon as Ava was finished.

Porter didn't speak a word to her the entire way home, and he immediately went to the shower as soon as they walked in the door. He was still in the shower, and she tensed when she heard the water shut off. Five minutes later, he was standing in the doorway in a pair of shorts and nothing else. He was tanned and lean and, she thought a bit hysterically, utterly lickable. She glanced at the floor as he cleared his throat.

"I'm sorry about earlier, Maggie."

"That's okay," she said. "I'm sorry you got hurt."

"It's nothing," he said. "It'll be healed by morning."

"Will you – are you and your brother going to…." She felt sick to her stomach that she had caused a rift between Porter and his brother.

"We're fine," he said. "He already texted me, and we're fine."

"Good, that's good." She continued to stare at the floor,

listening to the creak of the boards as Porter shifted from foot to foot.

"Anyway, I just wanted to apologize for fighting with my brother in front of you and acting like a complete idiot. I'm not normally like that."

"I know," she said. She supposed she didn't really know that, but Porter always seemed easygoing and laid back until tonight. She shivered a little as she remembered the way he licked her throat and the rough growl of his voice when he demanded she tell him she was his.

What was wrong with her? Porter was suddenly being just as possessive and weirdly territorial as Vaughn, but instead of making her uncomfortable and frightened, it was turning her on to the point where she could barely think straight. There was definitely something very wrong with her. Why would Porter's possessiveness fill her with lust when Vaughn's only made her feel ill?

Because you know that Porter's a good guy. Because you know he would never hurt you and because you want to belong to him.

Shut up, she snapped at her inner voice. *I don't even know him. Just because he's helping me and his family is nice doesn't mean I want to be with him. Just shut up.*

"I'm also, uh, sorry for what I said to you earlier. I didn't mean it. Sometimes my brother gets under my skin, and you know…."

Her stomach twisted, and she swallowed down the sudden nausea before nodding. "Right, of course. Don't worry about it, Porter. I knew you didn't mean it."

"Okay, well, I'm going to go to bed. It's pretty early, but I'm tired."

"Sure," she said as she pulled nervously at her too-small top. "Okay. Have a good sleep, Porter."

"Thanks, you too."

PORTER WOKE THE MOMENT SHE ENTERED HIS ROOM.

"What's wrong?" he asked as she stood next to his bed.

"Nothing. I was just thinking about what you said earlier at your parents' place, about how I was yours." She smiled sweetly at him. She wore his shirt again, and she tugged at the hem of it as he stared at her. He could smell the delicious scent of her need, and his cock reacted instantly, swelling and hardening as he struggled to ignore his lust.

"I didn't mean it," he said.

"Didn't you?" she asked.

"What are you doing in my room, Maggie?" His voice was hoarse.

"I think it's time I paid you. Don't you?" She hopped onto the bed and straddled him, licking her lips when she felt his erection through the blankets.

"I said I didn't want this."

"I know, but I think you're lying. This is what you want, isn't it?" she said. "You like that I've never been fucked before. Don't you, Porter?"

"Yes," he said.

She smiled. "You want to be the first to fuck me."

"Yes," he repeated.

"I want that too," she breathed before kissing him.

He groaned and crushed her against his chest as his wolf snarled and growled within him.

Take her! Claim her now so that no other can have her. She is ours.

His wolf was right. Vaughn was only one of many who would want her innocence. He would claim her now. He would take what was rightfully his, and all others would know she belonged to him.

He tore off her shirt. She was naked underneath, and she gasped in a combination of surprise and desire when he kneaded her breasts roughly.

Enough! Our mate is ready! Take her now! His wolf roared at him.

He pushed Maggie off of him with a harsh growl and slid naked from the bed.

"Porter? What's wrong?" she asked as she stared at his erect cock.

"Get on your hands and knees."

She obeyed him immediately, and he growled in approval before touching her bare ass. She inhaled sharply, and he slapped her ass lightly. "Spread your legs."

She spread her thighs, and he stared at her wet, pink slit. He could see her swollen clit, and she made a breathless moan when he reached out and cupped her pussy. He rubbed his fingers against her clit.

"If we do this, Maggie," he said softly, "this will belong to me."

He pulled her backward on the bed until he was pressed between her legs. He rubbed his erection over her dripping slit, growling in delight when she moaned and squirmed against him.

He guided his cock to her tight entrance before gathering a fistful of her hair and tugging on it. "No one else, Maggie. No one looks, no one touches, and no one fucks this sweet little pussy except for me. It will always belong to me. Do you understand?"

"Yes!" she cried eagerly. "Yes, I understand! Please, Porter."

"Please, what?"

"Please fuck me," she said.

With a soft growl, he thrust his cock into her. She stiffened and cried out, her body trying to reject the sudden invasion. He dropped over her, trapping her between his body and the bed as she panted harshly.

"No," he growled into her ear. "You're mine now."

"Porter, wait…"

"It's too late, Maggie," he whispered. "I can't stop."

He thrust in and out of her, his breath coming in harsh pants and his wolf howling at him to claim the woman beneath him. He thrust harder as his balls tightened and his cock swelled. With a rough growl, he bent his head and sunk his fangs into the back of Maggie's shoulder as he climaxed deep inside of her.

She cried out and collapsed on the bed. Porter stared at the bite on her shoulder before lifting his head and howling in triumph. Maggie was his now, and God help the shifter who tried to take her from him. He'd kill anyone who -

He sat up straight in the bed with his heart pounding and his cock stiff as a board and stared wildly around the room. The dream was so real and vivid that for a moment, he expected to see Maggie in the bed with him. He made a harsh moaning cry as shame flooded through him. What the fuck was happening to him? He'd been so rough with her in the dream.

The soft knock on the door made him jerk. It opened, and Maggie stepped into the room. "Porter? Are you okay?"

He stared blankly at her, and she moved toward the bed. "Are you all right?"

"I – what?" he said as he bunched the blankets up to hide his erection.

"You were howling. Did you have a bad dream?" she asked hesitantly.

"Yeah," he said.

"Do you want to talk about it?" She moved to sit on the side of the bed, and he groaned and scrambled back from her.

"Don't, Maggie!" He nearly shouted at her, and she flinched her face reddening.

"I'm sorry," she said.

He shook his head, fresh shame filling his body at the look on her face. "No, I'm sorry. I didn't mean to yell. Just – I'm okay, you should go back to the living room."

"Okay." She smiled at him and nearly ran from the room.

He collapsed against the bed with his body sweating and his head pounding and stared blankly at the ceiling.

"It was only a dream," he whispered. "Only a dream. She's not yours."

CHAPTER 6

"The Roasted Bean, Colin speaking. What can I brew you?"

"Hi, Colin. It's Maggie."

"Maggie! Holy shit, it's been a week! I've been calling your cell phone every day. Where are you?"

Maggie stared out the window of Porter's apartment. "I'm at a friend's place."

"Why haven't you been to work?" Colin asked. "What's going on?"

She heard a door closing, and the tell-tale squeak as Colin sat in his office chair. She had already decided just to tell her boss the truth, so she took a deep breath and said, "I had some trouble with a guy I was dating."

"What kind of trouble?" Colin asked.

"He, um, he didn't know how to take no for an answer," she said.

"Jesus, are you hurt?"

The genuine concern in Colin's voice took her by surprise. Colin was kind, and she liked him as a boss, but she hadn't expected him to be worried about her.

"Yes, I'm okay. I just, well, I had to go into hiding for a while."

"Shit," Colin said.

"I'm so sorry," she said. "I should have called you, but I didn't have my purse or my cell phone."

"It's okay," Colin said. "I'm just glad you're not hurt. Is that why the cop's been here looking for you?"

Terror seeped through her. "Did he – what did he look like?"

"Short with black hair and eyes," Colin said. "He said you were in danger, and he needed to find you."

"That's the guy I was dating," Maggie said. "Has he been in recently?"

"Nah. He was in for about three or four days in a row, but the last few days, I haven't seen him."

"Thank God," Maggie said.

"Maggie, if this guy is harassing you and he's a cop, can't you go to the police station and file a complaint?"

"It's complicated," she said. "Anyway, I just wanted to call you and tell you I'm sorry for just disappearing. I loved working for you and I -"

"Loved working for me? Are you quitting?" Colin asked.

"Well, I thought I was – I mean, I just disappeared without saying anything, so I just assumed I was fired," Maggie said.

"Of course you're not fired," Colin said. "It's not your fault, Maggie."

"That's – that's so nice of you," Maggie said.

Colin laughed. "I'm not the dick that the employees think I am."

"I don't think that," Maggie said.

"Good. Now that I know you're alive and well, I'll add

you back into the schedule. Can you work Saturday? I need someone to cover the evening shift – three to eleven."

"Yes," Maggie said. She was sure that Porter would disagree with her going back to work, but she needed the money. She had rent and bills to pay.

"Perfect. I've got you marked for Saturday, and I'll adjust the following week's schedule. Just check the board when you start your shift on Saturday. Okay?"

"Yes, thank you again, Colin. I appreciate this."

"You're a hard worker and great with the customers, Maggie. Trust me – I'm happy to have you back. See you later."

"Bye, Colin."

Maggie hung up the phone as a feeling of relief washed over her. She still had her job. She cocked her head and listened carefully for a moment. The shower was no longer running, and her relief turned to apprehension. She'd lived with Porter for a week now, and each day grew more uncomfortable than the last. He was avoiding her.

At first, she told herself she was just paranoid, but it grew harder to deny with each passing day. Ever since the barbecue at his parents' place, he was distant and quiet. He worked nearly every night at the bar and then stayed in his bedroom until late in the afternoon. Trying to be helpful, she cooked dinner every night. He was polite and appreciative, but he ate quickly and then left the apartment. She was almost always awake when he returned from work, but she stayed on the couch and didn't try to speak to him.

She rubbed her forehead before walking to the kitchen. A pot of beef barley soup was on the stove, and she stirred it then set the table. When Porter joined her in the kitchen, she smiled tentatively at him. "Hi. How was work last night?"

"Good," he said. "That smells delicious."

"Thank you. It's almost ready."

"That's good," he said. "I, uh, I have to go to work early tonight."

Just like every night, she thought but didn't say. She tried not to stare at him as he poured himself a glass of juice. He wore his usual jeans and t-shirt. The shirt clung to his lean abdomen, and she told herself that she absolutely couldn't see even a hint of his six-pack through it. A rush of warmth tingled in her belly, and she cursed inwardly. Whatever desire Porter had felt for her was gone now. She needed to get that through her thick skull.

She spooned some of the soup into two bowls before taking the biscuits out of the oven. She placed them on the table and sat down as Porter joined her. He ate some soup, and she said tentatively, "Does it taste okay?"

"It's really good," he said. "You're a great cook, Maggie."

"Thanks."

"You know that you don't have to cook, though, right?" he said. "I can make dinner for myself."

"I know," she said. "But I like to cook, and you've been so kind to me that I want to repay you somehow."

A grimace crossed his face, and her cheeks burned as she stared at her bowl of soup. God, she needed to stop bringing up the subject of repaying him. It just made her think about her original offer to him and how he had rejected it.

So, he doesn't want your virginity. That's a good thing, right? Did you want to give it up to some shifter you barely know?

"So, uh, I got some good news today," she said.

"Oh yeah?"

"Yes. I called the coffee shop and talked to my boss. I still have a job."

He gave her a look of surprise. "You do?"

"Yes. I told him what happened, and he said it wasn't my fault and that I wasn't fired. I have a shift on Saturday."

Disapproval crossed his face. "It isn't safe for you to go back to work."

"I think it is," she said. "I need my job." She hesitated and then forged ahead, "I thought I would go to my apartment tomorrow and grab some stuff. Maybe even try staying there."

"No," he said immediately.

"If I keep the door locked and -"

"He broke down your door the last time, remember?" Porter said.

"I know, but it's been a week, and my boss said that Vaughn hasn't shown up at the coffee shop in a few days. Plus, didn't you say that Davis has been checking my apartment a few times a day and hasn't seen any hyenas?"

"It's not safe," Porter said.

"I can't keep intruding on your life," she said.

"You're not."

"I am," she said. "I know that me living here is disruptive and -"

"It's fine," he said.

"It isn't. When you're home, you don't leave your bedroom, and I know you've been leaving early on purpose."

"I've been leaving early because it's busy at work," he said. "I don't mind having you here."

He was lying. She could see it in the grim lines of his face and the way he refused to look her in the eye.

"I need to start taking care of my problems," she said quietly. "It's very nice of you to let me stay here and nice of your brother to provide protection for free, but I can't take advantage of that forever."

71

"You're not staying at your apartment," he said. "End of discussion, Maggie."

His cheeks reddened at the look on her face. "Sorry," he said. "I know you're an adult and can make your own decisions, but I think you need to stay with me for a little longer. Give it another week, okay?"

She nodded. "Okay."

She wondered if she imagined the look of relief on his face. "I am going to pick up some of my stuff, though and my car. I'll need it to get to work."

"I'll go with you."

"You have to go to work," she said.

"I'll take you to your apartment tomorrow. Promise me you won't go there by yourself," he said.

She hesitated, and he scowled at her. "Promise me, Maggie."

"I promise."

———

"You have a nice place," Porter said. Maggie's apartment was small but tidy, and it had a warm and cozy vibe to it that his lacked.

"Thank you." She studied the door to her apartment as Porter closed it. "I can't believe my landlord fixed the door already. Honestly, I was a little worried that all of my stuff would be stolen. He isn't known for his promptness in making repairs."

"Davis spoke to him last week. He can be very persuasive when he wants to be. He also cleaned up the blood in the kitchen," Porter said.

"Really? That's so nice of him. He didn't have to do that," Maggie said. "I should do something to thank him."

"Like what?" Porter asked sharply. Jealousy and anger crowded into his chest.

"I thought I might make him cookies or buy him a gift card to the coffee shop," Maggie said. "What's wrong?"

"Nothing's wrong," he said. "Why would you think something's wrong?"

"You're growing a beard," she said, "and your eyes are glowing."

He closed his eyes and took a deep breath. His wolf had surfaced the moment Maggie talked about Davis. It was freaking out over even the thought of Maggie talking to the affable lynx shifter, and he tried to soothe it.

She's not interested in Davis. Cut it out already.

After a moment, his wolf retreated, and he opened his eyes. Maggie studied him, and he rubbed at the scruff on his jaw. "Sorry. I'm a little tired today."

"It's fine."

He sniffed the air, and she glanced nervously at the window. "Can you smell the hyenas?"

"Yes," he said, "but it's faint and probably because he was in your apartment last week."

She immediately crossed to the window and opened it, fanning the air with her hands. He grinned inwardly as she peered out the window. "I don't see his car or anything. Maybe it's safe for me to -"

"You promised," he said. "Another week, remember?"

She nodded, and the anxiety rising in his belly subsided. He really shouldn't be pushing her so hard to stay with him. The last week was pure torture, and avoiding her was more and more difficult. His wolf constantly whined when he wasn't around Maggie and made it nearly impossible to sleep or think straight. More than once, Porter had considered spending time with her just to calm his wolf and allow him some peace.

Unfortunately, being with Maggie might make his wolf happy in the short term, but it would eventually make it worse. Right now, his wolf was only demanding to be around Maggie. If Porter gave in to his demands, it wouldn't be long before his wolf wanted more. He wouldn't be content with just seeing and smelling her. His wolf would want to touch and kiss.

He'd want to mate.

A shiver went down his back. The idea of mating with Maggie was intoxicating. He was sleep-deprived, irritable, and goddamn horny. Afraid Maggie would hear him in his small apartment, he couldn't even masturbate to take the edge off. It didn't help that she was immediately covered in the sweet scent of her arousal every time he did go near her.

It's fading. Each day she wants you less.

He ignored his inner voice. Not that it was wrong about her lust fading but acknowledging that Maggie's desire for him was ending made him anxious and unsettled. He wanted her very much, but even if she agreed to join him in his bed, she would only be doing it to pay her debt.

Obviously, they had chemistry, but she didn't want a relationship with him. She would give him her virginity because she thought she owed it to him, not because she wanted him to have it. That thought made him feel sick, and he jerked away when he felt Maggie's soft hand on his arm.

"I'm sorry," she said before backing away. "You looked a little pale."

"I'm fine," he said. "Do you need help packing some clothes?"

She shook her head, and he sighed inwardly with relief. Going into Maggie's bedroom with her was a terrible idea.

"I won't be long," she said.

"Okay."

She disappeared down the hallway, and he moved to the window and studied the street below. She was going to work tomorrow, and he hated it. Knowing she would be alone and vulnerable set his teeth on edge. He had considered taking the day off work so he could sit in the coffee shop during her shift, but Arlo already had the weekend off, and he needed to be there. He had called Mal while Maggie was in the shower earlier. Mal assured him they'd have someone watching her, but he still didn't like the idea.

He sighed and checked his cell phone before staring at the street again. He just had to trust that Mal would keep her safe.

———

"It's so good to have you back at work, Maggie."

"Thanks, Simone." Maggie smiled at the short blonde woman. "It's good to be back. Did you lock the cash in the safe?"

"I did." Simone followed Maggie to the door. "Is there something wrong?"

Maggie shook her head. "No, why?"

"You look tense, and you keep staring at the parking lot."

"I'm good." She waited as Simone set the alarm and then followed her outside. Simone locked the door and stuck the keys into her purse.

"You working tomorrow?"

"No, my next shift isn't until Tuesday morning," Maggie said.

"I'm working Tuesday as well. I'll see you then, okay?"

"Yes. Drive safe."

"You too. Bye, Maggie."

Maggie scanned the parking lot again. The only two cars belonged to her and Simone, and some of her anxiety eased a little. Simone was parked close to the coffee shop, and she climbed into her car and waved before driving away.

Maggie hurried to her car and unlocked it. It'd been busy today, and it was a little nice to be back at work and back into a routine. There was no sign of Vaughn, and she'd even managed to relax halfway through her shift and forget about the hyena shifter. Maybe he really had given up.

"Hello, Maggie."

The hairs on the back of her neck stood up, and she whirled around, clutching at her car keys.

"It's been a while since you've been at work. We thought maybe you'd quit."

She stared at the two men standing in front of her. She knew they were both hyena shifters, and she tried to appear nonchalant and unafraid.

"Hello, Jake," she said.

Jake smiled at her. "You look good, Maggie." He nudged his companion. "Doesn't she look good, Hank?"

"Real good," Hank said.

"What do you want?" Maggie asked.

"Vaughn wants to see you. He's been worried about you."

"I don't want to see him," Maggie said.

"He asked Hank and me to pick you up. He's waiting for you at your place. You have a lot to talk about," Jake said.

"No, we don't. Tell Vaughn I never want to see him again."

Jake laughed. "Yeah, that's not going to work. He's a little upset with you."

"He's upset with me?" Maggie said. "He broke into my apartment."

"Only because you wouldn't open the door. You can't

blame a guy for being a little upset when his mate won't talk to him."

"I'm not his mate," Maggie said. "Leave me alone."

She turned quickly and jabbed her key into the lock. She cried out when Jake's hand wrapped around her arm, and he turned her to face him.

"I'm afraid I can't do that," he said as his eyes turned yellow and glowed softly. "You owe your mate an explanation for stabbing him in the thigh and then running away. It was an insulting thing to do, Maggie."

"Let go of me," she said as fear trickled down her spine. "Let go of me right now, or I'll -"

"You'll what?" Jake leaned down and grinned at her. She moaned softly at the sight of his fangs, and he barked loud high-pitched laughter. "Honestly, I don't even know what Vaughn sees in you, but -"

"Maggie, you ready to go?"

The low voice made them all turn. A man stood behind them. He had short reddish-brown hair, and he had a pierced eyebrow and tattoos covering his arms. He smiled at them, revealing a deep dimple in his left cheek.

"Who the fuck are you?" Hank asked.

"I'm Ronin. I'm a friend of Maggie's," the man said cheerfully. "Who the fuck are you?"

"Get lost," Jake said. "This doesn't concern you."

"I'm afraid it does," Ronin said. "Maggie's boyfriend asked me to pick her up tonight."

Jake's arm tightened painfully on her arm, and Maggie gasped.

"Boyfriend?" Jake said.

"Yep, a big old wolf shifter," Ronin said.

"You're dating a wolf shifter?" Jake said to Maggie.

"Jesus, are you stupid or just deaf?" Ronin asked. He

grinned at Maggie when she moaned in dismay. "It's a legit question. Hyena shifters aren't known for their brains."

Jake bared his teeth at him before dropping Maggie's arm and pulling aside his jacket. Ronin stared at the badge hooked to his belt as Jake said, "We're cops, asshole. Unless you want to be arrested and spend the night in jail, get the fuck out of here."

"Are you arresting me for my devilish good looks or my enchanting personality?" Ronin asked. "Also, that is one shiny badge. Do you polish it every night? You polish it every night, don't you?"

"Fuck off, little birdie," Jake said.

"Charming," Ronin said. He glanced at his watch. "As enjoyable as this conversation is, Maggie and I are heading over to Bud's. Her man is working tonight and wants to see her. He won't like it if she's late. You know how wolf shifters are."

Jake glanced at Hank. "Take care of him, Hank."

"Happily," Hank said. Growling deep in his throat, he started toward Ronin.

"Not a good idea, Hank," Ronin said.

Hank lunged for him, raising his fist to strike Ronin in the face. Ronin easily blocked the blow before punching the hyena shifter in the stomach. Coughing and gagging, Hank doubled over, and Maggie watched in terror as Jake reached under his jacket.

Moving with astonishing speed, Ronin pulled Hank's gun from his waistband and knocked him to the ground. He took two steps forward and pressed the gun against Jake's temple. Jake froze with his hand on the butt of his gun.

"Don't do that, handsome," Ronin said softly.

Jake dropped his hand slowly and stood completely still as Ronin reached under his jacket and took his gun. He tucked it into his belt before holding out his hand to Maggie. "Let's go, Maggie."

She took his hand as Ronin said, "Tell your friend Vaughn to stay away from Maggie."

"You're dead, bird shifter," Jake said as Ronin backed away with Maggie. "Do you hear me? You're dead."

"You'd be surprised at how often I hear that," Ronin said. He booted Hank in the ass as he passed him. "Keep kissing the pavement, sweetheart."

Jake snarled again at him, and Maggie watched in disbelief as Ronin blew a kiss to him. "This was fun, but I know you need to get home and shine up your pretty little badge. Have a good night, handsome."

He backed across the parking lot, keeping his gaze on both hyena shifters and holding Maggie's hand in a tight grip.

"Door's open," he said when they stopped in front of a car parked on the street. "Get in, Maggie."

She climbed into the car and watched as Ronin removed the clips from both guns before placing the clips and the guns on the pavement. He waved at the hyena shifters. "Toodles!"

He slid behind the driver's seat and started the car before pulling into the street. She stared wide-eyed at him as he said, "You okay?"

"Yes," she said. "Who are you?"

"Ronin Smith." He held out his hand, and she shook it. "I work for the security company."

"Oh," she said. "I – thank you."

"Don't mention it. Give me a second." He pulled out his cell phone and punched a button, holding the phone to his ear as he drove down the dark street.

"Hey, Mal. It's Ronin. A couple of the hyena shifters showed up at the coffee shop. No, she's fine. I took care of them. You still at Bud's? Okay. Is Kat there? Good. See you soon."

He hung up the phone and smiled at her. "Feel like having a drink, Maggie?"

"I'm sorry?"

"My lady is waiting for me at Bud's. Want to have a drink with us?"

"Um, okay," she said. "What about my car?"

"I'll pick it up tomorrow morning for you and drop it at Porter's place," Ronin said.

"Thank you."

"You're welcome," he said. "So, you ever been to Hawaii?"

PORTER WAS WAITING FOR THEM IN THE PARKING LOT OF Bud's when Ronin pulled in. The car had barely stopped when Porter yanked open the passenger door and cupped her face.

"Maggie? Darlin', are you okay?"

"I'm fine," she said. The touch of his hand sent warmth through her, and she didn't object when he unbuckled her seat belt and nearly yanked her out of the car. Her legs were shaking, and she wanted desperately to hug him, but she settled for patting his arm awkwardly. "I'm fine, Porter. Really."

He pulled her into his embrace, and she wrapped her arms around his waist, burying her face in his throat.

"I'm okay," she said.

"I knew you shouldn't have gone to work," he said.

"I have to work."

"You could have been hurt," he said. He pressed a kiss into her hair and hugged her so tightly it made her ribs ache.

"Ronin helped me," she said.

Porter twitched and abruptly pulled away from her. She had a feeling that he had forgotten about Ronin. The bird shifter was leaning against the car and grinning at them. Porter cleared his throat and took another step away from her.

"Thanks for helping Maggie, Ronin."

"No problem. Do you guys need a minute alone?" Ronin asked, his grin growing.

"No, of course not," Porter said. "Come inside, Maggie. You're freezing."

The bar was busy and loud. She followed Porter through the crowd of people. A man with a round belly and a flushed face sniffed at her as she passed by him. His nose wrinkled, and Porter growled at him before taking her hand. "Stay away from her."

"Like I'd go near a human," the man muttered.

Porter led her to a booth at the back of the bar. Mal and Willow sat on one side of the booth, and a dark-haired woman with green eyes sat across from them.

Ronin slid in beside her and kissed her. "Hey, Kitten."

"Hi. Mal told me what happened. You okay?"

"Nothing I couldn't handle," he said. He rested his hand on her thigh as she smiled at Maggie.

"Hi, I'm Kat."

"Hi, Kat. I'm Maggie."

"Nice to meet you." She slid across the narrow seat until she was pressed against the wall and urged Ronin to the middle. "Here, sit with us."

"Thank you," Maggie said. She started to sit next to Ronin and gave Porter a confused look when he growled and stopped her with a hand on her arm.

"No," he said. "Sit next to Willow."

"Why?" she asked.

"Just sit next to Willow," he repeated. He tugged her over to Willow's side of the booth. Mal had already moved over, and Willow snuggled up next to him before patting the spot beside her.

"Sit down, Maggie."

She sat beside Willow, and the petite brunette squeezed her arm affectionately. "Are you okay? You're very pale."

"I'm good."

Porter studied her face. "I'll bring you a drink."

"Just water," Maggie said.

He returned to the bar as Mal said, "Tell me what happened."

"So, you told him that Maggie was dating a wolf shifter?" Mal said.

Ronin nodded. "Yes, and I told him we'd be here tonight."

"Good," Mal said.

Maggie squeezed the table until her knuckles turned white. At the time, she was too frightened to comprehend that Ronin had told the hyena shifters they would be here. "Why did you do that? What if they show up here?"

"We want them to," Mal said. "It'll be a good opportunity for them to see you and Porter together."

"But what if they try to hurt Porter?" Maggie said. She could hear the hysterical tone in her voice, and Willow put her arm around her and squeezed lightly.

"It's okay, Maggie."

"It isn't," she said. "This is a stupid plan, and I should never have asked Porter to help. Vaughn and his friends are cops! They have guns! Porter is going to get hurt, and I'll never forgive myself."

"It'll be okay," Mal said. "Porter can take care of himself, and we're here too, remember?"

Maggie didn't reply. She felt sick to her stomach, and she suddenly hated herself for dragging Porter into her problem with Vaughn.

"Don't worry, Maggie," Willow said. "We promise it'll be okay."

"Hey, Bria's here," Ronin suddenly said.

Kat leaned around him and waved her arm in the air. "Bria, over here!"

A tiny brunette wearing skinny jeans pushed her way through the crowd. She sat next to Ronin and kissed his cheek affectionately. "Hey, Ronin."

"Hey, Stripes. How's it going?"

She rolled her eyes before leaning forward and smiling at Kat. "Hi, Kit-Kat."

"Hi, honey. I didn't know you were going to be here tonight. Where's Raden?"

"At home," Bria said briefly. "What are you guys up to?"

"We're starting a knitting club. Want to join?" Ronin said. "Membership fees are twenty bucks."

Bria laughed, but even Maggie could see the strained look in her eyes. "I'll think about it."

"Maggie, this is my best friend Bria," Kat said.

Bria smiled at her. "It's nice to meet you."

"It's nice to meet you too," Maggie said.

"Are you friends with Willow?" Bria asked.

"Actually, Maggie's dating Porter," Willow said.

"Really?" Bria said in surprise. She stared intently at Maggie and didn't notice Porter approaching their table.

"Since when did Porter decide to stop sleeping around with every female that gives him a come-hither look?"

Maggie glanced up at Porter. His usually tanned face was bright red, and he placed the glass of water in front of her and left without saying a word.

"Bria, what the hell?" Kat said.

Bria groaned loudly. "Jesus, that was a stupid thing to say."

"Way to make a booth awkward, Stripes," Ronin said.

"Maggie, I'm sorry," Bria said. "Sometimes, I speak without thinking first."

"It's fine," Maggie said.

Tori bounced over to the table, her tiny nose twitching prettily as she smiled at Bria. "Hey, hon. What can I get you?"

"I'll take a whiskey," Bria said.

Kat blinked at her. "Bria, are you okay?"

"It's been a long day, and I've just made an idiot of myself," Bria said.

"Anyone want a refill?" Tori asked.

"I'll have another beer," Mal said. "Thanks, Tori."

"Welcome, hon."

Maggie watched her head back to the bar. Jealousy surged through her when Tori leaned over the bar and rubbed Porter's arm. "What kind of shifter is she?"

"Rabbit shifter," Kat said.

Porter smiled at the pretty waitress, and Maggie tried to keep her jealousy from showing on her face. She must have been doing a terrible job because Willow squeezed her again. "She flirts with everyone, Maggie."

"Yes, she does," Kat said with a glance at Ronin.

Ronin laughed. "You know I like my ladies with claws, Kitten."

Kat wrinkled her nose at him as Tori returned with the drinks. She set them down and bounced away as Ronin said, "Our new friends are here."

Dread filling her body, Maggie glanced at the door. Jake and Hank had just walked through the door as well as two other men she'd never seen before.

"Are they all hyenas?" Willow asked.

"Too far away to tell," Mal said, "but probably. Hyenas stick to their own kind. Let me out. I want to talk to Porter for a minute."

Maggie and Willow slid out of the booth. Jake's hot gaze washed over her, and she tried not to shiver. Willow took her hand and gave it a reassuring squeeze as they sat back down.

"Don't worry, Maggie. We'll keep you safe."

She was more worried about Porter, but she tried to smile at Willow. "Thanks, Willow."

PORTER GLANCED AT HIS WATCH. IT WAS ALMOST TWO, AND the bar was nearly empty. The only people left in the bar were Maggie and the others, a group of horse shifters still gathered around the pool table and two female fox shifters flirting heavily with a coyote shifter.

Well, that wasn't entirely accurate. The four hyena shifters were sitting at a table, nursing drinks and talking to each other in low voices. About every few minutes, they would glance at Maggie. His wolf growled every time they did.

He swiped the top of the bar with the rag in his hand and smiled at Tori. "Go on home, Tori. I'll lock up."

"Thanks, hon. Everyone's paid up, and I told them the bar was closed." The bounce in the rabbit shifter's step was decidedly less as she put on her jacket. "It was busy tonight."

"Yes," Porter said as he studied the hyena shifters again.

"You know those guys?" Tori asked.

"No, why?"

"They were asking about you," she said.

"What did they ask?"

"What your last name was. How long you'd worked here."

"Did you tell them?" he asked.

She twitched her nose at him. "Of course, I didn't. Good night, Porter."

"Night, Tori."

Tori headed for the door, stopping to give the bouncer, Judd, a kiss on the cheek.

"Judd, can you walk Tori to her car?" Porter called.

Judd nodded, and the two of them left as Porter said in a loud voice, "Bar's closed, folks. Time to go."

He stepped out from behind the bar and straightened the stools as the horse shifters gathered their stuff and left. The two fox shifters and coyote shifter were weaving their way past him, and Porter grabbed the coyote shifter's shoulder.

"Hey, you driving tonight?"

He shook his head. "Nah. Got a cab waitin' for us." His words were slurred, and his eyes bloodshot. "Me and my ladies are gonna fuck in the back of it."

The foxes screamed drunken laughter before pounding the coyote on the back in a mock show of dismay.

"Good night, buddy," the coyote said before putting his arms around the foxes' shoulders.

As they headed out the door, Maggie's sweet scent surrounded him. He turned and smiled at her. "Hi there."

86

"Hi," Maggie said. "Uh, Willow said I should come over here and, um, make it look like we're, uh…."

She trailed off, licking her lips nervously and darting glances at the hyena shifters who hadn't moved from their table.

"Come here, darlin'," he said in a loud voice. She took a hesitant step toward him, and he put his arm around her waist and drew her up against him. He dipped his head and kissed her. Even though he could smell her anxiety, she responded immediately. Her lips parted, and she pressed her body against his eagerly before putting her arms around his broad shoulders. Her tongue darted out to lick tentatively at his lower lip. He made a low groan and cupped her ass with one hand.

He'd forgotten entirely that this wasn't real. After a week of denying his wolf and himself, being this close to Maggie was a heady drug that he couldn't get enough of. Her anxiety had disappeared, leaving only the powerful scent of her need for him. He kissed her deeply, pushing his tongue between her lips to explore and taste as she moaned. He nipped at her bottom lip and squeezed her ass before sucking on her upper lip.

Everything and everyone around them disappeared as he kissed her until she clung tightly to him and made low noises of need that set his nerves on fire. She moaned again, and he was tempted just to pick her up and carry her to the back room. He could fuck her quickly, fuck her and claim her so that the hyenas watching them would know without a doubt that Maggie was his. They wouldn't go near her if she bore his claiming bite.

The thought of Maggie bearing his bite mark sent a wave of almost unbearable lust through him, and he crushed her against his hard chest as his fingers bit into the soft cheek of her ass.

"Porter," she whispered against his lips, "too tight."

He released her as guilt washed over him. "I'm sorry, darlin'."

"That's okay," she said. She rubbed at her ribs before peeking around him. Her eyes widened. "They're gone."

He turned and looked for himself. Maggie was right. There was no sign of the hyenas, and he frowned a little as Mal and Willow joined them.

"Where did they go?"

Willow grinned impishly. "They left about two minutes into your hot-as-hell make-out session with Maggie."

Maggie turned a brilliant shade of red as Porter cleared his throat. "We had to make it look real, Willow."

"Oh, of course," Willow said. "You did a great job. Well done. I'm grading you both an 'A' for that. You left no doubt to anyone that you have the hots for each other."

"I'll say," Ronin said. He, Kat, and Bria had joined them, and he grinned at Kat. "On a scale of one to ten, how disturbed would you be if I said I was a little attracted to Porter right now?"

"Eh, I'd say a three," Kat said.

Ronin slid his arm around her waist. "Can I just say I love how open-minded you are, Kitten? Because if Porter fake kisses like that, his real kissing might be enough to make me consider trying out for the same team."

"Shut up, Ronin," Porter said.

Ronin laughed as Bria gave them a confused look. "I know I've had a lot of whiskey tonight, but what the hell are you guys talking about? Why would Porter be fake kissing Maggie?"

"It's a long story," Kat said. "Ronin and I will give you a ride home and tell you all about it."

"Can I stay at your place tonight?" Bria asked.

"Sure," Kat said. She smiled at the others. "Good night, guys. It was good to meet you, Maggie."

"You too. Thank you again, Ronin," Maggie said.

"Don't mention it," Ronin said.

They left the bar, and Porter cleared his throat. "I'll lock up, and then we'll go home, Maggie."

"Okay," she said.

"We'll wait," Mal said. He hooked his arm around Willow's waist and kissed the top of her head. "Do you mind, honey?"

"Nope," Willow said.

"You don't have to," Porter said. "I can handle it."

"There's four of them," Mal said. "If they try to take Maggie, you'll need my help. You know you will."

"If who tries to take Maggie?" Judd returned to the bar, giving them a curious look.

"Those hyena shifters might cause some trouble," Mal said. "Maggie used to date their leader briefly, and he's having trouble understanding that she's with Porter now."

Judd made a face and cracked his knuckles. "Fucking hyenas. Christ, there ain't nothin' worse than a hyena. I'll stick around, just in case."

"It's fine, Judd," Porter said. "I don't want to involve you in this."

"I don't mind. Besides, I can't have my potential new boss getting his skull cracked open by a few hyenas, can I?" Judd said.

Mal stared in surprise at him as Willow said, "New boss? What do you mean?"

ELIZABETH KELLY

"Aww, shit," Judd said. "Sorry, Porter. I thought your brother knew."

"Knew what?" Mal said.

Porter cleared his throat. "I'm thinking of buying the bar."

"What?" Willow gave him a look of delight before hugging him. "Honey, that's wonderful! Congratulations!"

"It hasn't happened yet," Porter said. "I'm still talking it over with Bud." He glanced at his brother. "What do you, uh, think?"

Mal clapped him heavily on the back. "I think it's great. You should do it."

"Thanks, Mal. Maybe don't mention it to Mom and Dad yet, okay?"

"I won't, but you know they'll be thrilled for you," Mal said.

"Yeah, I hope so. Anyway, give me ten minutes to cash out and lock up and then we can go, okay?"

"Sure," Mal said.

Porter glanced at Maggie before grabbing the cash drawer out of the register and heading to the back office. He sat behind the desk and closed his eyes for a few seconds. His wolf still howled at him to take Maggie, and he ignored it as he counted the cash. He needed to gain control before he was alone with her in his apartment. He focused on the money in front of him and did his best to forget how good it felt to have Maggie in his arms.

`90`

CHAPTER 7

"Are you okay?" Maggie asked.

Porter glanced briefly at her before returning his gaze to the road. "I'm fine. Why?"

"You look a little tired."

"So do you," he said.

"I didn't sleep well," she said.

That was the understatement of the year. When she and Porter had arrived home from the bar last night, she was more than tempted to ask him if they could continue what they'd started at the bar. Before she could, he had excused himself and gone to his bedroom. She had tossed and turned on the couch for most of the night before falling into a thin doze around three.

Porter turned left before giving her a quick smile. "I know you're worried about the hyenas, but don't be. It'll all work out."

She appreciated the thought, but she was certain that Vaughn would only cause more trouble. She sighed and stared out the car window.

"If you're too tired to do this, we can go home," Porter said as he stopped at a traffic light.

She shook her head. "No, I want to. It was nice of Willow to invite me over."

Porter laughed. "You know she's going to ask you to help her make centerpieces for the wedding, right?"

Maggie smiled. "I don't mind. I like that sort of thing."

"Yeah?"

She nodded. "Yes. I've always had an interest in arts and crafts."

His laughter made her flush with pleasure. God, she loved his laugh.

Porter was staring in the rear-view mirror, and she frowned a little at the look on his face. "What's wrong?"

"We're being followed," he said.

She twisted in her seat to stare out the back window. "What? Are you sure?"

He nodded, and she gave him an anxious look. "How did they know where you lived?"

"They probably followed us home last night from the bar," he said.

She moaned in dismay, and he patted her leg a little awkwardly. "It's okay, Maggie. We want them to see us together, remember?"

"I remember," she said.

She had thought this would be so simple. Find a shifter to pretend to be her boyfriend so that Vaughn would leave her alone. Only, she hadn't counted on starting to feel something for Porter. If anything happened to him, she'd never forgive herself.

"It'll be okay," he said again as he turned right. He drove down the street and pulled into the driveway of a modest home with dark grey brick. "We're here."

"Are they still behind us?" she asked.

He nodded. "Yeah, they parked a few spots back. Let's go inside."

They stepped out of the car, and Porter crossed to her side and took her hand. He pressed a kiss against her forehead before leading her up the sidewalk to the front door. The door opened, and Mal smiled at them.

"Hey. Come on in."

They followed him inside. As soon as the door shut, Porter said, "They followed us here."

"Not surprising," Mal said. "Well, that's not exactly a bad thing. Willow and Ava are in the kitchen. Why don't you take Maggie there and then meet Bishop and me in the living room?"

Porter nodded, and Maggie followed him down the hallway to the kitchen. Willow and Ava sat at the table. Cream-coloured pillar candles, small green wreaths, and spools of dark green ribbon covered the table.

"Just in time!" Willow said. "We're about to start the centerpieces. Pull up a chair, Maggie."

Porter still held her hand, and he squeezed it lightly. "I'll just be in the living room, okay?"

"Okay." She tried to smile at him, and he squeezed her hand again.

"Don't worry," he said.

She sat down across from Ava as Porter left the kitchen.

"What's wrong?" Ava asked.

"We were followed here by the hyenas," Maggie said.

"We should go out there and ask if they want to help," Willow said with a cheeky grin.

When Maggie didn't smile, Willow patted her arm. "It's okay, Maggie."

"It isn't," Maggie said in a low voice. "I – I thought this

would be so simple, but now I can't stop worrying that Porter is going to get hurt. It'll be all my fault if he does, and I'll never forgive myself. I should never have involved him."

"You needed help," Willow said. "Porter was the exact right person for you to find. He has a brother who owns a security company. It was fate, Maggie."

"If Porter gets hurt…." Maggie stared at the pile of candles in front of her as Willow glanced at Ava.

"He won't, honey," Ava said. "Porter's a wolf shifter, and he can take care of himself."

"I guess," Maggie said. She sighed and picked up a candle. "So, what are we doing here?"

"You don't have to help," Willow said. "You can just visit with us while we make them."

"No, I'd like to," Maggie said. "Just show me what to do."

"Oh my God," Willow said. "I suck at this."

It was over an hour later, and Maggie laughed when Willow held up her hand. A long ribbon was wrapped around two of her fingers, and she shook her hand before holding it toward Ava. "Help me, Ava!"

Ava set aside the wreath and pulled on the ribbon. "Did you glue this to your fingers?"

"I might have," Willow said with a sigh. "Why did I think it was a good idea to use super glue?"

Ava laughed. "I have no idea. Hold on, let me see if I can peel it off."

As she picked and pulled at the ribbon on Willow's fingers, Willow eyed the centerpiece Maggie had just finished. "Damn, that looks so good, Maggie. How many have you finished?"

"This is my fifth," Maggie said as she rearranged the greenery around the bottom of the candle. She retied the ribbon in the center of the candle and eyed it critically. "Is it crooked?"

"It looks amazing," Willow said. "I've only finished one, and look at it."

She pointed to the candle, and Maggie tried not to laugh. "It's, um, unique looking."

"Yeah," Willow sighed. "We should have had Ginger come over. She's like you with this stuff – a natural."

"She's working today," Ava said absently as she continued to pick at the ribbon.

"Who's Ginger?" Maggie asked.

"She's my bridesmaid. She's a sweetheart – you'll love her. She's a nurse like Ava, and she's dating Fenton, one of the employees at the security company. Ouch!"

"Sorry," Ava said. "I think we're going to need nail polish remover to get this ribbon off."

"God, I'm hopeless at this. Maybe we should have just eloped," Willow said.

"Mara would have been heartbroken," Ava said.

"What about your parents, Willow? Do they live here in the city?" Maggie asked.

"They passed away a few years ago," Willow said.

"I'm sorry," Maggie said.

"Thank you," Willow said. "I miss them a lot. I'm happy Mal has such a big family, and they're so accepting of me. I imagine growing up in foster care, you know what it's like to be lonely, huh?"

Maggie just shrugged and grabbed another candle. She liked Willow a lot, and the tiny brunette seemed open-minded, but she didn't think it was a brilliant idea to reveal she was already halfway to obsessed with Porter and his family. Normal people didn't latch on to other people's family like that. She'd known that she was lonely, but just that one evening spent with Porter's family made her realize just how messed up she was.

"Mara liked you a lot," Willow said.

"Did she?" Maggie asked. She flushed a little at the apparent eagerness in her voice, but Willow didn't seem to notice.

"She did. All of Porter's family liked you."

"Heath, maybe a little too much," Ava said.

"Uh, I just like Heath as a friend," Maggie said quickly.

"We know," Willow winced as Ava peeled off a layer of ribbon. "It's obvious that you're hot for Porter. Did you two go home and have 'hang from the ceiling' sex last night?"

Maggie stared open-mouthed at her. "O-of course not."

"Really?" Willow said in surprise. "After what happened last night in the bar, I was sure you would."

"I – that was just, I mean it wasn't real."

"It looked real to me," Willow said.

"We didn't have sex last night," Maggie said in a low voice. "Porter doesn't like me that way. He was just putting on a show."

Both Willow and Ava grinned at her, and she cleared her throat. "What? He doesn't like me."

"That's not what Mal says," Willow said.

"Or Bishop," Ava said.

"What do you mean?"

"They're shifters, remember?" Willow said. "They can smell all sorts of things. Both Mal and Bishop can smell how much you and Porter want to sex each other up."

"Oh my God." Maggie stared at the table as Willow gave her a curious look.

"It's not that big of a deal, honey. Shifters can smell all sorts of emotions. They're used to it, and Mal says lots of times they just block it out."

"Porter is a shifter," Maggie said.

"Uh, yeah, he is," Willow said.

"That means he can smell my – when I'm…." She dropped her head into her hands. "Oh my God, I'm such an idiot."

"Of course, you're not," Willow said. "Frankly, I think it makes things much easier. Shifters don't have to guess when we want to get into their pants. It cuts out the boring small talk, right?"

"I'm so embarrassed," Maggie said.

"Don't be," Ava said. "Porter wants you just as much as you want him. There's nothing to be embarrassed about."

Maggie didn't reply, and Willow squeezed her arm comfortingly. "It's no big deal, Maggie. Really. Hey, why don't you guys go out for dinner with Mal and me tonight? No doubt those rotten hyenas will be following you, and it'll be good for them to see you on a date."

"Sure," Maggie said. "If it's okay with Porter."

"I'm sure it will be." Willow studied the ribbon stuck to her fingers. "Maybe I'll paint my nails green to match the ribbon that will still be stuck on there."

Ava laughed and stood. "C'mon, Willow, let's find the nail polish remover."

───────

MAGGIE POURED HERSELF A GLASS OF WATER AND DRANK half of it before dumping the rest in the sink. She stuck the glass in the dishwasher and smoothed her hair a bit nervously. Mal and Willow would be here any minute for their double date, but she couldn't stop thinking about what Willow had said earlier.

Porter knew when she lusted after him. He could smell it. Fresh embarrassment flooded through her as she boosted herself up onto the counter and swung her legs idly. She'd had trouble looking Porter in the eye since they'd left his brother's place a few hours ago. She supposed that wasn't necessarily a bad thing. The smell of her embarrassment had to overpower the scent of her lust for him. Right?

Of course, considering what Bria had said about him in the bar, he was used to women radiating lust whenever he was around. Her stomach tightened as she remembered the look of embarrassment and shame on Porter's face. It bothered her that he was ashamed of his past.

So, tell him you don't care.

Maybe I do.

Her inner voice snorted. *Nice try. You don't give a rat's ass who he's slept with. Besides, just think about all that practice he's had in the bedroom. I bet he eats pussy like a champ.*

Her mouth dropped open. She was utterly shocked by her dirty thoughts. She'd had three serious boyfriends before she met Vaughn, but she hadn't let any of them perform oral sex on her. In some ways, it seemed more intimate than the act of sex, and she wasn't comfortable with giving or receiving oral sex.

Maybe it's time you gave it a try. Tell Porter you'll suck his dick if he eats your pussy.

Porter walked into the kitchen, and she quickly dropped her gaze to her thighs. Her pulse thudded rapidly, and there was no denying that the thought of Porter's dark head between her thighs sent fireworks of lust shooting through her. She had a hysterical urge to fan the air in front of her and shoved her hands into her pockets.

"Maggie? Before we go out, I think there's something I should do first," Porter said.

"What's that?" she asked.

"Wolf shifters, well, they do this thing where they, um, mark their mates. It's normally only done when they're," he hesitated and then forged ahead, "having sex with a woman, but I think it could help."

"Mark me?" Her palms were sweating, and she rubbed them against her jeans.

"Don't worry, it's only temporary, and humans can't smell the marking, only other shifters. It will help convince the hyenas that we're dating," Porter said.

"How do you mark?" she asked. If she were lucky, Porter would tell her that they needed to have a quickie for him to mark her.

Is that how you want your first time to be? A quickie on the kitchen floor? Jesus, girl, I know you're hot for Porter but have some self-respect.

She ignored her inner voice as Porter cleared his throat. "Well, basically, I just, uh, rub my face against you. I know that sounds dumb, but…."

"Like you did the night of the barbecue?" She raised her gaze to him. His face was a little flushed, and his look of embarrassment eased her own a little.

Now it was his turn to look away. "Uh, yeah. Like that."

"Okay, if you think it will help."

"I do." He moved toward her, and she smiled tentatively. "What should I do?"

"Just tip your head back. I'll mark your neck," he said.

"Sure." She tipped her head back, staring up at the ceiling, and he took a deep breath before brushing the strands of hair away from her smooth skin.

"Ready?"

"Yes."

He moved in a little closer. She widened her thighs automatically so he could fit his body between them and tried to ignore the images it immediately conjured up. The counter was the perfect height. If they were both naked, he could fuck her and –

Porter made a low noise in the back of his throat that was almost a growl. Her eyes widened, and she wished she could just sink into the floor and disappear. She was suddenly so damn horny for him that her pelvis was aching. There was no doubt he could smell it.

"I'm sorry," she said.

"For what?" His voice was hoarse.

"Uh, I don't know," she said stupidly.

He bent his head and rubbed the stubble on his cheek across her throat. She made a startled little noise and jerked against him.

He stopped immediately. "I'm sorry, did that hurt?"

"N-no," she said. "It didn't hurt."

She took a shaky breath as Porter leaned in again. This time, he cupped the back of her neck to hold her steady before repeatedly rubbing his face against her throat. She tried to stifle her soft moan of pleasure. It was ridiculous to find this so erotic. He was doing nothing more than rubbing his face against her, but waves of pleasure coursed through her body, and her core throbbed dully. Forgetting he was standing between her legs, she squeezed them together to stop the ache. He made his own soft noise when her knees pressed uselessly against his hips.

His hand tightened around her neck, and he switched to

the left side, rubbing and nuzzling her skin. It burned, but the pleasure of his touch overshadowed the slight pain. When he accidentally brushed his lips across her skin, she was helpless to stop her loud moan. He made a low growl in his throat before lifting his head.

"I'm done."

"Are you sure?" She stared at him, knowing her desire was reflected in her eyes and not caring. "Maybe you should mark a few other places, just to be safe."

His eyes glowed as he said, "That's a good idea."

"Yes, a very good idea," she moaned.

"Unbutton your shirt, Maggie," he said.

Her fingers trembling, she unbuttoned her shirt and watched in fascination as his eyes shone with a fierce light. He leaned forward and brushed his face against her upper chest. She had to touch him - she couldn't stand it any longer - so she threaded her fingers through his thick hair as he made another low growl.

She had no idea if she pushed him toward her breasts or if he went there on his own, but she arched her back and made a soft moan of approval when he rubbed his stubble over the tops of them.

"Maybe just a little more," he said against the swell of her breast.

"Yes," she agreed. "Yes, please, Porter."

He reached for the front clasp of her bra and unhooked it before peeling back the cups from her breasts. He groaned at the sight of her hard, rose-coloured nipples. She moved her hands to the counter and squeezed it harshly as the ache in her pelvis grew.

"Lean back," he murmured.

She did what he asked, feeling the upper cabinets digging into her shoulder blades as he gripped her thighs and bent his dark head. When his stubble slid across her sensitive nipple, she cried out and arched her back again. She wanted his mouth so badly. She wanted to feel his lips tugging on her aching flesh. She was just about to plead for him to do it when he sucked her nipple into his hot, wet mouth.

"Oh my God!" She hooked her legs around his waist, pulling him firmly against her.

His hand cupped her right breast, and he traced circles around her nipple with his rough fingers before tugging on it lightly. He teased her left nipple with his tongue, licking its tip then biting gently.

"Oh!" She bucked her hips against him, and he wrapped his hands around her waist and pulled her flush against him. He rubbed his erection against her core. She cursed inwardly at the thick material of their jeans and made a soft mewing sound of need.

He kissed her hard, sweeping his tongue between her lips as his hands kneaded and massaged her breasts. He plucked at her swollen nipples as she moaned into his mouth and kissed him back with a fierceness that seemed to surprise him.

Aching and needy, she tugged at his shirt. He helped her pull it over his head before pushing her shirt down her arms. It pooled, forgotten, on the floor as she stared at his naked chest. Her cheeks burning, she pressed her mouth against his hard, warm flesh. He squeezed her breasts, moaning when she tasted him delicately with her tongue.

"I want you, Maggie," he rasped.

"Yes," she said against his throat before licking him again. "Yes, Porter."

PORTER'S WOLF GROWLED HAPPILY AT MAGGIE'S SOFT 'YES'. He tried desperately to calm him down. Her acknowledgement didn't mean she wanted to be taken to his bed, despite what his wolf thought.

He needed to be absolutely sure, and he was about to ask her when she nipped him sharply on the throat. His wolf howled madly at the sting of pain, and Porter's pelvis thrust helplessly against Maggie's crotch.

Mine! Give her to me! His wolf snarled.

Porter growled, a low feral sound of pure need, and picked up Maggie. She wrapped her legs around him and bit him again. He squeezed her ass, pressing her firmly against his erection before giving her a gentle nip to her shoulder.

She jerked against him, and he grinned at her. "You're not the only one who bites, darlin'."

A growl of surprise erupted from his throat when she dipped her head and bit him for a third time. This was the hardest one yet, and he threaded his hand in her hair and pulled her head back.

She gave him a sweetly innocent look. "I'm sorry. Did that hurt?"

He laughed before pressing his mouth against hers. She returned his kisses, brushing her mouth against his with small delicate touches that drove him crazy. He tried to deepen the kiss, growling with frustration when she wouldn't allow it.

He started toward the bedroom. His wolf was nearly frantic with need, and he rubbed his jaw against her throat again. He didn't hold back - she belonged to him, and she and everyone else would have no doubt of that. She made a soft gasp of pain as the rough hair teased her sensitive skin.

"Porter? You guys ready?" His apartment door slammed shut, and Porter froze at the sound of his brother's voice.

He stared at Maggie. She returned his stare with wide eyes, and he quickly said, "I – uh – we just need a minute."

"We don't have a minute." Willow walked into the kitchen. "The reservation is for…."

She stared blankly at their half-naked bodies entwined together before a wide grin crossed her face. "Oops! We got a minute."

She backed out of the kitchen as Maggie groaned with embarrassment.

"We don't have a minute, Willow," Mal said impatiently. "What are they doing in there?"

"Making out," Willow said.

"They're what?"

"Making. Out." Willow repeated as Maggie buried her face in Porter's throat.

"We aren't making out!" Porter shouted. "I was just marking her for tonight so that the hyenas know we're together."

Maggie wiggled in his arms, and he set her down. Without looking at him, she hurriedly dressed as Willow made a snort of disbelief.

"Neither of them is wearing a shirt," she informed Mal. "He's marking her all right - marking her bosom."

Mal burst into laughter, and Maggie's face flamed bright red.

"Shut up, Willow!" Porter said as he yanked his shirt over his head.

"Hey, we're all adults here," she said gleefully.

"You're embarrassing Maggie," Porter snapped.

There was silence. "I'm sorry, Maggie," Willow said.

"Uh, it's okay," Maggie said. She'd finished dressing, and she touched the bright red marks on her throat and chest.

Porter grimaced. "I'm sorry. I was too rough with the marking."

"It's fine. It's probably more convincing, right?"

"Right," he said. His cock was still semi-hard, and he turned his back to Maggie and adjusted it, willing it to go down.

Maggie's face was red when he turned around, and she stared intently at the cupboards.

"Are you ready?" he asked gruffly.

"Yes."

Ignoring his wolf's howling to take Maggie to the bedroom and finish what he started, Porter jerked his arm in the direction of the door. "After you."

"So, when are you going to tell Mom and Dad about buying the bar?" Mal asked.

Porter shrugged. "Not sure if it's going to happen."

"Why not?"

"Because Bud keeps hiking up the asking price," Porter said. "I've had three meetings with him over the last month, and each time he raises the price."

"Why?"

"Who knows. You know how Bud is." He took a sip of beer before admitting, "I got into a shouting match with him at our last meeting, and we haven't talked about it since. I don't even know if he'll sell it to me now."

"Is that what's wrong with you?" Mal asked before taking a drink of beer.

"What do you mean?"

"You've been off all night. I assumed it was because of the tension between you and Maggie." Mal glanced casually across the crowded restaurant. The hyenas sat in a booth on the opposite side of the restaurant. They made no effort to hide their presence.

"There isn't any tension between us," Porter said before drinking the rest of his beer.

"Bullshit," Mal said. "If you're trying to convince the hyenas that you two are in love, you're doing a piss-poor job of it."

Willow and Maggie had excused themselves earlier to the ladies' room, and Porter glanced at the hallway that led to the restrooms. "It's going fine."

"No, it isn't," Mal said. "Maggie might smell like you, but you're hardly playing the part of the doting boyfriend."

"Drop it, Mal," Porter said.

"All I'm saying is that it's obvious that you two like each other, so why the tension?"

"Maggie doesn't like me."

Mal laughed and took another drink of beer. "Seriously, Porter?"

Porter sighed. "Fine. She might, uh, want me, but that's all it is. She's just using me to keep her safe from the hyenas."

"Which you agreed to," Mal pointed out.

"I know."

"So, what's the problem?"

"When she approached me in the bar, she was in pretty bad shape. She was scratched up and exhausted, and starving. She came to the bar because she was looking for a shifter to protect her, and she," he hesitated, "offered me her virginity in exchange for helping her."

There was silence, and he picked at the label on his beer bottle before glancing at his older brother. Mal didn't look surprised, and Porter sighed. "How did you know?"

"Maggie accidentally let it slip to Willow and Ava. Willow told me."

"Of course, she did," Porter said. "So, you know that I turned her down."

"Yes," Mal said.

Porter studied him. "That surprises you, doesn't it?"

Mal leaned forward. "Honestly? A little."

Hurt rippled through him, and he glared at Mal. "Jesus Christ, Mal. What kind of guy do you think I am?"

"Not a bad guy," Mal said. "But even you have to admit that you're a playboy. Hell, how many women have you slept with?"

"None of your business," Porter said stiffly. "Besides, you weren't exactly a monk before you met Willow."

"True," Mal said, "but we're not talking about me. I'm not saying there's something wrong with your behaviour. You're a grown man, and you're free to sleep with whomever you want. But you've got to know that you have a bit of a reputation for," he paused, "being a little too carefree when it comes to enjoying a woman's company."

Shame burned through Porter. The number of women he'd slept with had never bothered him before. But that was before he met Maggie. Before her sweetness and her innocence had set his blood on fire for her and only her.

"I'm not a bad guy," he said.

Mal gave him a look of surprise. "What? Porter, I know that. That isn't what I'm trying to say. All I'm saying is that since Maggie walked into your life, you've been different. You're usually so easygoing and upbeat, and now you're acting like," he paused and smiled a little, "me. Maggie's gotten under your skin, hasn't she?"

Porter rubbed his forehead. "No. Yes. Fuck, I don't know. At the barbecue, I could smell Heath's scent on her, and it sent my wolf into a goddamn frenzy. He's constantly howling and whining at me to spend time with Maggie. It's driving me mad, Mal."

Mal gave him a sympathetic look. "I know the feeling, trust me. Maggie seems to like you, so what's the problem?"

"I already told you," Porter said. "She tried to bargain for my help with her virginity. If I sleep with her now, she'll think I'm only doing it as some kind of damn payment."

"Is it?" Mal asked.

"No!" Porter growled at him, and Mal held up his hands.

"Okay, okay. Sorry. So, you need to convince her that it's more than that."

"She won't believe it," Porter said.

"Why wouldn't she?"

"Why would she?" Porter said. "Bria told her that I was a man whore, remember? Why would she think that she'd be anything more than another notch in my goddamn bedpost?"

He slammed his hand down on the table. "Bria called me and apologized, but I wasn't even angry with her. She was right about me fucking anything that moves, and Maggie deserved to know the truth about me."

"People can change, Porter," Mal said.

"Maggie is sweet and innocent, and I'm not the right guy for her. She deserves someone better than me."

"Jesus, you're practically overflowing with bullshit tonight," Mal said.

"Can we just drop this?" Porter said. "I can't sleep with Maggie, end of story."

Willow and Maggie walked toward their booth, and Mal nodded. "Yeah, we can drop it. But you need to do a better job tonight of pretending you're dating her. You're not convincing the hyenas of anything."

"Yeah, okay," Porter muttered.

HER STOMACH TIGHT AND HER THROAT ACHING, MAGGIE SLID into the booth next to Porter. They'd only been at the restaurant for fifteen minutes, but she had the beginning of a headache, and she could feel tears threatening. Porter had refused to look at her since Willow caught them in the kitchen, and she could feel the tension radiating from his body. He had kept a healthy distance between them and made sure not to touch her at all as they ordered drinks and food.

She supposed it was why she nearly fell out of the booth when Porter put his arm around her. He pulled her up snugly against his lean body and kneaded her neck gently before pressing a soft kiss against her mouth. "Welcome back, darlin'. I missed you."

"I – I missed you too," she said. Her lips tingled from just that brief kiss, and she stared wide-eyed at him.

He smiled at her before moving his hand to her thigh and stroking it slowly. His fingers slipped between her legs, and for one heart-stopping moment, she thought he was going to cup her crotch. Shamefully, her legs widened, and she saw a dark glimmer of lust in his eyes before he squeezed her thigh almost playfully and then took her hand. His gaze flickered past her, and she flushed.

The hyenas. He was putting on a show for the hyenas.

She squeezed his hand and made herself smile when he linked their fingers and brought her hand to his mouth to kiss her knuckles. "Have I told you how pretty you look tonight?"

"Thank you," she said. Knowing she was being stupid but unable to help herself, she leaned forward and pressed her mouth against his again. She was just doing her part. That was all. She let her mouth linger on his and could barely suppress her moan when the tip of his tongue darted out and licked her upper lip before he retreated.

Willow nudged Mal. "Cutest couple ever."

"Last week, you said Ginger and Fenton were the cutest couple ever," Mal said.

Willow shrugged. "They've got some competition." She took a sip of wine as the server approached with their food. "Thank goodness. I'm starving."

She cut a piece of chicken and popped it into her mouth. "So, Maggie, do you believe in ghosts?"

CHAPTER 8

Porter pulled out of the bar's parking lot and headed down the dark street. It'd been two days since their fake date with Mal and Willow. He'd spent most of it in a haze of lust so deep it was nearly suffocating. There was no sign of the hyenas in the last two days, and he hoped that they had given up. He *needed* for them to give up. He couldn't keep living with Maggie. Couldn't keep pretending that he didn't want her so badly, he was nearly drowning in it.

It didn't help that her lust for him was back. It covered her and never really disappeared completely. She had made them dinner before work tonight, a sweet ritual that he looked forward to more than he should. Unfortunately, he could barely eat. The smell of her need pulsing over him in thick, relentless waves had made his appetite for food disappear. He groaned and lifted his foot from the gas pedal, letting his car slow down to below the speed limit. He was in no hurry to get home. Maggie would be on the couch, and the temptation to just pick her up and carry her to his bed was becoming more difficult to ignore.

There was a flash of lights behind him, and he muttered a

curse when the police car turned on its siren briefly. He glanced at the speedometer before pulling the car to the curb and shutting it off. He grabbed his registration from the glove box as the police officer tapped on the window with his flashlight. He lowered the window, blinking when the bright glare of the flashlight shone in his face.

"License and registration," the cop said.

Porter handed him both, and the cop shone the flashlight on his identification. The cop was shorter with black hair, but his body was thick with muscle. Porter inhaled deeply, and alarm tingled down his spine. The cop was a hyena shifter.

"Evening, officer. What seems to be the problem?" he said.

"You were speeding," the copy said.

"Pretty sure I wasn't." He knew he wasn't. He was going under the speed limit.

"Step out of the car, please, Mr. Burke."

His wolf growled softly as Porter unbuckled his seat belt and opened the door. He climbed out of the car and leaned casually against it. He was over a foot taller than the hyena, but that didn't mean shit. Hyenas were mean and vicious fighters, and he wasn't about to forget that this particular hyena carried a gun.

He studied the cop's name tag pinned to his uniform. "I wasn't speeding, Officer Bales."

"No?" The cop said. He handed Porter his identification and, keeping his right hand on the butt of his gun, moved back until he was standing next to the taillights. He studied the left one.

"Your taillight is out."

"No, it isn't."

Porter growled when the cop suddenly hit the taillight with the handle of his flashlight. The glass broke, littering the pavement with red glass. The cop's boots crunched in the broken glass as he returned to Porter.

"What the fuck, asshole?" Porter growled again. "You're paying for that."

The cop tucked his flashlight into his belt. "Tell me something, Mr. Burke. Do you enjoy taking what doesn't belong to you?"

Porter studied him silently before giving the cop a tight grin. "Vaughn, I assume?"

The cop smiled. "She's told you about me."

"She might have mentioned something about a psycho hyena who doesn't know how to take no for an answer."

Vaughn growled under his breath, and Porter gave him an impudent grin but didn't say anything else.

"Maggie is mine," Vaughn said. "Stay the fuck away from her."

"I'm afraid I can't do that," Porter said with an easy grin. "It's kind of hard to stay away from a woman when she's your girlfriend."

Vaughn growled again, and his hand tightened on the handle of his gun. "Are you fucking her?"

"That seems like a pretty personal question," Porter said. "You always this nosy about your ex-girlfriends?"

"She's not my fucking ex, dickhead," Vaughn said as his olive-coloured skin turned red. "She's my mate, and if you've fucked her, if you've taken what belongs to me, I'll rip your head off."

Porter laughed. "I'd like to see you try. You know what I am, and you also know I'll tear you apart."

"Maybe I'll just shoot you in the fucking head instead," Vaughn snarled.

Fear bloomed in his belly, but Porter made himself laugh

again. "You're going to shoot an unarmed man? Hyena shifters are all the same – fucking cowards."

Thick black fur sprouted on Vaughn's face, and he made a high-pitched yodelling laugh that set Porter's teeth on edge. "You think because you're a wolf that you can just mark my mate, and I'll walk away? Maggie belongs to me, and the only dick she's going to be sucking is -"

"Shut the fuck up!" Rage clouded Porter's head. The image of Maggie on her knees in front of the despicable hyena, even just the idea that she would let him touch any part of her, sent his wolf into a frenzy of anger. He growled as his fangs dropped, and dark fur grew on his face. "Maggie is mine. Not yours. Mine."

His body welled, and his wolf snarled in triumph when a brief look of fear flitted across Vaughn's face. Porter's fear had disappeared completely. His wolf was very close to the surface and felt no fear at all despite the gun at Vaughn's hip. He wanted to fight. His wolf wanted to shed his silly human camouflage and do what he was meant to do - protect his mate.

"What do you say, Vaughn? Are you going to shoot me like the fucking coward you are, or is it going to be a fair fight?" Porter snarled.

Vaughn backed up a step. He hadn't removed his gun from the holster, but his hand was still wrapped tightly around it. Headlights flashed behind them as a car pulled up behind Vaughn's. Vaughn grinned when five men stepped out of the vehicle and moved silently forward.

Porter's nostrils flared. They wore dark pants and t-shirts, and all of them were hyenas. He recognized two of them – they were the ones who had tried to hurt Maggie in the parking lot after work. He bared his fangs at them as all five gathered behind Vaughn in a loose circle.

"Hello, Jake," Vaughn said. "Took you long enough to get here."

Jake barked laughter. "Sorry, Boss. Had a bit of an issue at the precinct. Took Hank and me a little longer to clean it up than we thought. Need some help?"

"Of course, he does," Porter said. "Hyenas can't do anything by themselves, can they?"

"Shut the fuck up, wolf shifter," Jake growled.

"Why don't you make me," Porter said. His fear was back, and he cursed inwardly when Jake sniffed in his direction.

"He's acting tough, but he's scared shitless."

Vaughn brayed laughter. "We can do this the hard way or the easy way. Walk away from my mate, and we'll let you live. Simple as that."

"She's mine," Porter said in a low voice. At the mention of Maggie, his wolf had surged forward again, and this time he welcomed the beast. His wolf wasn't afraid of the six hyenas, and he grinned in hard satisfaction when one of the hyenas sniffed the air and squealed anxious laughter.

"Boss, what the fuck is wrong with him?" the hyena said nervously. "He can't fucking think he can take all of us on."

"Shut the fuck up!" Vaughn said. He turned his black gaze to Porter. "Make your choice, wolf shifter. Is that stupid little bitch worth dying over?"

"She's mine," Porter repeated in a low voice. "I'll kill you and your friends before I let you anywhere near her."

"The hard way then," Vaughn said.

Porter howled into the cold night air as his spine cracked and his muscles swelled. His jaw was starting to lengthen and distort, and he howled again as his wolf rose to the surface. He would kill all of the mangy hyenas, and then he would go home and claim Maggie. He would take her as his mate and –

The sharp retort of gunfire rang out and pain, immense and immediate, tore through his thigh. It knocked him off his feet, and he hit the pavement, his head banging painfully against the hard asphalt.

His wolf whimpered with pain before growling. Porter muttered a curse and clapped his hand over his thigh. It gushed blood, and when he tried to stand, his leg collapsed under his weight and drove him back to the pavement.

He closed his eyes and called for his wolf. His wolf came forward eagerly despite the pain radiating through his body. Before he could shift, a hard fist connected with his face. It smashed into his nose, and he felt more than heard the crack when it broke. Blood poured out of his nose and into his mouth, and he spit it out as the hyenas shrieked laughter.

They had surrounded him in a tight circle, and Vaughn stuck his gun into his holster before winking at him. "I've got to get back to work, but my boys here are going to show you what happens when you cross me. Goodbye, wolf shifter. I'll make sure to tell Maggie that you died like a coward."

He walked away, and the circle closed in around Porter. He heard the crunch of tires as Vaughn drove away, and he snarled at the hyenas who stood above him. Jake laughed. His fist was covered in Porter's blood, and he shook his hand lightly before nodding to his friends.

"C'mon, boys, let's make this slow and painful."

They fell on him, kicking and punching and tearing at his flesh with their sharp fangs. Their laughter deafened him as they rained blows down on him. A foot connected with the gunshot wound in his thigh, and bright pain flared through his entire body. A fist punched him twice in the stomach, stealing his breath. He gasped for oxygen, his lungs screaming in protest, and he curled into a ball as his kidneys took a heavy kick. Pain shrieked through him, and darkness descended over his vision. He fought desperately against it. If he blacked out, they'd kill him for sure.

He called for his wolf again, but the battery of blows and the pain prevented the shift from happening. His wolf snarled and fought against the bonds of his human constraints as he tried to battle his way free.

Another vicious blow to his temple and Porter's tenuous grasp on consciousness floated away like a feather in the wind. As the darkness swallowed him, he was only vaguely aware of the loud, angry roar of a predator and the terrified shrieking of the hyenas surrounding him.

THE POUNDING WOKE MAGGIE FROM HER FITFUL DOZE. SHE sat up on the couch, staring groggily at the clock on the wall. It was just after five in the morning, and fear blossomed in her belly. She hadn't heard Porter come in, and she always woke up when he arrived home.

More pounding on the front door, and Davis called her name through the door. She nearly fell off the couch and stumbled her way to the door, unlocking it and yanking it open. She gave the lynx shifter a terrified look as he stared grimly at her.

"Davis? W-what's wrong?"

"It's Porter," Davis said. "The hyenas attacked him, and he's at the hospital. Get dressed, Maggie."

"Is he…"

She couldn't bring herself to say the words as Davis gave her an impatient look. "He's alive but hurt badly. Hurry, Maggie."

Tears flowing down her cheeks, she turned and ran to the bathroom for her clothes.

PORTER'S FAMILY AND BISHOP AND WILLOW WERE IN THE ER waiting room. The fear that gnawed nervously at her belly the entire ride to the hospital turned into a rushing roar that made her feel faint. She swayed a little as Willow rushed toward her.

"Maggie! Sit down, honey."

Davis held her firmly by the arm and led her to one of the plastic chairs. She dropped into it as Willow sat down next to her. She didn't think she imagined the accusing glares of Porter's family, especially his sisters and his grandfather, as Willow put her arm around her shoulders.

"Willow, is he – is he okay?" she whispered.

Willow nodded. "He's okay, honey. He was shot in the leg, but the bullet went right through."

"Oh my God," Maggie moaned as more hot tears leaked down her face. "Oh my God, Willow."

"He's okay," Willow repeated. "They beat him up pretty badly, but Judd saved him."

Maggie stared at her blankly before glancing up. Mal and Bishop were standing next to a large man who looked familiar to her. After a moment, her frightened mind placed him. He was the bouncer at Bud's.

"Judd was there?" she said.

Willow shook her head. "Not at first. He was driving home from the bar and saw the hyenas beating Porter in the street. There were five of the dirty assholes. Not a fair fight at all."

"How – how did he…." Maggie stared at the man who had saved Porter's life.

"Shit, a few hyenas ain't nothin' for a bear shifter," Judd said.

Mal squeezed his shoulder. "Judd, I can't say thank you enough. If you hadn't been there -"

"It was just dumb luck," Judd said. "I usually take Second Street to get home, but there was construction. Thank fucking God."

"Did you hurt any of them?" Ellet asked.

Judd shook his head. "Nah, they scattered like the cowards they were when I started pulling them off Porter."

"Ava? How is he?" Bishop put his arm around the redhead when she joined them.

Ava wore scrubs, and she rubbed absentmindedly at her belly as she smiled at Bishop. "He's better. He's been seen by Dr. Wilcox, and he's already starting to heal. He has a concussion, so they'll do an MRI just to be on the safe side. They patched up his thigh. He has some broken ribs, and they think a bit of internal bleeding, but Dr. Wilcox isn't going to take him into surgery. Porter's starting to heal on his own, so he doesn't think it's necessary."

"Thank God," Mal breathed.

"He's resting right now. Mara and Roland are still with him, but Dr. Wilcox will do more X-rays in a few hours. If he keeps healing the way he is, he'll probably be released by tomorrow."

She glanced at her watch. "My shift is over at seven, Bishop. Do you want me to meet you at home?"

"I'll wait for you and drive you home," Bishop said.

"Okay," Ava said.

She leaned her head against Bishop's massive chest, and he kissed her forehead as Heath said, "When can we see him?"

"In a couple of hours," Ava said. "He's awake but pretty groggy from the pain. They're going to keep him in the ER for now because there's a shortage of beds upstairs."

"Mom?" Mal hugged his mother when Mara appeared. She looked pale and drawn with fine lines around her eyes, but she smiled at him and returned his hug.

"Hi, Pudding."

"How is he?"

"He's okay."

Maggie stared at the floor, barely feeling Willow's reassuring squeeze. The looks of resentment from Porter's siblings were bad enough. She couldn't stand seeing the same look on Mara's face. She had only met Porter's mother once, but she was already unnaturally attached to her. Knowing that Mara hated her now made her want to vomit and cry simultaneously.

"Maggie?"

Mara's soft voice made her cringe, and she stared grimly at the floor as Mara's feet, clad in tennis shoes, appeared in front of her.

She stood up and wrapped her arms around her torso to try to stop her visible shaking.

"Maggie? Look at me," Mara said softly.

She raised her head but kept her eyes closed as more tears slipped down her cheeks. "I'm sorry, Mrs. Burke. I'm so very sorry," she said.

"It's not your fault."

Her eyes popped open, and she stared in shock at Porter's mother. There was no anger or bitterness on Mara's face. In fact, she gave her a warm look of concern, and when she stroked her thin shoulder, Maggie burst into harsh sobs.

"Oh, my love," Mara said before pulling her into her embrace. Maggie wrapped her arms around the wolf shifter's waist and cried as Mara rubbed her back. "Don't cry, my love. Don't cry now."

"Why don't you hate me?" Maggie sobbed.

Mara pulled back. "Why on earth would I hate you?"

"Because this is all my fault," Maggie said. "Porter's hurt because of me and – and – and…."

She burst into sobs again, and Mara wiped at the tears that were pouring down her cheeks with the heel of her hand. "Hush, my love. It's not your fault."

"It is!" Maggie said. "It's all my fault!"

"It isn't," Mara said. "Now, stop crying. Porter wants to see you, and it will upset him if he sees you crying."

She wiped again at Maggie's face as Maggie said, "Porter wants to see me?"

"Of course, he does," Mara said. "You'll have to be quick because he'll heal faster the more rest he gets, but he's been asking for you since he woke up."

Still holding Maggie's hand, she led her into the ER and past the nurses' desk. She pulled back the curtains surrounding Porter's bed, and Maggie made a low moan of dismay. The bed's upper half was raised, and Porter sat with pillows supporting his back and neck. His face and upper body were a mass of torn flesh and bruises. He had a swollen nose, and his right eye was swelled shut and black from bruising. Roland sat in a chair next to the bed, and a nurse injected something into the IV embedded in Porter's left hand.

"A little something for the pain, Porter," she said.

"Thanks, Ginger," Porter said. The nurse patted his arm and left.

Maggie tried not to cry as Porter smiled at her. "Hey, darlin'."

"Oh, Porter," she said.

He held out his hand. "Come here."

She ran to the bed and took his hand, squeezing it lightly. "I'm so sorry."

121

"It's not your fault," he said.

Tears slipped down her cheeks. "It is."

"It isn't," he insisted. His voice was raspy, and he slowly blinked as he touched her face with one hand. "Don't worry about it."

"Don't worry about it?" She laughed jaggedly. "You almost died because of me, and you're telling me not to worry about it?"

He glanced at his parents. "Can you give us a minute?"

They nodded, and Mara drew the curtain closed as Porter patted the bed. "Sit beside me, darlin'."

She eased her butt onto the bed, biting her lip when Porter winced before grabbing his ribs. He took her hand again and stroked the palm with his thumb. "Please don't cry, darlin'."

"You almost died," she said.

"I didn't," he said. "I'm fine. I'm already starting to heal. The doctor says I'll probably be able to go home by tomorrow."

"If Judd hadn't been there -"

"He was," Porter said. "Don't think about it."

"Right," she said with another bitter laugh. "I'll just stop thinking about how I almost got you killed. Easy."

His hand wrapped around her waist, and he urged her forward until her forehead was resting against his. "Please don't blame yourself. I volunteered to help you. I knew the risks."

She cupped his face gently. "I should never have involved you in this."

He turned his face and kissed her palm. "If you hadn't, I would never have met you."

She didn't reply, and he kissed her palm again. "Will you do something for me?"

"Anything," she said.

"Kiss me."

She drew back and stared at him. "What?"

"Kiss me, please."

She leaned forward and pressed her mouth against his. She started to pull away, and his hand gripped the back of her neck, holding her firmly in place as he returned her kiss. His tongue traced her lips, and she parted them so he could slide it into her mouth. He made a low groan, and she immediately pulled away, giving him a look of anxiety.

"Did I hurt you?"

"No," he said. "I needed that."

"You need rest," she said.

He grinned at her, and her pulse thudded erratically. What was wrong with her? He had nearly died, and she'd spent the last few hours terrified for him, but just one kiss had brought her lust roaring to life.

"Lie down with me," he said.

"No," she said. "You need to heal."

"I'd heal better if you were in bed with me," he said.

She stared at him in astonishment. "Porter, you're acting crazy."

He just shrugged, and she studied him a bit closer. His visible pupil was huge, and he grinned again at her. "Climb into bed with me, darlin'. Let me make you feel good."

"You're stoned," she said suddenly.

He laughed. "No, I'm not."

"You are," she said. "You don't know what you're saying."

"Sure, I do," he said as his gaze slipped to her breasts. "Will you take off your shirt? I want to see your pretty little breasts."

She shook her head. "You need to go to sleep now."

"Stay with me, please?" he said as his uninjured eye slipped shut.

"I'd better not," she said.

"Yes," he mumbled. "I need you. Don't leave me. Promise."

He squeezed her hand as his good eye opened, and he gave her a child-like look of pleading. "Promise you won't leave me, Maggie."

She leaned forward to kiss his forehead. "Go to sleep now, Porter."

PORTER OPENED HIS EYES AND STARED BLANKLY AT THE unfamiliar ceiling. His leg burned, and his ribs throbbed, but the skull-thumping headache had disappeared. He shifted slightly and groaned.

Mal's face appeared above his. "You okay?"

"Where's Maggie?" Porter rasped.

"She's fine. Are you okay?"

"I'm thirsty."

"Here." Mal held a Styrofoam cup with a straw to his mouth, and he drank a few sips. It soothed his dry throat, and he cleared it roughly as Mal set the cup on the table beside his bed. He glanced around the empty hospital room, dull panic flaring in his belly when he didn't see Maggie.

"Where's Maggie?"

"She's at the cafeteria with Willow and Becky. She didn't want to leave, but she hadn't eaten all day, so Willow forced her to go to the cafeteria."

"Can you raise the bed?" Porter asked.

There was a low hum, and he held his ribs as the bed raised into a sitting position. "Thanks."

"How do you feel?"

"Better," Porter said. "My head doesn't hurt anymore."

"Good. You've been sleeping for most of the day," Mal said. "You've got an MRI scheduled in about an hour, but they did a second set of X-rays while you were out, and your ribs and femur are healed."

"Were they broken?" Porter asked. The events of the last few hours were still a bit hazy.

"Your ribs were, and the bullet cracked your femur. Those fucking hyenas worked you over pretty good."

"Yeah, tell me about it."

Mal suddenly squeezed his arm. "Jesus, Porter, it scared the fuck out of me when Judd called. You looked like shit when I got to the ER."

"I'm all right, Mal," Porter said.

"Yeah, because Judd showed up. If he hadn't...." Mal gave him a grim look. "I'm assigning Garth to watch you."

"I don't need a babysitter," Porter said.

Mal grimaced. "Too bad. I'm not letting this happen again."

"It was Vaughn," Porter said. "He pulled me over, broke my taillight and then threatened to shoot me in the head if I didn't stay away from Maggie. He was the one who shot me in the leg. He left and let the other hyenas go after me."

"Jesus Christ," Mal said.

"The guy is crazy," Porter said. "I could smell it on him."

"All the hyenas smell a little crazy," Mal said.

"Yeah, but this was more than just their normal madness," Porter said. "He really does think that Maggie is his mate. He can't get anywhere near her, Mal. Do you understand? If he does, he'll hurt her badly."

His wolf growled, and Porter winced when the beast tried

to push to the surface. Mal squeezed his arm again. "Hey, stay calm. You don't want to shift right now."

Porter nodded and took a few deep breaths as his wolf retreated. "Are Mom and Dad still here?"

Mal shook his head. "No. I made them, and everyone else go home to get some rest. Becky refused to leave, though. She freaked out when I told her to go home with Mom and Dad and nearly shifted right here in the hospital room."

Porter smiled a little. After Mal, he was closest to his baby sister, and he wasn't surprised that she refused to leave.

"Mom and Dad will be back after dinner," Mal said.

"Okay." Porter glanced at the door. He was anxious to see Maggie. He vaguely remembered seeing her earlier, but he wanted to confirm that she was here and okay.

"Can you text Willow?" he asked. "Tell her I'm awake and ask her to bring Maggie back."

"Sure," Mal said. He reached for his phone as the door opened, and Becky stuck her head into the room.

"Porter!" She ran across the room and climbed into the bed beside him. She kissed his cheek and put her arm across his chest, squeezing gently as she rested her head on his shoulder.

"Hey, Becks."

"Do you feel better?" she asked.

"Yes."

"Good," she said as Willow and Maggie entered the room.

Porter smiled at Maggie. She gave him a small smile in return before staring at the floor. Her face was pale, and she had dark circles under her eyes.

"Hi, Porter," Willow said. "Holy crap – you look like twenty-five percent better than you did when we went to the cafeteria. This shifter's healing thing is super damn cool."

She kissed his cheek affectionately as Maggie stood at the end of the bed.

"Thanks, Willow. Hi, Maggie."

"Hi, Porter."

"How are you?"

"I'm perfectly fine. Stop worrying about me. Just concentrate on healing," she said.

"Maggie, I -"

"Mr. Burke? I have your dinner." A woman wearing scrubs walked into the room. She set a beige-coloured tray on the hospital tray next to the bed before leaving.

Mal lifted the lid and sniffed at the food. "Ugh, it doesn't smell that great."

"He should still eat," Maggie said. "Porter, I'd better go. Your family will be back soon, and you need to eat and get lots of rest."

He frowned at her as she turned to Willow. "Do you think you could give me a ride back to Porter's apartment?"

"Yes," Willow said.

Mal shook his head. "Not alone, Willow. I'll go with you."

"Sure," Willow said. "We'll grab a bite to eat before we come back to the hospital. Porter, want me to sneak you in some real food?"

"God, yes," he said.

"I got your back," Willow said with a grin. She held out her hand to Becky, "C'mon, sweetie."

"Nope," Becky said. "I'm staying right here."

"Go with them and have something to eat, Becks," Porter said.

"I ate at the cafeteria," Becky said. "I'm not leaving."

She snuggled closer and glared at Mal when he frowned at her. "Porter needs rest."

"I know," she said. "I'm not stupid."

"Becky -"

"It's fine," Porter said. Maggie had moved to the door, and he strained to see her around Becky's dark hair. "Maggie? I'll see you tomorrow, okay?"

She gave him a sweet smile tinged with sadness. "Good-bye, Porter."

He frowned again as she slipped out of the room. Willow followed her, and Porter tapped Becky on the back. "Can you give me a minute with Mal?"

Becky slid off the bed. "Yes, but I'm not leaving with him."

"I know, kiddo," he said.

She leaned over and kissed his cheek again. "I love you, Porter."

"I love you too, Becks."

She left, closing the door gently behind her, and Porter stared grimly at Mal. "Maggie's going to run. Promise me you won't let her."

Mal studied him before nodding. "I promise."

MAGGIE PACED RESTLESSLY IN THE LIVING ROOM. AFTER MAL and Willow dropped her off, she had packed her suitcase and waited for the sun to go down. Ronin sat in a dark grey car in front of Porter's building, and she checked out the window again. The streetlights were on, and she could see his car still parked on the street. His shift would be over soon, and as soon as he pulled away, she would sneak out the back entrance of the apartment building.

Willow said someone named Fenton would be watching the building tonight, and she hoped like hell that they hadn't shown him a picture of her. She could slip down the alley between Porter's building and the next, but she would still be exposed on the street for a few minutes. It would be dark, but no doubt Fenton was a shifter and could see in the dark.

She bit her lip and considered her suitcase for a moment. She'd be less noticeable if she left her suitcase, but she couldn't leave it. That would only give her an excuse to see Porter again in the future, and that was a terrible idea. Besides, she wasn't going back to her apartment. She was going straight to the bus station and getting the hell out of the city. She needed her stuff. She only had enough money for a bus ticket and a few nights at a motel, not buying an entirely new wardrobe.

What if you don't find a job right away? You'll be homeless in a strange city.

She didn't care. She couldn't stay here any longer. She couldn't put Porter in danger anymore. Yes, he looked much better even by the end of today, and she had no doubt that he would be completely healed in a few days, but what if Vaughn went after him again? What if he shot him in the head instead of the leg the next time?

Her stomach clenched, and she rushed to the bathroom. She had eaten a muffin in the cafeteria after Willow badgered her into it, and she threw it up before flushing the toilet and rinsing her mouth. Her stomach still rolled with nausea, and she wanted to cry. If Porter had died...

Don't think about that!

Yes, it was best not to think about it. The thought of Porter dying nearly paralyzed her with fear, and she needed to get moving. She couldn't stay here any longer.

She returned to the living room and hesitated for a moment. She should leave Porter a note, but what would she say? That she was sorry, and she thought maybe she was falling in love with him? That if he died, she would go crazy?

She snorted and moved toward her suitcase. Porter cared about her and wanted to sleep with her, but he wasn't in love with her. Even if she did leave a note confessing her love, it would just make her look like an idiot. She'd only known him for a few weeks – people didn't fall in love that quickly, and the way she felt about Porter both frightened and excited her.

It doesn't matter. He'll die if you stay with him. Leave, Maggie. Leave right now!

She checked out the window again. Ronin's car was gone, and she took a deep breath before grabbing her suitcase. Time to go.

There was a knock on the door, and she screamed softly and staggered back. Her suitcase bumped against her legs, and she dropped it before tripping over it and landing on her ass with a hard thud.

There was another knock, and Willow's cheerful voice said, "Maggie? It's Willow."

Her heart thudding in her chest and the coppery taste of fear in her mouth, Maggie shoved her suitcase behind the chair in the corner before standing and moving shakily to the door.

She hesitated with her hand on the door handle. "Willow? What – what are you doing here?"

"Open the door, Maggie," Willow coaxed.

She opened the door. Along with Ava and a woman who looked vaguely familiar, Willow stood in the hallway.

"Is Porter okay?" Maggie asked.

"He's fine," Willow said. "His nose is all healed up, and the swelling in his eye is gone. It's still bruised, but that'll probably be gone by tomorrow. Oh, and his brains are perfectly fine. The MRI came back clear."

"That's good," Maggie said with relief.

"It is. Invite us in, Maggie."

"This, uh, this isn't a good time, Willow."

"Sure, it is," Willow said with a grin. She pushed her way past Maggie. "I've brought wine. It's always a good time for wine."

A tall blond man with goldish green eyes appeared in the doorway. Maggie took a step back as Ava, and the slender dark-haired woman moved past her.

"Maggie, this is Fenton," Willow said. "He's on watch duty tonight."

"Um, hi," Maggie said.

"Hello," Fenton said. "Mind if I come in and take a look around?"

"Uh, there's no one else here," Maggie said.

Fenton just stared at her, and after a few seconds, Maggie moved aside. The man moved with the grace of a large cat, and she wasn't at all surprised when Willow said, "Fenton's a cheetah shifter."

The shifter disappeared into Porter's bedroom before returning and moving into the kitchen. He reappeared after a few minutes and moved into the living room, checking the locks on the window and studying the street below him.

"Okay, I'll be downstairs. Call me if you need anything." He spoke to Maggie, but he stared at the dark-haired woman.

"We'll be fine, Fenton," she said. She patted his broad chest, and Maggie watched as he leaned down and pressed a kiss against her mouth.

"Stay in the apartment, love. Text me when you're ready to leave, and I'll come upstairs and walk you and Ava to the car. Okay?"

"Yes. Thank you, honey."

Fenton left, and the woman held her hand out to Maggie. "Hi, I'm Ginger."

Maggie shook her hand. "I think I saw you earlier in the ER."

"You did." Ginger eyed the bag in Willow's hand. "You gonna crack open that wine or what, Will?"

"Yep," Willow said.

Maggie followed the three of them into the kitchen. Ava searched through the cupboards until she found some wine glasses and set them on the table. Ginger carried a bag, and she produced a large container of cookies out of it and put them next to the wine glasses.

"I made cookies yesterday. Here, Willow, let me help you with that," she said.

She grabbed the bottle of wine from Willow and quickly opened it as Willow withdrew a second bottle. "Sparkling apple juice," she said to Ava before opening it and pouring some into a glass.

"Sit down, Maggie," Ava urged.

Maggie glanced at the clock on the microwave before sinking into the chair next to Ava.

"I thought you were having dinner with Mal," she said, "before you went back to the hospital."

"I did," Willow said. "But most of Porter's family were there, and I had plans with Ava and Ginger. We're celebrating and thought you would like to join us."

"That's nice of you, but I'm pretty tired, and I was thinking of heading to bed early," Maggie said.

"Well, at least have one glass of wine with us," Willow said.

"What are you celebrating?" Maggie asked as she sipped at the wine. It made her already upset stomach even worse, and she set the glass down abruptly as Ginger bit into a cookie.

"This morning was Ava's last shift. She is officially on maternity leave," Willow said. "That's definitely a call for celebration."

"I couldn't agree more," Ava said with a soft grin. "My back and feet ache way too much for twelve-hour shifts."

Willow set her glass down and grabbed Ava's legs, lifting them into her lap before rubbing her feet. "Poor Ava."

Ava groaned happily. "I'd tell you that you don't have to do that, but, oh my God, it feels good."

Willow laughed. "Happy to help, honey."

Ginger passed the container of cookies to Maggie. "Have a cookie."

"No, thank you." Maggie glanced again at the clock on the microwave.

"Got somewhere to be?" Willow asked.

"Uh, no. I just…"

Willow glanced at Ava. Ava reached out and patted Maggie's hand. "Honey, you know what happened today isn't your fault, right?"

"Yes, it is," Maggie said.

"No, it isn't," Willow said.

Anger crept in, and Maggie embraced it. It was a welcome change from the fear and despair. "Yes, it fucking is. It's all my fault, and it drives me crazy that none of you see that."

She glared at Willow. "Porter nearly died last night. He was shot and beaten, and if Judd hadn't been there, he would have died. You think I want to sit here and fucking drink wine with you when the man that I lo – when Porter nearly died! You're just as crazy as fucking Vaughn!"

She slammed her fists down on the table. Her wine glass

tipped over, and wine splashed across the table. She stared dully at it as Willow said, "Do you feel better now, honey?"

Maggie burst into tears. She heard the scraping of a chair, and then Ava crowded up against her. She put her arms around her, and Maggie buried her face in her shoulder and sobbed. She was so tired of crying, so damn tired of being weak, but she couldn't stop. Ava rocked her gently back and forth, stroking her hair and murmuring soft words of comfort until Maggie's tears slowed to a stop. She took the tissue pushed into her hand, and wiped her face and blew her nose.

"Oh, God, I'm sorry," she said as she stared at the large damp spot on Ava's shirt.

"It's fine," Ava said. "It's not the first time I've been cried on. Do you feel better?"

"Yes," she said. Oddly enough, she did. She had cried buckets since this morning, but the burst of anger and the subsequent crying jag had finally eased some of the tension and the nausea swirling in her belly.

"Good," Ava said.

Ginger mopped up the spilled wine. She poured Maggie another glass and set it in front of her.

"Thank you," Maggie said. "I'm sorry I yelled at you, Willow."

"Don't be," Willow said. "You needed to let off a little steam. You were wound tighter than a drum. It's good to yell and cry sometimes. Especially when you can medicate with wine and cookies after."

Maggie sipped at her wine and accepted the cookie that Ginger offered her. She bit into it before smiling at her. "It's good."

"Thanks," Ginger said.

"So," Willow said, "where were you going to go?"

"What do you mean?" Maggie gave her a cautious look.

"Before we got here, where were you planning on going?"

"I, uh, I wasn't."

Willow just smiled at her, and Maggie sighed. "The bus station. I need to leave the city."

"You can't leave," Willow said.

"I have to. It's too dangerous for Porter if I stay here."

"You think Vaughn wouldn't find you?" Willow said. "He would, and then what? You'd be alone and defenseless."

"I can disappear," Maggie said.

"Can you?" Willow said skeptically. "Not to be a Debbie-downer, but I feel like just disappearing is a lot harder than the movies make it look. Unless you know a guy who makes fake IDs and crap like that?"

Maggie shook her head. "No, but if the city is big enough, I can disappear in it."

"This is a big city," Willow pointed out, "and you haven't been able to hide from Vaughn."

"I won't put Porter in danger anymore," Maggie said. "I can't."

"He won't be," Ava said. "Bishop and Mal will have someone watching him at all times. This won't happen again."

"Vaughn's not going to give up," Maggie said. "We can't be watched forever. I can't live forever with Porter. Eventually, he's going to want to find a – a girlfriend and live his life without worrying that some crazy hyena is going to murder him."

"I think he's already found himself a girlfriend," Ginger said.

Willow grinned at Ginger. "How did you know that Porter has the real hots for Maggie?"

"He was hopped up on pain medication at the hospital.

You would not believe the stuff people tell us when they're drugged. It was rather adorable the way he was going on and on about Maggie and her perfect breasts."

Willow burst into laughter as Maggie's face flamed red. "Oh God, he didn't."

"He did," Ginger said. "His dad nearly turned as red as you are now, but Mara couldn't stop giggling."

"Mara and Roland were there?" Willow said with delight. "Oh, this just gets better and better."

Maggie buried her face in her hands as Ginger said, "He also told his mother that he was going to claim Maggie and give Mara and Roland a bucket of grandpuppies."

"What did Mara say?" Willow asked.

"She just laughed and said to check with Maggie first that she wanted to be claimed and wanted his pups."

"Do you want babies, Maggie?" Willow asked.

Maggie stared at her. What the hell was happening?

"Do you?" Willow prompted.

"I, well – Porter was high on medication." She seized onto that thought with desperation. "He didn't mean anything he said."

The three of them didn't reply, and she cleared her throat. "We can't do this forever. I need to come up with a solution that doesn't involve putting Porter in danger."

"Bren," Ava said suddenly.

Maggie gave her a curious look. "What's a bren?"

"Not what – who," Ava said. "He's a detective."

Maggie shook her head. "No. I can't go to the police. Have you forgotten that Vaughn is a cop? He's told me numerous times that they protect their own."

"Bren is different. I promise you," Ava said. "We can at least talk to him and tell him what's going on."

She scrolled through her phone, and Willow touched her arm. "Ava, are you forgetting something?"

"What?" Ava gave her a blank look.

"Vaughn saved Bren's father from being assassinated."

"He's the Senator's son?" Maggie said. "God, no. We can't talk to him."

"We can," Ava insisted. "I get the feeling that Bren isn't that close to his father. We know for a fact that he doesn't feel the same way about shifters as his father does. He wouldn't have saved Bishop's life if he did."

"He saved Bishop's life? When?" Maggie said. She had only met Bishop a few times, and the grizzly shifter was so quiet that she didn't have a sense about him at all other than that he was fiercely protective of Ava. Still, she couldn't imagine him needing anyone to save his life. He was close to seven feet tall and solid muscle. She could only imagine what he looked like when he was in his grizzly form.

"He did," Willow said as Ava continued to scroll through her contacts. "A while back, Kat's man Ronin was in some trouble with a mad scientist who was doing all sorts of awful experiments on him."

"Why?" Maggie asked.

"Well," Willow hesitated, "let's just say that Ronin has some special abilities. Anyway, there was a virus going around that was turning shifters into these terrible mutant monsters, and the mad scientist dude thought Ronin was the key to the cure. He kidnapped Ronin and Kat, and Bishop, Mal, and Fenton rescued them. Bren was kind of involved – it's a long story – and he showed up in the nick of time and saved Bishop's bacon from another grizzly shifter."

"Oh," Maggie said.

"He's a good guy," Willow said, "but maybe not the right person to talk to about this."

137

"He is," Ava said. "Listen, we don't have to tell him who the cop is. We can just tell him what's happening and ask him for his advice. You should talk to him, Maggie."

Maggie hesitated before nodding. "Uh, okay. As long as we don't say Vaughn's name."

"We won't," Ava said.

She sent off a quick text and took a sip of her sparkling apple juice. "I can't believe I didn't think of this before."

Her phone buzzed, and she scanned the screen.

"That was quick," Ginger said.

"Bren's got a crush on Ava," Willow said.

"No, he doesn't," Ava said absently. She texted quickly before smiling at Maggie. "We're going to meet with Bren on Saturday. Okay?"

"Okay," Maggie said.

"Well, I think we've had enough hyena talk for one day," Willow said. "Who wants to talk about the fact that I'm getting married in two weeks, and I still don't have my wedding dress."

"That seems to be cutting it close," Maggie said.

"Well, I have my dress, but the alterations still aren't done," Willow said. "I found the perfect dress, but as usual, my boobs were too small to fill it out." She brightened. "I ordered these fake boob things to stick in my bra, but Mal took one look at them and said no way."

Ava laughed. "You don't need to pad your bra, Willow."

"You should have seen them, though," Willow said as she stared at her chest. "They made my chest look three times bigger, but Mal was weirded out just because they were the colour and texture of raw chicken."

Ginger laughed. "Oh my God, Willow. Only you."

"It doesn't matter anyway," Willow said. "I accidentally left them sitting on the dresser, and the cats stole them and stuck them under Mal's pillow for safekeeping. Mal found them in the middle of the night, and it freaked him out so much that he tossed them in the garbage."

She took a swallow of wine. "The seamstress swears the dress will be ready in the next couple of days, but I'm starting to worry. Oh, and I still haven't decided on the cake, and the flower shop wants me to come in and look at some of their sample bouquets. I'm starting to hate my procrastinating nature."

"I can help you," Ava said. "Now that I'm done work, I have plenty of free time."

"You're the best, honey," Willow said. "You know I'm going to take you up on that, right? I meant to do all of this stuff last week, but then Martin showed up, and I was busy chasing around his ex-wife for like three days."

She glanced at Maggie. "Martin is a ghost."

Maggie cleared her throat. "You really see ghosts, Willow?" They had talked about it on their double date, but she wasn't confident that Willow wasn't pulling her leg.

"I really do," Willow said. "This one should have been super easy. Martin just wanted me to tell his ex-wife that he was sorry for all the pain he caused her in the divorce. But his ex-wife refused to believe me, even when I told her stuff that only Martin would know."

"How did you convince her?" Ginger asked.

"Luckily, her second husband is totally into the para-normal and believes in ghosts. He helped me convince her," Willow said. "But not before she called the police on me twice."

"The police?" Ava laughed. "Oh God, did you get arrested?"

"Of course not. I ran off as soon as she called 9-1-1. I've

been doing this for years, remember? I know when to get the hell out of Dodge," Willow said.

"That's true," Ava said. She yawned and then gave them an embarrassed look. "Sorry."

"That's okay," Willow said. "Are you ready to go home?"

"I think I'd better. I told Bishop I wouldn't be late, and I only had a short nap this afternoon."

"I'll text Fenton and ask him to come upstairs," Ginger said. She pulled out her cell phone as Willow smiled at Maggie.

"Do you feel better, honey?"

"I do, thanks."

"Good. Listen, I'm spending the night, so are you cool with sleeping in Porter's bed while I take the couch?"

"I – you don't have to spend the night," Maggie said. "I'm not going to leave."

"I know," Willow said. "Even if you tried, Fenton would stop you. He's got the vision of a," she paused and laughed, "cat. I'm still going to stay the night, though, so there's no point in arguing with me. I always get what I want. Don't I, Ava?"

"Yes, you do," Ava said with a small grin. "You definitely do."

CHAPTER 9

"**A**re you sure I can't get you anything?" Maggie asked worriedly.

Porter shook his head before trying to adjust the pillow propped behind his back. He made a show of grabbing his ribs and letting a twinge of pain cross his face even though it didn't hurt at all. Maggie immediately rushed forward.

"Here, let me help you." She helped him lean forward on the couch and reached behind him to reposition the pillow. Her soft breasts brushed his shoulder, and he gritted his teeth against the sensation. He inhaled deeply. Her lust wasn't there, anxiety and worry coated her instead, and he felt a moment's guilt that he shook off.

He pretended to be still hurt and in pain to keep Maggie safe. If she thought he couldn't manage alone, she wouldn't take off and leave him. His suspicions were correct about her trying to run. Willow had only just gotten there last night in time to stop her. Maggie would have disappeared if Mal hadn't asked Willow to plan that fake girls' night. He shuddered at the thought, and Maggie straightened.

"Do you need more pain medication?"

He shook his head and shifted again, giving another fake wince. "No, I'm okay. Thank you."

"You're welcome." She bit at her bottom lip. "Are you sure you should have been released from the hospital? You seem like you're in a lot of pain."

"I'm sure," he said. Maybe he'd better tone it down a notch with the wincing. Really, the only part of him that still hurt was his thigh. He had some light bruising left on his face and ribs, but they weren't even painful to the touch. He limped slightly on his thigh, but that would be gone by tomorrow. Of course, he had affected an exaggerated shuffle when he walked, making Maggie rush to help him. He refused to admit that having her slender body pressed up against his with her arm slung around his waist made him almost dizzy with the need to fuck her.

"Do you want to watch some TV?" she asked hesitantly. "I have to work in the morning, but I don't mind staying up for a while longer."

"No, that's okay. I'm pretty tired, and you look exhausted too," Porter said. "Would you mind helping me to my bedroom, though?"

"Of course not," she said. "Do you need help getting off the couch?"

He didn't, but he nodded. "Yes, please."

She planted her tiny feet, and he leaned forward as she slid her arms under his arms and linked her hands in the middle of his back. Her head pressed lightly against his chest, and he resisted the urge to bury his face in her silky hair.

"On the count of three, okay?" Her voice was muffled against his shirt. "One, two, three."

She heaved him up, putting surprisingly little pressure on his ribs. He was a bit taken back by her strength. She was small but sturdy.

"Okay?" she puffed.

"Yes," he said. "Thank you."

"Of course. Let's get you into the bedroom."

His wolf growled happily at the thought of Maggie in his bedroom. She'd slept in his bed last night. While she was busy in the kitchen, he'd gone to his bedroom to change into his shorts and t-shirt and immediately smelled her scent in his bed. His face turned red as he and Maggie slowly shuffled across the living room and down the hall. He had rolled around on the bed, rubbing and sniffing the sheets like a damn dog until some of Maggie's scent was on him.

"Porter, are you okay?" Maggie slowed to a stop.

"Fine," he said.

"Your face is kind of red." She gave him another worried look as he smiled at her.

"I'm good."

"All right," she said doubtfully.

When they were in the bedroom, she helped him sit down on the bed. He flinched and rubbed his ribs as she backed toward the door.

"If you need anything in the night, just call me," she said.

He was struck with sudden inspiration. "Actually, do you think you could stay in here with me tonight?"

Two spots of red formed high on her cheeks, and she licked her lips. "Stay here? In your bed?"

"Yes," he said. "I probably will need help in the night getting to the bathroom, and it'll be a lot easier if you're right here."

"Oh, well, I'm a light sleeper, so if you just call for me...."

He gave her his most charming smile. "Please, Maggie? The bed's plenty big for both of us, and I promise I won't do anything," he paused, "inappropriate."

The red in her cheeks grew brighter, and she stared at the floor. "Um, okay. I'll just change and be right back."

"Thanks, Maggie. I appreciate this."

She nodded and left his bedroom quickly. He climbed into bed and pulled the covers to his chest. He wanted Maggie in the bed with him because he wasn't confident she wouldn't try to sneak out during the night. Sure, Fenton was parked in the street below him, but he didn't trust that the cat shifter would see her. The best way to make sure she didn't leave was if she was in his bed with him. That was his only reason. It certainly wasn't because he was dying to have her soft warmth in his bed.

MAGGIE TUCKED HER TOOTHBRUSH BACK INTO THE HOLDER next to Porter's. It looked a little too right sitting next to his, and she rolled her eyes at how stupid she was being before studying herself in the mirror. Her cheeks were red, and her eyes were over bright. She took a few deep breaths.

Nothing was going to happen. Porter was obviously in a lot of pain, and he only asked her to sleep in his bed because he needed help. She knew that, so why were her nipples like hard pebbles against the soft fabric of Porter's shirt? Why was her pussy pulsing and throbbing like it thought it might have a chance of being filled with something hard and thick?

She shivered all over as her nipples tightened even further. She plucked the shirt away from her breasts. Maybe she should put her bra back on. She frowned. She was being ridiculous. Porter didn't want her tonight. He'd been shot and beaten two days ago. While shifters might have healing powers, the way he was limping and grabbing his ribs suggested he was in a lot of pain. Thinking about asking him to fuck her now was both selfish and stupid.

"Just control yourself," she muttered to herself as she left the bathroom and walked to his bedroom. She usually just wore Porter's shirt to bed – which, considering she had a perfectly good pair of pajamas tucked into her suitcase, was ridiculous – but she couldn't give up his shirt. It felt good to wear it. It made her somehow feel closer to him. Tonight though, she had thrown on a pair of shorts under his shirt. It felt a little too dangerous to be in his bed wearing nothing but a shirt and panties.

Porter was in bed with the covers drawn to his waist. The bedside lamp bathed him in a soft glow, and her mouth went dry as she studied his chest. His upper body was hairless, which struck her as a little funny – he was a wolf shifter, shouldn't he be hairy as hell? – and she wondered if he waxed. A giggle threatened to escape, and she covered it with a manufactured cough. Her horniness was making her act like an idiot.

"You okay?" he asked.

"Uh, yes. Just fine," she said. She slid into the bed and pulled the covers up to hide her erect nipples. She could do this. It was just sleeping in a bed beside a deliciously handsome wolf shifter who made her pussy drip just by looking at her.

Maggie! Stop thinking about that!

"Um, good night, Porter."

"Good night, Maggie. Thank you again."

"You're welcome."

He clicked off the light, and she clutched nervously at the covers before shifting to her side until her back was to Porter. She curled into a small ball and stared unblinkingly at the wall. After a few minutes, her night vision kicked in, and she could make out the laundry hamper and the dresser. Beside her, Porter breathed deeply and evenly. He was probably already asleep. She shifted onto her back and stared at the ceiling. After ten minutes, she rolled to her side again and counted the knobs on the dresser's drawers. Eight knobs – two on each drawer. She squinted at the laundry hamper as she tried to squirm into a more comfortable position.

Porter's bed was comfortable, but her skin felt too tight and itchy. Just the brush of Porter's shirt against her too-sensitive nipples made her fidget with pleasure and annoyance. She flipped onto her back again and plucked the shirt away from her breasts. She moved her legs restlessly and tried to push her head into a more comfortable position on the pillow.

Was it her imagination, or could she feel the heat of Porter's body? No, she decided, it wasn't. He had a queen-sized bed, but it wasn't like he was sleeping on the edge of his side. She stared irritably at the ceiling. He could have given her a little more room, for God's sake. She was lying right on the edge to try to avoid his hard body, and he was sprawled out like he owned the damn bed. She squirmed again. Maybe she could poke him a few times in his sore ribs. That would probably make him move.

Seriously? You want to cause him pain just because you can't control your damn libido?

She cursed under her breath and turned to her side. What was wrong with her? She had to get up for work in exactly six hours, and she would be dead tired if she didn't get to sleep soon. She kicked at the covers a little. Maybe if she uncovered her feet, she'd be more –

She let out a breathless squeak when Porter's hard arm wrapped around her waist. He yanked her over to him until her back was pressed firmly against his chest and her ass was snug against his groin.

His warm breath stirred her hair as he said, "Are you always such a wiggle worm in bed?"

She giggled nervously. "Wiggle worm?"

He nuzzled her hair as his arm tightened around her waist. "Yes, wiggle worm. Go to sleep, Maggie."

"I'm trying." She started to squirm again, but Porter held her firmly.

"Just relax and go to sleep," he said.

"Okay," she said. She forced her tense muscles to relax, and he made a low noise of approval when she softened against him. Her ass was pushed right up against his crotch, but no delicious hardness pressed against her ass cheeks. She had zero effect on him, and disappointment drowned out the tendrils of need and excitement. He didn't want her.

She closed her eyes as Porter's breath brushed against her neck in a steady and slow rhythm. Jesus, he was asleep again already. She tried to slide away from him and gasped when Porter threw his leg over hers and pinned her restless legs to the bed. He moved his arm until his hand cupped her throat gently, his forearm hot and hard between her breasts.

"Go to sleep, wiggle worm."

Being called a wiggle worm shouldn't turn her on the way it did, but her pussy was definitely wet, and her nipples were as hard as glass. Of course, maybe it was less Porter's words and more the way he had her pinned to the bed and the feel of his warm breath in her hair. She tried to move, and he rubbed his thumb along the side of her neck.

"Sleep, darlin'," he breathed into her ear.

Still no hardness pressing against her ass, and she sighed and allowed herself to melt into Porter's embrace. He didn't loosen his hold on her, and she thought she would start to feel suffocated and trapped. To her surprise, his firm grip gave her a feeling of contentment, and she closed her eyes before yawning softly. His thumb continued to stroke her skin, and she made a happy little noise of satisfaction as she drifted into sleep.

———

PORTER WOKE TO THE SOUND OF HER SOFT LITTLE MOANS. HE blinked at the bright light that shone through the window as Maggie moaned again. She was still curled up in his arms with her firm little ass pushed up against his hard cock. It'd been a real test of his willpower last night to hold her while she squirmed and wiggled against him. The only reason he hadn't gotten an erection and tried to fuck her was because he promised he would behave. Or maybe it was the exhausted look in her eyes despite the sweet scent of her need. She'd had a rough few days, and she needed her rest. His craving to fuck her overpowered his desire to take care of her.

But, fuck, she was warm and soft, and her skin was silky smooth against his. Her shirt had ridden up, and he could feel her satin thighs pressed against his rough ones. She rubbed her ass against his cock, and he groaned softly as she arched her back. He was cupping her right breast, his thumb repeatedly rubbing over her hard nipple. He felt a moment of shame for groping her in his sleep, but then her ass rubbed against his cock again, and rational thought fled.

Maggie belonged to him, and it was time she and everyone else knew it. He bent his head and marked the side of her neck. She gasped, and her eyelids fluttered open. She peered over her shoulder, blinking sleepily at him, and he smiled.

"Morning, darlin'."

"Porter?" she asked. "What time is it?"

"Time for you to be fucked."

Shit. He hadn't meant to say that. His wolf had growled out the ridiculously cheesy line before Porter could stop him. Maggie flushed, wetting her lips as desire flickered through her blue eyes. The scent of her need was overpowering now.

Quickly, before she could stop him, he tugged down the loose neckline of her shirt and tucked it under her perfect breasts. Her nipples were deliciously hard, and he plucked at the right one with his fingertips as she inhaled sharply.

"Does that feel good, Maggie?" he asked before moving to her left nipple and giving it a sharp little tug.

"Oh!" Her back arched again, and he thrust his pelvis against her ass, wanting her to feel how hard he was for her.

"Does it?" he growled.

"Yes," she whimpered. "It feels really good."

He smiled and marked her throat again as he kneaded her pale breasts and stroked her nipples until she was moaning and circling her ass against his dick. He kissed her throat, licking his way to her ear before nuzzling the soft waves of her hair out of the way.

His hand moved to her thighs, and he pulled lightly on the top one. "Open your legs, darlin'."

"Porter," she moaned. "We can't. You're hurt."

"I'm fine," he said. "Open your legs so I can see how wet your pretty pussy is for me."

She shuddered at his words, and her tightly closed thighs loosened. He took advantage of her trembling muscles and pulled her thighs open, draping her top one over his hip and hooking her foot behind his calf. He pushed his hand inside her shorts and her panties and cupped her warm pussy. She was wet. Dripping wet. He made a low growl of approval and stroked her swollen clit.

"Your sweet pussy is ready for my dick right now, and I've barely touched you," he said. Even he could hear the arrogant satisfaction in his voice, and she groaned in embarrassment before trying to tug his hand away. He tightened his grip on her, his fingers pressing against her pussy with firm possessiveness.

"Don't be embarrassed," he whispered before licking the soft spot just below her ear. "I want you wet and dripping for me, darlin'. It'll make it easier for you when you take my cock for the first time."

She moaned and squirmed against him when he pressed on her clit. "Porter, please."

"Look at me," he demanded. She turned her head, and he kissed her roughly, forcing her lips apart so he could claim her mouth. His tongue pushed into her warm mouth, and he explored her with heavy, bold licks that would leave no doubt in her mind that she belonged to him.

"Do you know how happy it makes me that the only cock you'll take in your tight pussy is mine?"

She shook her head, and he brushed his mouth against hers again. "It makes me very happy. Your pussy is all mine, no one else's. Say it."

"Yours," she whispered. "It's yours."

"Good girl," he said. He rewarded her obedience by rubbing her clit lightly. She squealed and moaned, her hips wiggling and squirming to try to find more friction.

"So greedy, my little wiggle worm," he said. "I think you want me to fuck you right now."

"Yes," she said. "Yes, I want that."

"Want what?" he asked.

She hesitated, and he pinched her clit gently. Her hips jerked against his hand, and she gave him a wide-eyed look of desire.

"What do you want, Maggie?" he repeated.

"I want you to fuck me," she said.

He pinched her clit again, and she made a harsh, desperate sound of need. "Porter!"

"You need to come first," he breathed into her ear. "You need to be very wet and ready for my dick."

He rubbed her clit, circling it with the tip of his finger before pressing rhythmically against it. Her hips rose and fell, desperately seeking relief. He smiled when her body stiffened. He couldn't wait to see how she looked as she climaxed. She would be so beautiful, so –

The ringing of her cell phone nearly jarred them both off the bed. He snatched his hand away from her pussy, feeling stupidly guilty for some reason. She blinked at him before reaching for her phone. She almost knocked it off the nightstand, and cursing under her breath, she hit the answer button.

"H-hello?" Her voice was husky with need, and his wolf made a low growl of anger. It didn't want anyone hearing her that way but him. His wolf growled again, and Porter soothed him absently as Maggie sat up hurriedly. She yanked up her shirt before throwing back the covers.

"Oh shit! I slept in! I'm so sorry, Simone. I'll be there in twenty minutes." She ended the call and jumped out of bed before running for the door.

"Maggie! Wait!" Porter said.

She stumbled to a stop in the doorway. "I'm sorry, Porter. I forgot to set my alarm, and I'm late for work. I have to go – I, I need my job. I'm sorry."

"No, I'm sorry," he said. "This is my fault."

"It isn't," she said, "but I do need to go."

He slid out of bed and grabbed for his jeans. "I'll make you a quick breakfast."

"I don't have time," she said.

"You can eat it in the car," he said.

She gave him a small, distracted smile and ran out of the bedroom.

"MAL, TAKE WILLOW HOME," MAGGIE SAID.

Mal shook his head. "No, it's fine."

Maggie smiled at him before glancing at Willow. The tiny brunette was curled up at the opposite end of the couch, sound asleep. "Willow's fallen asleep, and you both have to work in the morning."

Mal glanced at his watch. "Porter will be home in another couple of hours. We can wait."

"I'm not going to leave, Mal," Maggie said. "I don't need you and Willow to babysit me."

He studied her silently, and she sighed. "It's eleven-thirty at night. I know better than to try to leave now. Besides, Fenton's outside and you and I both know I can't sneak by him."

"You can't," Mal said. "You shouldn't even try."

"I'm not going to," Maggie said. "I promise."

"Running away is a terrible idea, Maggie."

"I know," she said. "I was just scared and feeling guilty over what happened to Porter."

"And now?"

"I still feel guilty, but I know it was a stupid idea. I'm not going to leave."

Mal checked his watch before standing. "I'm going to trust you, Maggie. Don't make me regret it."

"I won't," Maggie said.

She watched as Mal crouched next to the couch and smoothed Willow's hair back from her face before gently shaking her shoulder. She stared blearily at him before giving him a soft smile. "Hi, honey."

"Stand up, Willow. It's time to go home."

"Is Porter here?" Willow asked as Mal helped her stand.

"Not yet, but he'll be home soon."

"We can't leave Maggie," Willow said before yawning.

"She's promised me she's not going to leave," Mal said as he helped Willow into her jacket.

Willow squinted at Maggie. "Don't leave, Maggie."

"I won't," Maggie said. "I'm going to bed."

Willow nodded before yawning again. "Okay. Night, Maggie."

"Good night, Willow." She followed them to the door of Porter's apartment and hugged Willow. "I'll see you later. Bye, Mal."

"Bye, Maggie."

They left, and Maggie shut the door and locked it. She rubbed her hand over her forehead before heading into the kitchen. She made herself a cup of tea and sat down, staring into the steaming liquid.

She had a terrible time concentrating at work today. She made so many mistakes with coffee orders that Simone finally switched her to till. She asked Maggie what was wrong, and she lied and said that she was tired. Telling Simone that she was too horny to think straight didn't seem like a brilliant idea.

She sipped at her tea. She had almost fucked Porter this morning. She *would* have fucked him if her damn phone hadn't rung. Sleeping with Porter used to feel like a bad idea, but now she couldn't think of why it was such a bad idea. If she gave Porter her virginity, then that asshole Vaughn would leave her alone. It was a win/win situation.

You're in love with Porter. If you sleep with him, you'll

*never want to leave. Porter wants you, but don't kid yourself
into thinking that he feels the same way about you. You're just
another conquest for him, Maggie. He sleeps around, remember? He's never once talked about a serious girlfriend. He
isn't interested in a relationship.*

No, he wasn't. She knew that, and she had always told
herself that she wanted her first time to be special and to
mean something to her, but that was before Porter touched
her. Before he told her that her pussy was his and he was the
only one allowed to fuck her.

*So, he's good with the dirty talk, and you like it. Doesn't
mean you should give up your v-card to him.*

It'll get Vaughn off my back.

*Now you want to sleep with Porter just so that Vaughn
doesn't want you anymore? You would use Porter like that?*

He doesn't care. He's getting what he wants too.

Yeah, but –

She slammed her hand down on the table so hard that tea
slopped over the edge of the mug and splashed on the table.
She had to stop thinking about it. The back and forth was
driving her crazy.

She mopped up the spill and took another sip of tea.
She'd worked a full eight hours at the coffee shop today, and
when she was done, Mal and Willow were waiting for her.
Porter wasn't supposed to go into work today, Bud had told
him to stay home and recuperate until Monday, but one of the
other bartenders had called in sick. Arlo wouldn't be able to
keep up with the Friday night rush, and in desperation, they
had called Porter.

Willow had invited her back to their house for dinner.
After dinner, she'd helped Willow finish making the last of
the centerpieces for the wedding and helped her organize the
seating plan for the reception. Mal and Willow had insisted

on following her home and going into the apartment with her, but they'd only been there for an hour or so when Willow fell asleep.

She checked her cell phone. Porter hadn't texted her at all today. Maybe he regretted what he had said and did to her this morning. She wished he hadn't gone into work. He was still in pain last night, and she hadn't checked if he was feeling better this morning.

He felt well enough to fuck you.

God, yes. She closed her eyes and thought about how Porter touched her this morning. The raspy groan of his voice when he told her that her pussy was all his. Just thinking about it made her wet and needy all over again.

She dumped her mug of tea down the drain before heading to the bathroom. She brushed her teeth and changed into Porter's shirt. As she passed his bedroom, she paused and opened the door before peering at his unmade bed. She'd never fall asleep if she didn't take the edge off. She crept into his bedroom, glancing guiltily behind her before slipping off her panties and leaving them on the floor.

She crawled into his bed and pulled the covers to her waist. She buried her face in Porter's pillow and inhaled deeply. It smelled like him, and just his scent made her pussy throb with need. She relaxed against the pillows and slid her hand between her thighs. She would masturbate and give herself an orgasm. Porter wouldn't be home for another couple of hours. He'd never know that she touched herself in his bed.

CHAPTER 10

Porter slipped silently into the apartment. The bar was surprisingly slow for a Friday night, and Arlo had encouraged him to go home early. He suspected Arlo's urging to go home was a combination of guilt for calling him in when he was supposed to be recuperating and irritation at Porter's inability to make a correct drink all night. His need for Maggie and his urge to claim her was all he could think about. He wondered for a moment if he was going insane. It certainly felt like he was.

His mind had wandered repeatedly to this morning when he had nearly taken Maggie's innocence. He should have felt guilty about it, he should have been berating himself for losing control, but instead, both he and his wolf were dying to finish what they'd started.

He sighed and kicked off his boots before hanging his jacket in the closet. Mal had texted him just before leaving the bar to let him know that he and Willow were headed home. Maggie had promised his brother she wouldn't leave the apartment, but just knowing that she was alone had Porter quickly agreeing when Arlo told him for the third time to go home. It wasn't that he didn't trust her. He just worried that her guilt over what happened to him would overpower her common sense.

He deliberately avoided looking at the couch as he crept through the living room and toward the bedroom. If he saw her lying there, he would take what was his.

He swallowed thickly and moved to his bedroom. The door was open, and he frowned a little. He was sure he had shut it before he left. He usually tried to keep Maggie's scent out of his room, although he had fucked that up royally this morning. Surprisingly, he could still smell her in his room, could still clearly scent her arousal. His wolf began to growl.

Go back and take her. Give me my mate!

He'd turned back to the living room when he heard her soft moan of need from his room. His cock hardened in response as he quickly entered his bedroom. His jaw dropped, his wolf howled, and he stared in stunned silence at the bed. The room was dark, but he could see Maggie clearly. She was lying in his bed, the covers pushed down to her waist, and her eyes closed. As he watched, she made another soft little moan. He nearly came in his jeans when her back arched, and she uttered a gasp of pleasure.

She was touching herself. She was lying in his bed, and she was touching herself. His wolf snarled at him, angry that his mate was forced to find her own pleasure. Porter stripped off his shirt.

His wolf was right. Maggie was his, and he wasn't going to stand by and watch as she used her fingers to come all over his bed. Not that he minded the idea of her sweet cream marking his sheets, but he wanted to be the one to bring her there.

As she arched her back again, he moved toward the bed. "Hello, Maggie."

She screamed breathlessly and yanked her hands out from under the covers, fumbling for the bedside lamp as he stood at the end of the bed.

"Porter, wh-what are you doing home?" She gave him a guilty look as he smiled lazily at her.

"It was slow at work. I came home early."

"Oh. Do you – are you feeling better?"

"Completely healed," he said. "Why are you in my bed?"

She turned bright red and grabbed for the covers when he pulled them off of her with a hard yank. She wore just his shirt, and she tugged it down nervously before sitting up.

"I wasn't feeling well, and your bed was more comfortable than the couch, so I thought I would lie down in it for a while."

"Is that right?" His eyes glowed in the dim light of the lamp, and she stared wide-eyed at him.

"Y-yes. What are you doing, Porter?"

He crawled up the bed. He stopped at her tightly closed thighs and bent his head to her crotch. He inhaled deeply, and she blushed furiously when he gave her a knowing smile.

"I should go," she said as he straddled her thighs and rested his hands on the headboard. She was trapped between his arms, and she gave him another look of embarrassment.

"What were you doing in my bed, darlin'?" he asked.

"I – nothing."

"That isn't true, is it?" he growled.

Before she could stop him, he took her hand. She moaned when he slipped her first two fingers into his mouth and sucked on them.

"Porter…"

"So sweet," he growled. "Tell me what you were doing."

"I – I was touching myself," she said.

"Were you thinking about me?"

"Yes." She licked her lips. "I was pretending it was your hand touching me."

"That's unfortunate. I'm not putting my hand between those soft thighs."

"I really should go now, Porter. I'm sorry." Disappointment mixed with embarrassment crossed her face and she struggled to get out from under him.

She squeaked in alarm when he abruptly pulled her shirt over her head. She crossed her arms over her naked breasts. "What are you doing? You – you don't want me."

"That's not true." He bent his head and marked her neck roughly before brushing his mouth against hers. "I said I wouldn't use my hand, darlin'."

She continued to stare at him blankly, and he wanted to smile at her innocence. Her confusion told him what he wanted to know, and he used his knee to push her thighs apart. "My mouth, though, it wants to be all over your sweet pussy."

She moaned, and he grinned at her. "Have you had a tongue in your pussy, Maggie?"

He knew the answer, but he wanted her to say it. He wanted to hear that he would be the only one who would ever taste her sweetness.

"No," she whispered.

"Do you want my tongue in your pussy?"

She nodded, and he kissed her again. "Say it."

"I can't."

"Yes, you can."

She hesitated and then whispered, "I – I want your tongue in my pussy, Porter."

"Good girl," he murmured approvingly. "Move your arms."

After a moment's hesitation, she dropped her arms. He

pushed her onto her back and stared at her breasts. Her nipples were hard, and she shuddered all over when he bent his head and took one into his mouth. He sucked firmly, his hands stroking her ribs and then her hips as she squirmed under him and clutched at his head. When both nipples were swollen and red from his mouth, and she made loud moans of need, he kissed his way down her stomach. He nibbled and licked her soft skin as he pushed his large body between her thighs.

He used his shoulders to push her thighs apart further, kissing the top of one soothingly when she visibly tensed. He stared at her warm core. She was waxed smooth with just a small patch of dark hair at the top of her sex. The lips of her pussy were swollen and wet, and he could see the tiny pink bud of her clit peeking out between them. He marked her inner thighs roughly, kissing the burn away when she gasped.

"Porter, I -"

He could hear the nerves in her voice and knew instinctively that she was about to call a stop to this. He licked her swollen sex slowly. She cried out as her entire body twitched, and she dug her hands into the sheets.

He licked her again, this time letting his tongue linger on her swollen clit. He growled happily when a surge of wetness coated his mouth, and she made a sharp, hungry cry of need. He pulled back and waited. After only a few seconds, her hands touched his head, and her pelvis arched upward.

"Porter, please," she moaned.

"Look at me, Maggie," he demanded.

Her eyelids fluttered open, and she gave him a hazy look of desire. Keeping his eyes on her face, he leaned down and placed a light kiss on the top of her pussy.

"Mine," he said in a slow and deliberate voice.

She flushed and pressed her hands against the back of his skull in a silent plea.

"Say it, Maggie."

"Yours," she said.

"Again."

"Yours. Please, Porter," she begged.

He marked the top of her pussy. His wolf growled with satisfaction at the red mark it left on her pale skin before he marked both her inner thighs again. Her fingers were curling and uncurling at her sides, and he pushed the wet lips of her pussy apart with his thumbs. He stared at her exposed clit as his wolf howled with delight. He licked her swollen clit with a slow sweep of his tongue. She moaned breathlessly, her thighs first tightening around his shoulders and then loosening as he sucked on her sensitive clit.

"OH!" Her hips arched, and her hands threaded through his thick hair and yanked almost painfully.

Moaning his name repeatedly, she thrust her pelvis against him as he slid one thick finger into her tight opening. She tensed, her thighs pushing against his broad shoulders, and he sucked her clit until the tension was gone from her body and her thighs were splayed apart. He moved his finger in a gentle back and forth motion and licked and sucked at her swollen button until her entire body arched off the bed, and she screamed in pleasure. He licked away her cream and stroked her thigh soothingly until she collapsed, trembling against the bed.

"Porter?" she whispered when he started to drop small kisses on her knees.

"Yes, Maggie?"

"Wh-what are you doing? Aren't you going to come up here and – I mean - shouldn't we be…"

He grinned wickedly at her. "I'm going to fuck you, darlin'. But I'm not done with your sweet pussy yet."

She shivered all over and moaned when he licked her warm core.

"I can't – I can't have another one like that," she said. "Not right away."

"I think you can." He massaged the inside of her thighs before marking them again. "Besides," he cupped her pussy possessively, "this belongs to me, remember?"

She didn't reply, and he rubbed her clit with his thumb, ignoring her squirms of protest until she was moaning her need to him and making soft, muttered pleas.

"Maggie," he said quietly.

"I remember!" she cried out. "Just please, Porter! I need you!"

"I know, darlin'." His wolf growled with satisfaction as he bent his dark head between her thighs once more.

Porter settled his body over Maggie's nearly twenty minutes later and marked her throat. She was trembling and panting beneath him, and he groaned when his cock brushed against her wet pussy. His dick was so hard it hurt, and his wolf howled at him to take the woman beneath him.

Wait! Just wait! he snapped and leaned down to kiss Maggie's mouth.

She returned his kiss and gave him a dreamy, contented look. "I came so many times, Porter. I feel really good."

A grin crossed his lips as he stared down at the blissful face of his mate. "I'm glad, darlin'." He stroked a strand of hair back from her face. "I want to fuck you, Maggie."

"I want that too," she said.

"Are you sure? Absolutely sure?" he asked.

She nodded and touched his face lightly. "This is exactly what I want."

He shifted against her, letting the head of his cock probe against her opening, and she spread her thighs eagerly and arched her pelvis. He groaned loudly. He needed to put a condom on before he went any further. If he didn't –

She is our mate. Put our pup in her belly. It's what she wants, his wolf growled persuasively

He stiffened against her as Maggie rubbed her hands across his chest and biceps.

Show the hyena shifter that she is ours. He won't take her from us if she carries our pup in her belly.

His eyes glowed at the thought of the hyena shifter taking Maggie from him. His wolf was right. Maggie belonged to him, and she should be carrying his pup. He would fuck her again and again until her scent changed, and he was sure she was pregnant.

"Porter?" He jerked at the sound of Maggie's worried voice, and she made a soft cry of surprise when the head of his cock pushed into her.

"Jesus," he muttered as she touched his face tentatively.

"Do you have a condom?" she asked almost timidly.

His face reddened. He didn't move, just stared down at her, and she gave him an embarrassed look.

"I'm sorry. I'm not on the pill, and well, you know, safe sex is um, important, right?" she said.

He twitched and pulled away. "Yes, of course. I'm sorry, darlin'. Just give me a minute."

He sat on the side of the bed and pulled a condom from the top drawer of the bedside table. He tore open the package and rolled it on quickly before moving between her thighs again.

He must have had an odd look on his face because she swallowed nervously. "Porter, is something wrong?"

"No, not at all." He shook his head. "Everything's fine, Maggie."

"Are you sure? You look a little upset."

He smiled at her. "Just feel incredibly stupid for nearly forgetting to use a condom."

"That's okay." She rubbed his chest. "We're good now."

"Yes, we are." He kissed her firmly and then sucked on her bottom lip as she ran her hands over his warm back and pressed her pelvis against his.

"Are you ready, Maggie?" He cupped one breast and stroked her nipple with his rough thumb. His cock was back at her opening, and she spread her thighs and braced her feet on the bed before nodding at him.

He hesitated as doubt crept in. What if she thought he was doing this as payment for protecting her?

"Do it, Porter. Make me yours," Maggie said.

MAGGIE COULD SEE THE HESITATION AND DOUBT ON PORTER'S face as the head of his cock rested against her entrance. She suddenly knew with certainty that he was going to stop. She could see it in his face and feel it in the way his body started to withdraw from hers. Her pussy clenched at the thought of being denied and feeling anxious and needy, she pressed her mouth against his ear and said the one thing she knew would make him continue.

"Do it, Porter. Make me yours."

He growled, his eyes glowing in the darkness, and there was a sharp pinch as he pushed smoothly into her. She tensed and waited for the pain, but there was none. It felt a little strange, she decided. There was an unfamiliar and uncomfortable feeling of fullness, but already the discomfort was fading as her inner walls stretched to accommodate him.

"Maggie? Are you all right?"

Porter stared worriedly at her, and she smiled and touched his face. "Yes, it doesn't hurt."

"Are you sure? I can stop."

She smiled again. The look of almost desperate need on his face said otherwise, and she felt an odd trickle of power ripple through her.

"I don't want to stop." She moved experimentally under him, and his breath hissed out between his teeth. She could see his fangs, and she stared fascinated at them as he moved in and out of her in a slow, steady rhythm.

"Does it feel good for you, Porter?" she asked a little shyly.

He groaned. "So good, darlin'. You feel so fucking good."

That ripple of power went through her again, and she rested her hands on his hips. "Harder."

"Yes, harder," he muttered. He moved faster, the bed squeaking and the headboard banging rhythmically against the wall as a thick beard grew on his face. Maggie watched in fascination as he panted harshly and trembled above her. There was a feeling of warmth within her but nothing else. She was almost glad about that. She wanted to watch Porter come, wanted to see what her body could do to him and witness his loss of control.

She twitched and gasped when he pushed his hand between their sweaty bodies and rubbed her clit. It was still swollen and sensitive from his tongue and lips, and she cried out as the warmth within her turned into a blazing out-of-control burn.

"Porter!" She shouted his name, her hips rising and falling against his as he rubbed her clit and fucked her hard.

She screamed his name again as she came, and her pussy tightened around him. He called her name, and she opened her eyes to see his fangs distended from his mouth and his eyes turned a bright, vivid jade. He was staring at her shoulder, and she watched in shock when he suddenly turned his head and plunged his fangs into the soft meat of his arm.

PORTER'S WOLF HOWLED WITH RAGE WHEN HE SANK HIS fangs into his arm instead of Maggie's soft flesh. He tore his mouth free and howled hoarsely as he came deep inside of her warmth. Blood poured out of his arm, splashing onto the bedsheets and Maggie's pale flesh as he shuddered wildly before collapsing against her.

His wolf snarled at him. The primal need to claim Maggie still raged through him, and he fought bitterly against the shift as his wolf tried to break free. He wanted to bite Maggie and mark her as their mate forever. More hair sprouted on Porter's cheeks and forehead, and he was only dimly aware of Maggie's frightened cry.

He rolled off of her and curled on his side with his back to her. His fingernails dug into the palms of his hands, and he made a series of harsh barks as his body shuddered. Little by little, he took back control, and his wolf retreated, snarling and growling with anger.

"Porter?" Maggie's frightened voice made guilt course through him. He sat up and gave her a look of shame.

"Darlin', I'm so sorry. I didn't mean to scare you."

She sat up next to him and shook her head. "You didn't scare me."

She was lying. He could smell the fear on her.

"Please don't be frightened of me," he begged in a low voice. "I would never hurt you."

"I know you won't," she said.

He reached tentatively for her hand, relief flooding through him when she didn't flinch away. She squeezed his hand tightly. "You're bleeding badly."

"It'll stop soon," he said.

She shook her head. "Wait here for a minute."

She climbed out of bed and left the room. He disposed of the condom and then pressed the sheet against the bite in his arm. Maggie returned carrying the first-aid kit from the bathroom and climbed back into bed.

She opened the box and pulled out some gauze and tape before picking up a disinfectant wipe. She tore it open, and he dropped the sheet. The blood had slowed to a trickle, and he flinched at the burn of the disinfectant when she wiped the bite marks.

"I'm sorry," she said. She pressed gauze against the wound and quickly taped it into place as Porter muttered a curse.

"You have blood on you. I'm sorry."

"It's okay," she said. She used a clean gauze to wipe away the blood on her upper chest and left shoulder.

"Why did you bite yourself?" she asked.

"It was an accident," he lied. "Wolf shifters, uh, sometimes bite when they mate with other shifters but never with humans."

"You wanted to bite me?" she asked.

He nodded, and she frowned at him. "So, you bit yourself instead to stop from biting me."

"Please forgive me, Maggie. I'm so sorry."

"Porter, you have nothing to apologize for. You're the one

who was bitten, not me." She smiled at him and patted his bare chest. "Don't feel bad."

"I scared you," he said.

"Only for a second," she said.

He muttered a curse, and she squeezed his other arm. "It's okay."

There was a moment of awkward silence, and then she gave him a tentative smile. "I guess I should go back to the couch."

"No!" He winced and lowered his voice. "I mean, I want you to stay with me in my bed, but if you'd rather not, I understand."

"No," she said quickly. "I want to stay here with you, but I just wasn't sure if...."

He cursed inwardly. God, he had fucked up Maggie's first time so badly, and he'd never forgive himself.

As if she sensed what he was thinking, she cupped his face. "Porter, I don't regret this. It was everything that I wanted it to be."

"Are you sure?" he asked.

She nodded before smiling at him. "Well, maybe not the part where you bit yourself, but everything else was super awesome."

He grinned a little, and she gave him a look of relief. "There you are."

He leaned forward and kissed her. She kissed him sweetly in return and then smiled at him again. "We should change the sheets and go to bed. It's late."

When the fresh sheets were on the bed, he shut off the light, and they climbed into bed. He spooned her tightly as she relaxed against him. He cupped her breast and kissed the back of her shoulder. Already he wanted her again, but he couldn't risk it. What if he couldn't stop himself from biting her?

"Thank you, Porter," she said. "It really was amazing. I mean that."

He kissed her shoulder again. "For me too." He paused and said awkwardly, "I didn't take your virginity as payment for protecting you. You know that, right?"

She nodded. "Yes. I didn't give it to you for that reason."

"Why did you?" he asked.

"Because I," she hesitated before clearing her throat, "because I wanted you to be my first." She rubbed his arm. "Good night, Porter."

"Good night, darlin'."

CHAPTER 11

He woke to the feel of her soft ass rubbing against his erection. He groaned and tried to move away, but he was right on the edge of the bed. He shook Maggie a little roughly to wake her. She blinked sleepily as her firm ass pressed and rubbed against his dick before smiling over her shoulder at him.

"Morning, Porter."

"Uh, hi," he said.

She took his arm and tugged it over her body before pressing his hand against her breast. He automatically cupped it, his fingers playing with her nipple. She arched into his hand and moaned softly.

Stop it! You can't keep doing this. You're going to lose control and bite her, and then you'll be up shit creek without a paddle.

He started to withdraw his hand, and Maggie moaned in disappointment before grabbing his wrist and tugging his hand back to her breast. "Don't stop. Please."

She stared at him again, and he was lost by the look of

need in her eyes. Fuck it. He could take Maggie without biting her. She wanted him, and what kind of idiot would he be if he didn't give her what she wanted?

He pulled on her nipple, and she arched again, pushing her ass more firmly against his cock. He kissed the side of her throat before trailing kisses down her smooth shoulder. She rubbed his thigh with her soft hand as he traced circles around her belly button with the tips of his fingers.

When he moved his hand lower, she parted her legs eagerly, and his wolf growled in approval. Porter cupped her pussy, rubbing lightly at her clit until she was squirming and panting loudly. He wanted to fuck her again, *needed* to fuck her. He kissed her hard on the mouth before nipping at her bottom lip.

"I want you, Porter," she whispered.

"Are you sure you're not too sore?" he asked.

"I'm good. Please," she said as her fingers dug into his thigh.

He pressed one finger inside of her, watching her face carefully. Her pussy squeezed around his finger, and he groaned as she smiled at him. "I want you."

"I want you too," he said, "so much."

"Then take me," she demanded.

"Stay right there," he said. He sat up and grabbed a condom. When it was in place, he curled up behind Maggie again and wrapped his hand around her thigh. He pushed her forward a little and lifted her leg, holding it up as he positioned his cock at her wet entrance. One firm push, and he was deep inside her warmth. She gasped, and he kissed her neck again.

"Okay?"

"Yes," she said breathlessly. "Don't stop."

He moved slowly, watching his cock slide in and out of her as she awkwardly tried to match his rhythm.

"I'm sorry," she said as a tinge of red crept over her cheeks.

He marked the back of her shoulder roughly as he tried to focus. "It's good."

He let her leg rest over his and gripped her hip, helping her thrust back and forth. He groaned loudly. "Like that – good."

"I just," she gasped loudly as he made a harder thrust, "need more practice."

"Yeah," he groaned, "lots and lots of practice. Fuck! Don't squeeze, darlin'."

"No squeezing," she moaned as her inner walls squeezed him again, "got it."

"You don't," he half-growled, half-groaned.

She made a breathless little laugh that turned into a squeal when he moved harder and faster. He braced one hand between her shoulder blades and cupped her pussy with the other. He rubbed at her clit as he plunged in and out, and she cried out as her entire body shuddered around him.

"God," he moaned, "you're fucking killing me. Play with your beautiful tits, darlin'."

She cupped both her breasts, rubbing her nipples with her slender fingers as he groaned and panted behind her.

He rubbed her clit faster, pushing in and out of her in a quick, hard rhythm as she squeezed her nipples and made low cries of desire.

"Porter, I'm – I'm going to…."

Her body stiffened, and her pussy squeezed around him like a warm, wet vice. She moaned loudly, her head whipping back and forth on the pillow and her hands clutching her pale breasts tightly. He thrust furiously as her pussy squeezed him again. His wolf pushed to the surface just as his orgasm started. Panic mixed with desire as his fangs popped out, and his wolf snarled at him to claim Maggie. He stared at the smooth flesh of her back as his wolf pushed his head down toward her pale skin.

At the last minute, he whipped his head to the right and buried his fangs into his arm again as his climax roared through his body. He pumped furiously, tasting his blood in his mouth as his wolf howled with rage and disappointment. Blood was flowing out around his mouth, spattering across Maggie's side and hip. He pushed in deep one final time, his back arching as Maggie made a low sound of surprise. He shuddered wildly and pulled his mouth away from his arm. More blood poured out, and he pulled out of her wet warmth before sliding off the bed. He staggered a few feet away, one hand clamped over his bleeding wound as he pulled off the condom and threw it in the small trash bin. Maggie sat up and turned around.

"Oh, Porter," she said with dismay. "You bit yourself again."

"It's fine," he said.

She climbed out of bed and took his hand. "It isn't. You're really bleeding. Come to the bathroom."

She took his hand and led him into the bathroom before closing the lid on the toilet. "Sit down."

He sat, and she pressed a towel against the wound. When the blood slowed to a trickle, she cleaned it and wrapped a bandage around it before removing the bandage on his left arm. This one was almost healed, but she cleaned it with a disinfectant wipe anyway before giving him a solemn look.

"I'm sorry," he said. "I got blood on you again."

"I don't care about that," she said. His blood was already

starting to dry on her side and hip. "You have to stop biting yourself when we have sex, Porter."

"I know," he said. He took a deep breath. He was ashamed that he had bitten himself again, but at least, he thought with a slight note of bitterness, he hadn't nearly shifted. Maybe next time, he could control the urge to bite her.

If there is a next time. You think Maggie will want to keep fucking you if you bite yourself and bleed all over her every fucking time?

"I'm so sorry," he said.

She threw the bandage wrappers in the garbage and rinsed the towel out in the sink. Without looking at him, she said, "Maybe it's better if you just, uh, bite me."

"No!" he shouted, and she cringed away from him.

He cursed under his breath and stood up before pulling her into his embrace. "I'm sorry, I didn't mean to yell."

"It's okay," she said. He rubbed her lower back as she stared up at him. "I don't like that you keep hurting yourself."

"It doesn't hurt that much," he said.

"Well, then," she hesitated, "I don't mind if you bite me instead, Porter. I know I'm not a shifter, but -"

"No," he said again. "No, darlin'. I can't bite you. I *won't* bite you."

His wolf was nearly dancing a damn jig from excitement. He tried to ignore his eager clamoring that Maggie wanted him to bite her.

She doesn't know what it means! he snapped at his wolf.

"Okay." She cupped his face and smiled at him. "But I don't want you to stop, uh, sleeping with me because you're worried about my reaction if you bite me. If it happens, it's no big deal, okay?"

"I won't bite you, Maggie," he repeated.

She stood on her tiptoes and kissed his mouth. "I know. I just wanted you to know it's okay if you do."

She studied the drying blood on her side and hip. "I'm going to have a quick shower. Do you have plans for today?"

He shook his head, and she gave him a tentative look. "I'm meeting with Ava and a police detective named Bren this afternoon. We're going to, uh, talk to him about my problem with Vaughn."

"Mal mentioned it to me," he said. "You know that Bren is the son of Senator Matthews, right? The same Senator who Vaughn saved from being murdered."

She nodded. "I know it seems strange, but Ava said we don't have to tell him who Vaughn is."

"I guess," he said, "but I'm still going with you."

A look of relief crossed her face, but she said, "You don't have to come if you don't want to."

"I want to," he said. "Why don't you have your shower and I'll make breakfast."

"You could join me in the shower," she said.

He was beyond tempted to join her, but if he did, he'd definitely fuck her again, and his wolf was still too riled up and too close to the surface for that. He'd bite her for sure. "I'd better not. I know you said you're not sore, but I think we should give you a break."

"We could just shower together, nothing else."

"Maybe you could just shower, but I couldn't," he said with a slight grin. "You wet and naked is way too tempting, darlin'."

She flushed prettily, and he squeezed her bare ass before pressing a kiss against her mouth. "Just give me a few minutes to brush my teeth and use the washroom, and then you can hop in the shower, okay?"

"Okay," she said.

"What do you want for breakfast?" he asked.

"I'm not picky," she said. "But I am pretty hungry."

He nuzzled her throat affectionately. "Me too. I'll make a big breakfast."

———

THE WEASEL SHIFTER LOCKED HIS CAR AND WALKED SLOWLY up the sidewalk. He studied the small, white house before climbing the front steps of the stoop. He raised his hand to knock and hesitated. He didn't want to be here. Fuck, he wanted to be anywhere else *but* here. He didn't have a choice, though. The cop was his only chance at saving his brother.

He knocked before he could change his mind. The door opened almost immediately, and he stared at the hyena shifter. The shifter sniffed at him before grinning. "C'mon in, little weasel."

The hyena led him into the house and down a narrow hallway. He wrinkled his nose. Hyena's scent marked their territory, and the smell made him want to vomit. They passed by a doorway, and he paused and glanced into the room. Another four men were sitting in the room, two were playing a video game, and two were staring at their phones.

"Hurry up," the hyena barked at him.

He followed him down a second hallway and waited as the hyena knocked on the door at the end of the hallway before opening it. "He's here, Boss."

"Show him in."

Clearing his throat, he stepped into the room. It was a small office. Large pictures of the grassy plains of Africa covered the walls. The scent of hyena was nearly overpowering in the room, and he had to fight both his gag reflex and his urge to cover his nose.

"You like the pictures?"

He studied the hyena sitting behind the desk. He had short black hair and black eyes, and a 'don't fuck with me' attitude practically seeped from his pores.

"They're nice."

"Thanks. Took them myself. I've always wanted to see Africa, see where my people come from, and I finally did it. It was a great trip, wasn't it, Jake?"

"Yeah, Boss."

The hyena motioned to the chair that was in front of the desk. "Have a seat, little weasel."

He grimaced but sat in the chair as the hyena grinned. "You don't like being called a weasel, do you?"

"Not particularly."

"Why not? You're a weasel shifter. You shouldn't be ashamed of that."

"We don't have the best reputation," he said. "Just like hyenas."

The cop scowled at him. "Shut your fucking mouth about hyenas. You don't know shit about us."

He shut his mouth. Antagonizing the very cop who could save his brother was stupid.

The hyena leaned back in his chair and rested his hands across his flat belly. "I'm being rude to our guest. You want a beer, buddy?"

"I'm not your buddy," he said.

The hyena laughed. "Oh, I think you and I are going to become real close."

"Officer Bales, you phoned me and said you could help my brother. I'm here to talk about that. I don't want a drink. I don't want to be your -"

"You're being awfully rude to the man who can keep your stupid brother's ass out of prison, Mr. Calden." He paused and grinned at him. "Can I call you Arlo? You can call me Vaughn. There's no need for us to be so formal, is there?"

Arlo sighed and nodded. "Sure, fine, whatever."

Vaughn leaned forward and flipped open the file sitting in the middle of his desk. "Let's see. I have a police report here that says a young man, a Mr. Andrew Calden, was discovered at a frat party with a rather substantial amount of cocaine in his pocket. He is, of course, denying that it's his and says he was holding it for a friend."

Vaughn barked harsh laughter before grinning at Jake. "It's what they always say, isn't it, Jake?"

"Yes, Boss."

"The DA believes your brother had that cocaine with the intent of selling it. That's some serious prison time. You believe your baby brother, Arlo? Do you think he was just holding it for a friend, or does he have a drug problem?"

Arlo cleared his throat. "He has a problem."

Vaughn laughed again. "He most certainly does. Didn't he get into university on a baseball scholarship?"

"Yes," Arlo said.

"First in your family to get into university, am I right?"

"Yes."

"Your parents must be real proud of him. Or they were."

"They still are," Arlo said.

Vaughn cocked his head at him. "You telling me they believe their baby boy's story about it not being his?"

Arlo hesitated before nodding.

Vaughn rolled his eyes. "Of course, they do. I bet they'll be heartbroken when he loses that scholarship and is kicked out of university. I bet they won't like visiting him in prison instead of that fancy school."

Arlo winced before saying, "Can I ask you a question?"

"Be my guest."

"How did you know Andy was my brother? Why did you call me and tell me you could help?"

"Well, that's the million-dollar question, isn't it, Arlo?" Vaughn said. "Although I suspect you have half an idea of why I'm so willing to help out your drug-addicted weasel brother."

Arlo cleared his throat. "Porter Burke."

"Bingo!" Vaughn said happily. "Jesus, Jake, maybe weasels aren't nearly as stupid as we think they are. Why don't you tell me what your little bartender friend, Burke, has shared with you, Arlo?"

Arlo picked nervously at a small shaving nick on his throat. "I know that he's been having some issues with a pack of hyenas over a human. It didn't take much to figure out you're the hyena. He's dating your ex-girlfriend, and you don't like it. You tried to kill him the other night."

"Kill is a strong word," Vaughn said.

"You shot him."

"In the thigh. Wolf shifters heal quick."

"Your pack kicked the shit out of him. If Judd hadn't come along, they would have beaten him to death."

Vaughn waved his hand. "That's a bit of an exaggeration. They were just teaching him a lesson."

"What lesson?" Arlo said. "The woman isn't with you anymore. There's nothing wrong with Porter dating her."

He cringed back when Vaughn slammed his hands down on the top of the desk. His black eyes glowed and dark fur sprouted on his face. "The woman is my mate! She's mine, and he can't have her!"

His heart thudding in his chest, Arlo stared at Vaughn as the hyena sat back in his chair and closed his eyes. After a few minutes, the hair faded from his cheeks. He sat forward again and studied the file before lifting his gaze to Arlo. "To answer your question – I knew who you were because we've been doing a little, I guess you could call it research, on all of Burke's friends and family. It's good to know your enemy, don't you think?"

"Sure," Arlo muttered.

"Anyway, imagine my surprise when Thursday night your little brother popped up in the system. Calden isn't exactly a common name, so I had my good friend, Hank, do a little background check. Being a police officer comes in handy, doesn't it?"

Arlo didn't reply, and Vaughn smiled at him. "So, here you are, and here I am. Both of us with a problem that the other can solve."

"I can't convince Porter to stop dating Maggie," Arlo said. "We work together, but we're not like friends or anything. He's not going to listen to me. Besides, I don't even know why you want this girl. Even for a human, she isn't your kind's type. She's small and nervous and – and timid. You like your women to be stronger and bigger than you. Female hyenas rule the pack, and this Maggie chick can't rule anyone."

"Shut the fuck up, weasel!" Vaughn snapped. "You don't know anything about her. She's destined to be my mate, and that's all your little weasel brain needs to know."

His sudden fit of anger passed, and he smiled benignly at Arlo again. "I'm well aware that you aren't friends with the wolf shifter, but I'm sure there's some information you can share that I haven't discovered for myself."

"Like what?"

Vaughn shrugged. "Anything and everything you can think of, little weasel. I'll decide if it's relevant or not."

Arlo crossed his arms across his chest. "If I do this, what will you do for my brother?"

Vaughn grinned at him. "The cocaine found in your brother's possession will magically disappear from evidence. If they can't find the cocaine that was on your brother, they can't charge him for possession with intent to sell. Of course, it'll only disappear if you give me helpful information. So, why don't you start talking?"

Sweat dripped down Arlo's back, and he studied the floor of Vaughn's office. Fuck, Porter was nothing but good to him and always treated him well, but if Andy went to prison, it would destroy his parents.

"Time's ticking," Vaughn said.

Arlo blew his breath out in a harsh rush. "His older brother owns a security company. They're keeping both Porter and Maggie under watch. You won't be able to get near them again."

"We already know that, idiot," Vaughn said impatiently. "Tell me something that I can't fucking see with my own two eyes."

"Uh, he's got four -no, five – siblings and they -"

"Information we know," Vaughn said. "You need to start trying harder, or your brother will be staring at the inside of a prison cell, my weasel friend."

More sweat dripped down his back, and Arlo fidgeted in the chair. "He's worked at the bar for close to six years and, uh, he – he's thinking about buying it from Bud."

Vaughn cocked his head. "Is he?"

"Yes, they've been in negotiations for about a month now, but Bud keeps raising the asking price. I think Porter's a little pissed about it. They got into a screaming match about it a while ago. I heard them fighting in Bud's office."

"Is he still buying the bar?" Vaughn asked.

"I don't know. I don't think they've talked about it since the fight."

Vaughn studied him carefully. "That's good information, Arlo. Well done."

"So, you'll help my brother?" Arlo leaned forward eagerly.

"I will," Vaughn said.

"Thank you. Thank you so -"

"On one condition," Vaughn said.

"What do you mean?" Arlo asked.

"I'll make the evidence against your brother disappear so that Mommy and Daddy can rejoice in their baby boy's innocence if you feed me information on the wolf shifter."

"We're not friends," Arlo said. "I told you that before. We don't hang out together outside of work."

Vaughn gave him an irritable look. "I heard you the first time. But what I want from you is so simple that even a stupid little weasel like you can handle it. All I want is regular information on Burke's plan to buy the bar."

"That's it?" Arlo said.

"That's it. I'll make your baby brother's problem disappear if you hold up your end of the bargain. Can you do that, little weasel?"

"Yes," Arlo said quickly.

"Good. Then we're done here," Vaughn said. "Call me in a few days and give me an update."

"My brother?" Arlo said.

"Problem will be taken care of by Monday," Vaughn said. "Don't you worry about that."

Feeling an odd mixture of relief and nausea, Arlo stood and followed Jake out of the office. He breathed a sigh of relief when he was out of the house and hurried to his car. He climbed in and slammed the door shut before rubbing his forehead. He was going to kill Andy for getting him into this mess. This was the last time he was bailing out his goddamn ass.

What about Porter? What if the information you're giving that asshole hyena gets him killed? Your brother is a drug-addled fuck-up, and you've spent the last ten years giving up everything to try to save him. When will you realize it's impossible? Your brother doesn't give a rat's ass about you. Porter might not be your friend, but he's always been good to you and always treated you with respect. If he dies because of you, can you live with that?

He cringed and started the car before driving away. That wasn't going to happen. All Vaughn wanted was information. How would knowing about Porter buying the bar allow Vaughn to kill him? It wouldn't. Besides, Porter had his brother's security company watching over him. Vaughn couldn't try to hurt him again. If Andy went to jail, it would destroy his parents' and Arlo couldn't let that happen. His family needed him.

"Boss?" Jake sat down in the chair across from Vaughn.

"What is it?" Vaughn asked.

"Why are you helping the weasel? He didn't give us anything."

Vaughn laughed. "Of course, he did, Jake. You're just not bright enough to see it."

Jake scowled at him. "I'm bright enough to see that you're losing your fucking mind over a goddamn pathetic human. The weasel was right – she's too timid and useless to be your mate."

Vaughn growled loudly. "Watch your tongue, Jake. That's my mate you're insulting."

Jake leaned forward, "Boss, listen to me – I know you like this girl and think she's something special, but she isn't. You have to see that."

"I see her potential," Vaughn said. "She may appear to be weak, but I know she isn't. I want her because she's strong, and she'll make an excellent mate."

"No, you want her because you've got a thing about her being a fucking virgin," Jake said sullenly. "Which is fucking ridiculous because we both know she isn't one anymore. Not with the way she's been marked by that prick of a wolf shif -"

He made a strangled yelp as Vaughn shot out of his chair and leaped across the desk. He knocked Jake to the floor and wrapped his hands around his throat before squeezing hard. Jake clawed at his hands as his eyes bulged.

"Shut your fucking mouth, Jake," Vaughn said in a low voice. "Maggie hasn't allowed herself to be defiled by the wolf shifter. He may have marked her, but she's still innocent. She can deny it all she wants, but she is my mate, and there's no fucking way she's given herself to the wolf shifter. Do you understand?"

He eased the pressure of his hands enough for Jake to take a ragged, gasping breath.

"Do you understand, Jake?"

"Yes, Boss," Jake choked out.

"Good." Vaughn released him and stood gracefully before returning to his chair. Coughing and gagging, Jake sat up before dragging his body up and into his chair. He rubbed at his throat and gave Vaughn a dour look.

"Stop looking at me like that," Vaughn said.

"What do you care if he buys the bar?" Jake asked. "We should just fucking kill him and be done with it."

"I was sloppy before. I let my anger cloud my judgment. Killing Burke is the wrong move. If they found out we were involved -"

"We're cops. We can make it look like an accident or self-defense," Jake said before massaging his throat again. "Fuck, you're a goddamn hero cop, remember? No one would believe you killed him."

"I can't take the risk," Vaughn said, "and neither can you or our other pack mates. You know what they do to cops in prison."

"We won't get caught," Jake said. "Neither Maggie nor that fucking prick have even made a complaint at the station or filed a restraining order. They know it's pointless."

Vaughn shook his head. "We're not going to kill him. I have a better idea. Burke's tried to take my mate, and that's unacceptable."

"I still don't get how using that weasel for information is going to help," Jake said. "He don't know shit about nothing. I'll be risking my career by taking that evidence, and for what? A lousy little weasel who can't tell you dick all."

Vaughn laughed. "That' s where you're wrong, Jake. Just trust me. All right?"

Jake studied him before nodding in resignation. "Yeah, okay."

"Good. Now, you need to take the evidence against Calden's brother tonight. Make it disappear, but don't dump it. I want it kept in case the weasel needs a little more convincing to help us."

Jake stood and walked toward the door. He paused in the doorway when Vaughn called his name. "Yeah, Boss?"

"Don't fuck this up," Vaughn said.

"I won't, Boss."

MAGGIE AND PORTER CARRIED THEIR COFFEE TO A TABLE AT
the back of the coffee shop. Ava and Bishop were already
seated, and Porter grinned at Bishop as they sat down across
from them.

"Didn't know you were going to be here, B. Worried that
Ava will go into labour when you're not there?"

Bishop shrugged before glancing at Ava. "Something like
that."

Ava gave him a sweet but slightly exasperated look. "He
knows I'm with you, honey."

Bishop just shrugged again before sipping at his coffee.
"Yeah, I know."

Porter reached for Maggie's hand. "The detective has a
thing for Ava."

Bishop growled under his breath, and Ava poked him
lightly in the side. "Stop growling, and Porter, stop riling him
up. Bren knows I love Bishop."

"We're not going to tell him who Vaughn is, right, Ava?"
Maggie took a sip of coffee and held tightly to Porter's hand.
Her stomach churned from the single sip of coffee.

"That's right," Ava said. "Please don't be nervous,
Maggie. Bren is a good guy and – oh, there he is."

She waved wildly, and Maggie turned to look. A tall,
dark-haired man waved back before ordering a coffee. She
studied him as he paid for his drink and waited patiently for
his coffee. His dark hair was on the longer side, and he wore
a leather jacket with jeans and a t-shirt. She thought he might
be in his late twenties, but as he picked up his coffee and
drew closer, she decided he was closer to his early thirties. He
was clean-shaven with small laugh lines around his mouth

and light blue eyes, and he had a kind face. Some of her nerves abated a little as Ava stood.

"Hi, Bren." She hugged him briefly - Maggie wondered if she was the only one who heard Bishop's low growl – before smiling at him.

"Hi, Ava. It's good to see you again. You look great – pregnancy agrees with you."

Ava laughed. "People keep telling me that, but I'm not sure it's true."

Bren held out his hand to Bishop. "Hello, Bishop."

"Hey," Bishop said before shaking his hand.

Bren sat down between Ava and Maggie as Ava said, "Bren, I'd like you to meet friends of ours. This is Mal's brother, Porter, and Porter's girlfriend, Maggie."

"It's nice to meet you," Bren said and shook both their hands. He drank some coffee before saying, "So, you're having some problems with a police officer?"

"Yes," Porter said. "Maggie dated him for a short time, and now he's having trouble understanding that she doesn't want to be with him. He broke into her home and threatened her, and now he's stalking her. We have employees from the security company watching her 24/7, but he's not taking the hint."

"Is he a shifter?" Bren asked.

"Yes," Porter said.

"What kind?"

Porter glanced at Maggie. "Hyena."

"Are you a shifter?" Bren asked Maggie.

"No," Maggie said. "Plus, he's doing more than just stalking me. When he found out I was dating Porter, he pulled him over on his way home from work last week, and he shot him in the leg before he had his police buddies beat the crap out of him. Porter would have died if a friend from the bar hadn't shown up and saved him."

"Jesus," Bren said. "Did you report it?"

"No," Porter said.

"Why not?"

"It's complicated."

Bren frowned. "Tell me you've at least filed a restraining order against him."

"I haven't. What good would it do?" Maggie said. "He's a police officer, and he told me when we were dating that the police protect their own."

"They do, to a certain extent," Bren said. "But if he's threatening you and shot Porter, then that goes beyond protecting their own. They're not going to stand behind a guy who tried to kill a civilian."

"It's complicated," Porter repeated.

"What's the guy's name?" Bren asked.

"We can't tell you that," Porter said.

Bren frowned again. "If you don't tell me who he is, how am I supposed to help?"

"We were hoping maybe you could give us some ideas on how to handle this without filing restraining orders or reporting him," Ava said.

"Honestly, there isn't much beyond that," Bren said. "If I knew his name, I could talk to the captain about what's been happening."

"The thing is," Ava said with a glance at Maggie, "this guy is, well, he did something that makes him very," she hesitated, "uh, popular, I guess is sort of the word, and it might be more difficult than you think to have him reprimanded for his actions."

Bren studied Maggie for so long that she squirmed a little.

"Is his name Vaughn Bales?" Bren asked.

Maggie jerked and pushed her chair back before standing. "I have to go."

Porter stood and put his arm around her. "Darlin', it's okay."

"It's not okay!" Maggie said fiercely. "I knew this was a mistake! Now he knows, and he'll tell Vaughn that I'm scared and desperate and -"

Bren stood as Porter held Maggie a little closer. "Maggie? I'm not going to say anything. Sit down, please?"

Maggie sat down with a heavy thud. "Of course, you'll say something to him," she said dully. "The guy saved your father's life."

"How did you know it was Vaughn?" Bishop asked.

Bren sat down and took a drink of coffee. "I'm a detective. We're good with the small details."

Bishop grunted, and Bren smiled a little. "Well, I assumed that this police officer worked in the precinct in this area of the city, which happens to be my precinct. There are six hyena shifters at the precinct, and only one of them has done something that would make him – as Ava calls it - *popular*."

"Porter," Maggie whispered, "can we go?"

She was close to tears, and she gave Porter a grateful smile when he nodded. "Of course, darlin'."

"Maggie, wait," Bren said. "Just hear me out for a second, okay?"

Maggie hesitated before slumping in her seat. She stared at the table as Bren said. "Officer Bales saved my father's life, and while I'm grateful to him, it doesn't give him an automatic pass to be an asshole."

"Have you met him?" Ava asked.

Bren nodded. "My father had him come to the house for a thank-you drink/publicity stunt after Vaughn stopped the assassination attempt. He wanted both my brother and me to be there."

There was an undernote of bitterness in Bren's voice.

"What did you think of him?" Ava asked.

"He's arrogant," Bren said, "and I got a distinct impression that he regretted saving my father's life. But I can't blame him for that."

"So, having his life saved by a shifter didn't change your father's views on them?" Ava said.

"Not in the least," Bren said. "The press had a field day with it, of course. Article after article about how the shifter-hating Senator was saved from death by a shifter. My father's PR team put a nice little spin on it, though – for every article that talked about his life being saved by a shifter, they reminded the general public that it was also a shifter who tried to kill him."

"I remember," Bishop said. "They talked about how the Senator didn't personally hate shifters, and he was grateful his life was saved, but it still didn't negate the need for a shifter registry. They even put out multiple reports about how shifter-related crime was on the rise."

"That's my father," Bren said, that bitterness in his voice stronger this time. "Anyway, this Vaughn guy posed for all the pictures and said all the right things when they handed him the key to the city, but I'm certain he regrets what he did."

"He does," Maggie said. "He told me about it. He was assigned to the political rally, and he said he thought the guy was going after the mayor. He said if he'd known it was your father who was the target, he wouldn't have stopped him."

"Not surprising," Bren said dryly. "The assassination attempt is probably what won my father his second term. His popularity was waning, but after a shifter tried to murder him, the voters who were on the fence came back to his way of thinking in a hurry."

"So, what do we do now?" Porter asked.

Bren sipped more coffee. "Well, you're not incorrect in that it being Vaughn will make it a bit more difficult. He's well-regarded at the precinct and not just because he saved my father's life. I did a bit of research into him after the assassination attempt, pure curiosity on my part, and he has a squeaky-clean record for a hyena shifter. Normally those guys have lots of unnecessary force complaints in their records."

"Not surprising," Porter said.

"We have a couple of options," Bren said. "Porter can file a report on Vaughn, and you can file a restraining order against him. However, it'll seem a little odd that the incident happened last week, and Porter is just reporting it now. At the end of the day, it'll be Porter's word against his, and I'm betting that Vaughn will have his hyena buddies back him up as an alibi."

"What's the other option?" Porter asked.

"I'll speak to him," Bren said. "He's been on the force for as long as I have, and technically, I don't have any seniority over him. But if he knows that someone else is aware of the shit he's pulling, it might be enough to make him give up."

He gave Porter a thoughtful look. "Of course, he did try and kill Porter, so me speaking with him probably won't affect him at all. At the very least, you should file a restraining order against him, Maggie."

"I don't think it will even make a difference," Maggie said. "The only thing that will help is if I leave the city."

"No!" Porter said so loudly that the people at the next table turned to stare at him. He lowered his voice and said, "You can't leave, Maggie. He'll find you, and I won't be there to protect you."

"He won't find me," Maggie said. "I can disappear."

Porter took her hand and held it tightly as if he thought she might just get up and leave. "No, Maggie. Promise me you won't try to leave the city."

"At least let me talk to him before you make plans to leave," Bren said. "It might help."

"Okay," Maggie said. "Thank you, Detective Matthews."

Bren smiled at her. "Call me Bren."

CHAPTER 12

"Maggie, you're worrying me," Porter said.

"I'm fine." She handed him the last dinner dishes, and he loaded them into the dishwasher.

"You're not," Porter said. "You've been quiet all day."

"Just a little worried about our conversation with Bren this afternoon, I guess," Maggie said.

"I know, but I think it'll be a good thing if Bren talks to him," Porter said. "He might even convince Vaughn to leave you alone."

"Maybe," Maggie said.

Before he could reply, his cell phone rang. He fished it out of his pocket and studied the number before answering it. "Hey, Bud."

"Hi, Porter. How are you feeling?"

"Better, thanks."

"Good. Listen, I wanted to apologize for our fight the other day. Truth be told, I was a little unsure about selling the bar at all, but it has nothing to do with you," Bud said.

"Yeah, I get it," Porter said.

"Anyway, if you're still interested in buying the bar, I'm willing to go with the price you're offering."

"Really?"

"Yes. Alice reminded me that I ain't getting any younger, and if I want to spend time with our grandchildren, I can't keep spending all my time at the bar," Bud said. "So, if you're still interested, I got my lawyer to draw up the paperwork."

"I'm still interested," Porter said. "I'll just need to have my lawyer look it over first."

"Of course," Bud said. "I'll email you the paperwork now. Have your lawyer take a look at it, and if it's to your liking, we can meet in a couple of days to sign it. Sound good?"

"Sounds perfect," Porter said. "Thanks, Bud."

"You bet. Talk to you later, Porter."

"Bye, Bud."

Porter shoved his phone into his pocket and grinned at Maggie. "Bud's agreed to sell the bar to me."

"He has? That's wonderful!" Maggie said. "Congratulations, Porter."

"Thanks," Porter said.

Maggie followed him into the living room and watched as he logged into his laptop. "He's emailing me the paperwork now."

He checked his email and read through the paperwork before forwarding Bud's email to Heath with a short note of explanation. "It looks good to me, but I'll have Heath look at it to make sure, and then I'll get a bank draft and meet with Bud to pay him and sign the paperwork."

He closed his laptop and grinned at Maggie, who squeezed his shoulder happily. "We should celebrate."

"That's a great idea," Porter said. "Do you want to go out for drinks?"

Maggie shrugged as her face reddened slightly. "We could. Or we could stay in and celebrate."

She gave him a sweet look of need that made his wolf howl happily. "What did you have in mind?"

She held out her hand. "Join me in the bedroom, and I'll show you."

He took her hand, and she squeezed it lightly as they walked to the bedroom. They helped each other undress, but Maggie tugged his hand away when Porter cupped her breast. "This is about you tonight, remember? I want to make you feel good."

"You already do," he rasped.

She smiled at him and ran her fingers over his chest. "I like you, Porter."

"I like you too, Maggie."

She traced her hand over his lean abdomen, and he sucked in his breath when she wrapped her hand around his dick. She pumped him firmly, staring up into his face as he moaned.

"I want to try something I've never done before," she said.

"What's that?" Already he could barely think straight with Maggie's soft hand rubbing his dick.

Her gaze flickered to his erect cock. "I've never, uh, performed oral sex before. Will you let me try it on you?"

His hips bucked against her, and she licked her lips anxiously when his eyes glowed. "Fuck, yes."

She giggled nervously, and he groaned when she ran her thumb over the head of his cock. "I probably won't be very good at it."

"There's only one way to find out," he said.

She laughed, and he kissed her on the mouth. "I sound pathetically eager, don't I?"

She shook her head. "No. Sit down on the bed."

He moved to the bed and sat down as she kneeled between his legs. She leaned forward and kissed the middle of his chest before licking and nibbling her way down his abdomen. Already he was panting, and he cupped the back of her head, groaning when she squeezed his thighs with her hands.

"Please, Maggie," he said when she pressed kisses against the top of his left thigh.

She smiled at him before gripping the base of his cock with her soft hand. He could feel her warm breath on the head of his cock, and he released her head. He was afraid he would shove her mouth down over his cock if he didn't.

She took a deep breath before sucking experimentally on the head of his cock. He moaned loudly, his hips thrusting against her mouth, and she released him and raised her head.

"Okay?" she asked.

"Yes," he muttered. "Please don't stop."

She sucked on his cock again, and he couldn't stop himself from threading his hands through her hair and holding tightly. Panting harshly, he watched as she sucked him tentatively at first. His low groans of pleasure seemed to embolden her, and he thrust again lightly when she took more of him into her mouth.

"Stroke me with your hand," he instructed hoarsely.

She obeyed, twisting her hand in a light clockwise motion around the base of his cock as she sucked firmly. He moved her head up and down, controlling her movements with firm pressure and moaning when she opened her mouth wide and let him thrust back and forth.

He was close to coming already, and he watched Maggie's lips stretch around his width for only a few more minutes before he pulled her head away. He stared at her red and swollen mouth as she said, "Did I do something wrong?"

"No," he said. "I'm not going to last if you keep doing that, and I want to fuck you, darlin'."

"I want that too," she said.

He lifted her to her feet and leaned forward to suck one nipple into his mouth. She clutched at his head as her back arched. He teased both her nipples before reaching between her legs. She was soaking wet, and he pushed two fingers into her warm core. He curled his fingers and pressed against the front wall of her pussy before rubbing firmly. She immediately squeaked in alarm and pulled away.

"That felt weird," she blurted out.

He grinned, and she blushed. "I'm sorry. It wasn't bad or anything. It just felt…strange."

He pulled her closer and cupped her ass, kneading it lightly as he pressed kisses against her flat abdomen. "You have nothing to apologize for, darlin'."

He stood and kissed her hard on the mouth, sliding in his tongue to stroke against hers as she clung to him. He kissed her neck and traced her shoulder with his tongue. "Get on your hands and knees, darlin'."

She climbed onto the bed and balanced on her hands and knees. He stroked and kneaded her ass as she gave him a slightly self-conscious look.

"You're beautiful, Maggie," he said.

"Thank you," she said.

He rolled on a condom and urged her forward to the center of the bed before kneeling between her legs. He tugged her legs wider and reached between her legs to stroke her clit.

She moaned and ground her pussy against his hand as he stroked her lower back with his other hand.

"I can't wait," she said. "Please, Porter."

"Spread your legs, darlin'," he said.

She widened her legs even further, and he studied her wet, pink slit with appreciation as she rocked against his hand.

"Porter!"

He guided his cock to her wet entrance and pushed into her with one hard stroke. She moaned and arched her back as her ass pressed against his pelvis. He gathered her dark hair into a ponytail and tugged gently until her head lifted and she stared at the ceiling.

"Ready, darlin'?"

"Yes!" She wiggled against him, and he reached under her and cupped her left breast, pinching the nipple lightly until she moaned.

"Stop teasing!" She twisted her head and glared at him.

His wolf made a chuffing noise of amusement at his mate's demanding tone, and Porter squeezed her breast again before moving his hands to her hips. He held her tight and thrust deep. She squealed with pleasure and thrust back against him. She met each of his strokes with eager abandonment as her hands dug into the sheets. He drove in and out of her, his breath coming in harsh pants as she squeezed around him. Her pussy felt amazing, and he pushed on her upper back until her upper half was flat on the bed. He held her there as he fucked her roughly, his fingers digging into her hip as pleasure coiled in his belly.

Her small whimpers of pleasure turned to loud squeals when he reached under her and rubbed her clit. He kept her pressed into the bed with one heavy hand between her shoulder blades as he stroked and rubbed the swollen, wet nub. She fisted the sheets and twisted her head back and forth on the bed before her pussy clamped down around his dick, and she screamed his name. He could feel her orgasm rippling around his cock, and he howled loudly before thrusting wildly in and out of her. His balls tightened painfully, and he shoved himself deep inside of her warmth as his fangs descended. He bent over her, and his wolf howled happily when he pressed his fangs against the soft skin on the back of Maggie's shoulder.

Don't you dare! His inner voice shouted in alarm.

With the last of his willpower, Porter whipped his head to the left and sank his fangs into his forearm. He ignored his wolf's growl of rage as he climaxed hard inside Maggie. Warm blood filled his mouth, and he moaned and shuddered wildly before pulling out and collapsing on the bed next to her. He tried to hide his forearm as Maggie moved to her side. Her warm smile faded when she saw the drops of blood on the quilt, and she quickly sat up.

"Where are you bleeding?"

"I'm not," Porter lied.

She scowled at him, and with a low sigh, he pulled his arm out from under his body.

"Oh, honey," she said when she saw the blood flowing down his arm. "You can't keep doing that."

"It's not that bad," he said.

She sighed and slid off the bed before holding her hand out to him. "Come to the bathroom with me."

He took her hand and followed her out of the bedroom as his wolf snarled and growled at him.

"Sweet merciful heaven," Simone muttered to Maggie, "be subtle about it, but you need to check out the two abso-fucking-lutely gorgeous men who just walked in."

Maggie glanced up from the cash register and couldn't stop the smile from crossing her face. Porter and Mal had just walked into the coffee shop.

"The one on the left is about to find my number on his coffee cup," Simone said into her ear. Porter grinned at Maggie and waved before he and Mal sat down at a table near the window.

Simone elbowed her in the side. "Do you know him?"

"Yes," Maggie said. "He's, uh, my boyfriend."

Simone's mouth dropped open, and she stared at Maggie before holding up her fist. "*Damn*, girl. You're banging that guy? Nicely done."

Maggie blushed and wiped her hands on her apron. "Knock it off, Simone."

"You have to introduce me to his friend." Simone eyed Mal appreciatively.

"That's his brother, and he's getting married in a couple of weeks," Maggie said.

"Dammit," Simone said. "I don't suppose he has other single brothers?"

"Two, actually," Maggie said, "and I think they're both single."

Simone dramatically waved her hand in front of her face. "Get me some water. I'm feeling faint."

Maggie laughed and poked her in the side. "You're nuts."

"I know," Simone said. "But promise me you'll bring them here and introduce me."

Maggie grinned at her as Porter approached the counter. "Hi, Maggie."

"Hi, Porter. I still have about half an hour left on my shift."

"I know. Mal and I thought we'd grab a coffee while we waited." He smiled at Simone, who elbowed Maggie in the side again.

"Uh, Porter, this is Simone. Simone, this is my boyfriend, Porter."

"It's nice to meet you," Simone said. She held her hand out, and Porter shook it.

"Nice to meet you too."

"What would you like to drink?" Simone asked.

"Just two black coffees would be great." Porter pulled out his wallet, and Simone waved him off.

"It's on the house."

"Thank you." Porter smiled at Maggie. "Mom's doing a Sunday family dinner, and she wants you there as well. Do you want to go?"

Maggie hesitated and glanced at Simone. Simone took the hint and hurried away to pour the coffee as Porter said, "What's wrong?"

"I don't think I should go," Maggie said. She hadn't seen any of Porter's family since he was hospitalized, and she was certain they wanted to keep it that way.

"Why not?" Porter asked.

"I nearly got you killed," she said in a low voice. "I'm pretty sure your family hates me now."

"Of course, they don't," Porter said. "They don't blame you, and Mom specifically invited you to come to dinner today."

She bit at her bottom lip as Porter reached across the counter and took her hand. "Darlin', they don't hate you. I promise. Please come to dinner."

"I – okay," Maggie said.

Porter gave her his adorable boyish grin as Simone returned with the coffee. She fumbled the coffee onto the counter as she stared at Porter, and Maggie could barely hold in her giggles.

"Thank you, Simone. It was nice to meet you." He returned to the table with the coffees, and Simone made a low whistle.

"Maggie, if you don't introduce me to his single brothers, I swear to God I'll break the espresso machine and tell Colin you did it."

"You wouldn't!" Maggie said indignantly.

"Hell, yes, I would," Simone said.

"You're evil."

"Totally evil," Simone agreed.

"HYENAS STILL BEHIND US?" PORTER ASKED MAL AS THEY pulled into his parents' driveway.

"Yes." Mal checked the rearview mirror. "They just parked behind Davis' car."

Porter rolled his eyes. "Jesus, they need to give it up."

They climbed out of the car, and Porter took Maggie's hand before leading them into the house. Maggie was pale and fidgeting nervously as they walked through the house toward the backyard. He squeezed her hand and pressed a kiss against her forehead before murmuring, "Stop worrying, darlin'. Everything is fine."

She nodded, but the pinched look of worry didn't leave her face as they stepped into the yard. Roland stood by the door, and he hugged Porter roughly. "Hey, son. Feel better?"

"Yes, thanks, Dad."

Roland smiled at Maggie, and she twitched when he gave her a gentle hug. "Hi, Maggie. It's good to see you again."

"Uh, hi, Roland," Maggie said.

"Dad?" Ellet stood by the barbeque, and he waved at them. "Hey, guys. Dad, I think the barbecue is out of propane."

Roland headed toward Ellet as Heath, holding a beer in one hand, strolled toward them. He smiled at Maggie and went to hug her. Porter growled deep in his throat and put his hand on Maggie's arm, pulling her up against his body.

Heath rolled his eyes. "Relax, Porter. I can smell your scent all over her."

Maggie blushed furiously as Mal wandered over to Roland and Ellet.

"Mom and the rest of the ladies are upstairs," Heath said to Maggie. "They're doing something wedding related. Mom said to tell you to come upstairs and join them."

Porter pressed a brief kiss against her mouth. "Do you want me to walk you upstairs?"

Maggie shook her head before grinning at him. "Sweet of you, but I think I'll be okay walking upstairs by myself."

He growled teasingly at her and squeezed her ass as she turned and headed inside. His teasing growl turned to a real one as the door shut behind her, and he glared at Heath. "Stop staring at her ass."

Heath rolled his eyes again. "Seriously? I wasn't. Chill out – I know she's your woman."

Porter took a deep breath as Heath rummaged in the cooler and handed him a beer. "Sorry, Heath."

"It's fine," Heath said. He took a drink of beer. "I got your email with the paperwork for the bar. I took a quick look at it, but I'll look at it more in-depth at work tomorrow."

"Thanks. I appreciate that," Porter said.

"No problem. When are you telling Mom and Dad?"

"Once the paperwork is signed, and I've paid Bud," Porter said.

"They'll be happy for you. You know that, right?" Heath said.

"Yeah, I do."

"Good. Let me know when you're meeting with Bud, and I'll go with you," Heath said.

"I will. Thanks again," Porter said.

MAGGIE STEPPED INTO THE GUEST BEDROOM. MARA, JESSA, and Becky stood in the room, and she smiled timidly at them.

"Maggie!" Mara gave her a warm smile and crossed the room to hug her. "How are you, my love?"

"I'm good," Maggie said. "Um, how are you?"

"Good, thanks," Mara said. She looked Maggie up and down before inhaling deeply. Maggie flushed when a small smile crossed Mara's face. She hugged Maggie again. "It's good to see you again."

"It's nice to see you too. Thank you for inviting me to dinner," Maggie said.

"Of course, my love," Mara said. "You're always welcome."

Maggie cleared her throat before smiling at Jessa and Becky. "Hi there."

Jessa looked up from her phone and smiled. "Hey, Maggie."

"Hey," Becky said. She walked toward the door, brushing past Maggie. "I'm supposed to be there in ten minutes, Mom."

"I know, Bumblebee," Mara said as Becky gave Maggie a sullen look before disappearing out of the room.

Maggie swallowed heavily as Mara patted her arm. "Don't mind her, my love. She's just going through the typical teenager hormones, and Porter is her favourite sibling, so she's still a little grumpy about what happened to him. She'll warm up to you soon."

"It's okay," Maggie said. "She should be upset with me."

"No, she shouldn't," Mara said. "Don't talk that way. If her attitude doesn't improve, Roland and I will speak to her."

She put her arm around Maggie before smiling at Jessa. "JJ, will you do me a favour and drive Becky to her friend's house?"

"Sure." Jessa stuck her phone in her pocket. "I'll be back in twenty."

She left the room as the door to the guest bathroom opened, and Willow stepped into the room. She wore her wedding dress, and Ava trailed after her, holding the long train to the dress in her arms.

"Oh, honey," Mara said softly. "You look so beautiful."

"Thank you, Mara. Hi, Maggie," Willow said as she stood in front of the full-length mirror. Ava spread the train out behind her before standing next to her.

Maggie and Mara stared at her. The strapless white satin gown clung to her upper body and flared out at her hips, and simple lace edged the bottom as well as the train. Ava opened a box on the bed and pulled out the veil before fixing it to Willow's hair.

"I think you should wear your hair up," she said as she stared critically at Willow.

"I think so too," Willow said. "I know Mal loves it when I wear my hair down, but the veil works better with an updo. Mara, what do you think?"

"Up," Mara said. She stroked Willow's bare arm before smiling at her in the mirror. "I'm so happy you're marrying Mal, honey. You have no idea."

Willow smiled at her. "I'm happy too, Mara."

Mara cupped her face and kissed her forehead. "You're a part of our family now, Willow. You'll never be alone again. Do you understand?"

Willow blinked rapidly as a tear slid down her cheek. "Yes."

Mara wiped the tear away. "Now, don't you start crying like that or I will too, and Roland will think I'm even crazier than he already does when he sees my puffy eyes. I love you, honey."

"I love you too," Willow said.

She hugged the older woman firmly as Mara's pocket rang. She pulled out her phone and glanced at the number. "Oh, dear. It's Mrs. Parsons."

She hit the answer button. "Hello, Mrs. Parsons. What's that? He's out again? Oh, of course, dearest. I'll send one of the boys over right away. No, of course, we don't mind. Yes, I'm sure. Okay, yes – no, it's quite fine. Do not climb the tree. Bye, dearest."

She stuck her phone into her pocket and sighed. "Mrs. Parsons is our neighbour four doors down. Her cat is stuck in the tree again. Mrs. Parsons is eighty years old and keeps trying to climb the tree to get him. Roland caught her scaling the tree two weeks ago on his evening walk and had to rescue her. He climbed the tree and caught the cat for her. Since then, she calls every time her cat escapes. I swear this is the third time this week. We keep telling her not to let him out, but he's a wily little bugger. He sneaks past her when she's getting the mail. Anyway, I'd better run outside and get one of the boys to pop by her house and climb the tree before she does. I'll be back."

She hugged Willow again before leaving. Maggie smiled at Willow. "You look amazing, Willow."

"Thanks, Maggie," Willow said as she eyed herself in the mirror. She grabbed her boobs and adjusted them. "I still think I should stuff my bra. Give me a little extra oomph for the big day."

Ava laughed. "No, Willow. You're perfect just the way you are. I'm warning you now that I'll be checking your bra for rolled-up socks before you walk down the aisle."

"Traitor," Willow said. "Maggie, are you a yay or a nay on bra stuffing?"

"Nay," Maggie said. "More than a handful is a waste anyway, right?"

"I guess." Willow adjusted her boobs again before twisting to her right to stare at her butt. "At least my ass looks good."

"It looks fantastic," Ava said.

Maggie drifted closer and stared at the scar on the back of Willow's shoulder. It looked like a bite mark, and she hesitated only briefly before tapping Willow on the arm. "Willow? Can I ask you a question?"

"Sure," Willow said.

"How did you get that?" Maggie pointed to the scar.

"Mal bit me," Willow said as she smoothed her hand over the veil.

"Did it hurt?" Maggie asked.

Willow shrugged. "A little, but between you and me, I was in the middle of having the best orgasm of my life, so I didn't really notice."

"So, he only bit you once?" Maggie said.

Willow gave her an odd look. "Yes. There isn't a need to

do it more than once, is there? Ava, can you fix the back of the veil?"

"Just a minute." Ava stared at Maggie. "Maggie, has Porter bitten you?"

"No," Maggie said.

"Mara would know if he did," Willow said. "She knew the minute she smelled me that Mal had bitten me."

"What do you mean?" Maggie asked.

Before Willow could reply, Ava said, "Has Porter tried to bite you?"

"Why would he?" Willow said. "They're only pretend dating. Have you and Porter even had sex yet?"

"Has he tried to bite you?" Ava persisted.

"Uh, no, not really," Maggie said.

Willow stared at her. "What do you mean – not really?"

"He bites himself instead," Maggie said.

"He what?" Willow nearly shouted.

"He bites himself," Maggie repeated. Willow and Ava were staring at her with identical expressions of shock. Feeling self-conscious, she said, "Porter and I had sex on Friday and then, uh, a couple of times yesterday. Friday night, he bit himself in the arm while we were having sex. I was surprised, but he said that sometimes shifters bite each other during sex but not, um, humans. But each time we have sex, he ends up biting himself. Last night, he, uh, well, he pressed his fangs against me, and I thought he was going to bite me, but then he bit his arm again. I feel terrible about it, and I told him it's okay if he bites me, but he won't."

She paused before studying the scar on Willow's shoulder. "I guess he's afraid of scarring me."

"Holy shit," Willow breathed. She gave Ava a wide-eyed look of shock. "She doesn't know."

"I don't know what?" Maggie said.

"Honey," Ava said, "wolf shifters only bite their sexual partners when they, well, when they…."

"When they're claiming them," Willow said.

"What? What do you mean claiming them?" Maggie said.

"Claiming them as their mate," Willow said.

"So, if Porter bit me, that means he wants to date me for real?"

Willow shook her head. "No. Maggie, honey, listen carefully. A wolf shifter mates for life. They claim their mate by biting them. Once they've bitten them, their mate carries their scent on her skin for the rest of her life. It's a wolf shifter's way of telling other shifters to stay the hell away from their woman. A claiming bite is like a marriage between humans. Only there's no possibility of separation or divorce. Once a wolf shifter bites you, they'll love you and only you for the rest of their life."

Maggie took a staggering step back, and Ava grabbed her arm. "Maggie? Are you okay?"

"So, if Porter bit me," Maggie said, "then I'd be his mate for life?"

Willow nodded solemnly. "Yes."

"Oh my God," Maggie said. "I – oh my God."

"It's very serious," Willow said. "Mal lost control and bit me without my permission, and then he freaked the hell out about it. As he should have. A wolf shifter shouldn't bite a woman without their permission first. If Mara ever found out her kid bit me without asking permission, she'd kick his ass. Lucky for Mal, I was just as in love with him as he was with me, so it all worked out. But if I wasn't and I had left him – Mal would have gone crazy."

"I didn't know," Maggie said. "Yesterday morning, I – I told him it was okay if he bit me."

She gave Ava and Willow a look of horror, and Ava

rubbed her back. "It's okay, honey. Obviously, Porter knew you didn't understand what you were permitting him to do. He didn't bite you."

"He didn't, did he?" Willow said when Maggie didn't reply.

"No, he didn't. I swear," Maggie said.

"Thank God," Willow said. "Having two Burke men bite their mates without permission would be so freakin' bad."

"I think we have a bigger problem," Ava said. "Porter wants to bite Maggie, which means he's in love with her and thinks she's his mate."

"Shit, you're right," Willow said. "Maggie, do you love Porter?"

Maggie stared blankly at her. "I – what?"

"Are you in love with Porter? You lost your v-card to him, so obviously you think he's something special, but are you in love with him?"

"I – I don't know," Maggie said.

Liar!

She ignored her inner voice as Willow said, "So, this is super awkward, but I need to ask. You told us that Vaughn wanted you because of your virginity, right? Did you give Porter your virginity so that Vaughn would leave you alone?"

There was a sharp inhale behind her, and Maggie turned around. Porter stood in the doorway, and her stomach dropped at the look of hurt on his face.

"Porter," she said, "I -"

"Mom sent me up here to tell you that dinner is almost ready," Porter said. He walked away without waiting for their reply.

"Shit," Willow said. "Maggie, I'm sorry."

"It's okay," Maggie said.

"It isn't," Willow said. "I'll talk to Porter."

"No, don't," Maggie said. "I'll talk to him about it later."

Willow gave Ava a miserable look. "I didn't know he was standing there."

"I know, honey," Ava said.

"This is all my fault."

"It isn't," Maggie said. "Don't be upset, Willow. I should have told Porter about Vaughn wanting my virginity a long time ago."

She rubbed her forehead as Willow said, "When will I ever learn to keep my big mouth shut?"

"It isn't your fault," Maggie repeated. "We'd better get downstairs. They'll be waiting for us."

CHAPTER 13

"**P**orter, we need to talk," Maggie said.

Porter threw his keys on the table and tossed his jacket on the chair. "I'm tired, Maggie. I don't feel like talking."

"Well, that's too bad," Maggie said. "We need to talk."

Porter glared at her, and she folded her arms across her chest and gave him a defiant look. Dinner at his parents was highly awkward, and she knew that everyone could feel the tension radiating from Porter. They left almost immediately after dinner, and Porter didn't speak once the entire drive home.

"I'm tired," he repeated. "It's been a long day."

"Yes, it has, but I want to explain what you heard earlier."

"What's there to explain?" he growled. "Vaughn wanted you because of your virginity, so you gave it to me to keep him away. Why haven't you called him yet to tell him that you're not a virgin anymore? Or have you called him already, and that's just another lie you're telling me?"

"Stop it!" Maggie said sharply. "Not telling you that

Vaughn wanted my virginity wasn't lying to you. It didn't feel like something I could share with you and -"

"But you could share it with Willow and Ava?" Porter shouted.

"They only knew because I accidentally blurted it out when I first met them. Vaughn told me that all shifters wanted a woman who was a virgin, and I believed him, which is why I even offered the stupid thing to you as payment in the first place. I thought a shifter wouldn't be able to resist that. Ava and Willow told me the truth," Maggie said.

"Fine," Porter said. "It doesn't matter anyway. You got what you wanted from me, and now Vaughn will leave you alone. You can go back to your normal life now."

"I didn't sleep with you just to get rid of my virginity so Vaughn wouldn't want me," Maggie said.

Porter shrugged. "Whatever you say, Maggie."

"You dick!" Maggie shouted. She threw her purse on the table and glared at him as Porter gave her a look of surprise.

"Maggie, don't – "

"Be quiet!" Maggie said. "You're going to listen to me for two minutes, you stubborn jerk! Was there a part of me that thought if I weren't a virgin, Vaughn wouldn't want me anymore? Of course, there was. But after I offered it to you and you refused, I realized that you were right. I didn't want to give it away to someone I didn't care about. I didn't want to sleep with someone just in the hopes that it would get Vaughn off my damn back."

She ran her hand through her hair before glaring at him again. "I gave you my virginity because I wanted to. Because I like you a lot and because I am so attracted to you, I can barely think straight! It had nothing to do with Vaughn. After we slept together, I asked you if you took my virginity as payment for your protection, and you said no. I believed you,

Porter. I took you at your word because I trust you. Do you know how hurtful it is that you won't give me the same trust? I will tell you one last time - I slept with you because I wanted to. Do you believe me or not? If you don't, tell me and I'll leave. I'm not staying with someone who thinks I'm a liar."

Porter stared at her before slumping against the counter. "Yes," he said. "I believe you."

"Finally." Maggie pulled out a chair and sat down with a harsh thump. She stared at the floor and stiffened when Porter knelt on the floor in front of her and took her hands.

"I'm sorry," he said. "I'm sorry for yelling at you and for not believing you."

"And for being a dick," she said.

He smiled a little. "I'm sorry for being a dick. I should have realized that Vaughn wanted you for your virginity. You said you knew virgins were a big thing to shifters when you offered it to me. Honestly, though, I was a little shocked by your offer, and it went right over my head."

She reached out and touched his face. "Apology accepted. I hate fighting with you."

"I hate it too," he said before kissing the palm of her hand. "I'm sorry. I overreacted."

She studied him silently, and he kissed her hand again. "What?"

"Willow told me what it means when a wolf shifter bites a woman."

Porter's face paled, and he stood and backed away. She stood and followed him, backing him up against the counter.

"You keep trying to bite me whenever we have sex," she said. "Why?"

He hesitated before saying, "My wolf wants me to claim you as his mate."

"Your wolf," she said.

He nodded. "Yes. He, uh, thinks you're his mate."

"Only your wolf?"

"Yes."

She hid the dismay she felt at his answer. What did she think he would say? That he loved her and wanted to be with her for the rest of his life? God, they'd only known each other for a few weeks, and she'd caused him nothing but trouble. It was a damn miracle that he was even attracted to her. She should thank her lucky stars that he even wanted her at all.

Or maybe he wasn't. Her heart a quick staccato in her chest, she said, "Are you – are you even attracted to me or is it all just your wolf?"

"No, I'm attracted to you," Porter said. "I swear. I want you so much, Maggie. It's just my wolf is – well, he's impulsive and is sometimes ruled by his, uh, base urges."

"Base urges."

"Yes, eating and hunting and…mating."

"Right," she said. "So, when we have sex, it's your wolf who wants to bite me, not you."

"Yes," he said again.

"Okay," she said. "Okay."

"I'm sorry," he said.

"You don't need to be sorry," she said. "But I guess we should stop having sex. If you lose control and your wolf bites me, you'll be stuck with me forever."

He winced and reached out to pull her into his embrace. She thought about resisting before giving in and resting her head against his broad chest. She blinked back the tears as Porter pressed a kiss against the top of her head.

"I can control it," he said.

"By biting yourself instead of me," she said.

"I won't bite you during sex, Maggie. I promise," he said.

"But if you don't want to sleep with me again, I'll understand."

"I want to," she said as she discreetly wiped away the tears running down her cheeks. "But I don't want something to happen that you'll regret for the rest of your life."

"I can control it," he repeated.

She sighed inwardly, wishing he had said he wouldn't regret it. But that was stupid. *She* was being stupid. In fact, the smart thing to do would be to tell Vaughn that she wasn't a virgin anymore. He'd leave her alone, and she could get back to her normal life again.

Without Porter.

She flinched involuntarily at the thought of never seeing Porter again. He hugged her tightly and kissed her forehead.

Yes, without him. He didn't want her for anything more than sex – he had just admitted it to her. So why wasn't she calling Vaughn? Why was there a part of her that hoped Porter would change his mind if she just stuck around long enough?

You're pathetic. You know that, right?

Yeah, she knew.

"I guess I should text Vaughn," she said. "You're right that if he knows I've had sex, he won't want me anymore. This can all end tonight."

"No," Porter said.

She frowned at the weird anxiety in his voice, but when she tried to look at him, he pressed her face against his chest.

"No," he repeated. "Contacting Vaughn is a terrible idea."

"But you said -"

"You shouldn't contact him. What if instead of losing interest, he gets angry?" Porter said.

"I think it's worth the risk," Maggie replied.

"It isn't," Porter insisted. "Listen, at least give Bren a

chance to talk to him, okay? He might convince Vaughn to leave you alone."

"I don't think it'll work," Maggie said. She broke free of Porter's grip and lifted her head to stare at him. "I don't have to see Vaughn. I can just text or…"

Porter gave her an anxious look. "What's wrong?"

"Your fangs are out," she said softly before touching his jaw, "and you've grown a beard. Are you upset with me?"

"What? No, of course not," Porter said as he retracted his fangs with a soft pop. "Just promise me that you won't contact Vaughn – not yet."

She hesitated and then nodded. "Okay."

He gave her a look of relief. "Thank you, Maggie."

She touched his face. "I know it's early, but I was thinking of going to bed. Are you – do you want me in your bed, or should I go to the couch?"

"I want you in my bed," he said. "If you want to be there."

"I do," she said.

He took her hand, and she followed him out of the kitchen.

PORTER LEANED AGAINST THE HEADBOARD AND STARED AT the door of the bedroom. Maggie was in the bathroom, and he wondered if she would join him in his bed. His wolf growled at the thought of Maggie sleeping on the couch. He froze at the sudden thought that maybe Maggie was texting Vaughn right now. Maybe she had decided to contact him anyway. If Vaughn found out she wasn't a virgin and lost interest, Maggie would leave him forever.

Take her phone, his wolf growled persuasively. *Take her phone, so she can't leave us.*

He started to climb out of the bed before he realized how ridiculous he was being. He couldn't take Maggie's phone in a bid to keep her here. She wasn't his prisoner, for fuck's sake.

She needs us to protect her. It's for her own good, his wolf growled.

Jesus, he was going insane. His wolf's advice was starting to sound almost reasonable. He ran his hand over the scruff on his jaw before resting his head against the headboard and closing his eyes.

He had lied to Maggie earlier. He'd looked her right in the eye and lied to her, and he felt terrible about it. But he couldn't tell her the truth. If he told her that it wasn't just his wolf who wanted her as his mate and that he loved her and wanted to spend the rest of his life with her, she'd run screaming. Only an insane shifter fell in love with a woman he barely knew.

Your brother did.

Yeah, he did, and look how Willow reacted when he bit her. Willow was the most open-minded human he knew when it came to shifters, and she still nearly ran when Mal told her that he loved her and wanted to be with her for the rest of his life. Watching how Mal suffered as Willow tried to decide if she wanted to be with him forever was burned into Porter's memory. He didn't want to suffer the same fate, nor did he want to put Maggie through the same painful decision.

He couldn't tell her that he loved her – not yet. He would tell her in another few weeks when it didn't seem quite so fucking weird.

You don't have a few weeks! She wants to leave, remember?

His fangs popped out at the thought of Maggie leaving him, and he groaned before clapping his hand over his mouth. Fuck, he needed to get control of himself. Maggie wouldn't contact Vaughn, at least not until after Bren spoke to him. In the meantime, he would think of perfectly valid reasons why she shouldn't tell Vaughn she was no longer a virgin. He would convince her that he loved her over the next few weeks, and if he were lucky – she'd realize that she loved him too.

What if she doesn't? What if she never loves you the way you love her?

Bite her! His wolf snarled. *Bite her, and none of this will matter. She is our mate and belongs to us!*

Maggie walked into the bedroom. She wore his shirt again, and she pulled self-consciously at the hem of it before joining him in the bed. He was still sitting up, and she sat cross-legged next to him.

He gave her a tentative smile. "Hi."

"Hi," she said in a low voice.

He smoothed her hair back from her face. He desperately wanted to make love to her, but he wasn't sure that was what she wanted despite what she said earlier. "Are you ready to go to sleep?"

"No," she said steadily. "That isn't what I want."

"Are you sure?" he asked.

She nodded and moved until she was straddling him. "I'm positive. Unless you don't want this?"

He didn't reply. Maggie wasn't wearing panties, and her warm pussy rested directly against his dick. It immediately hardened, and she made a soft sound in the back of her throat. "I guess I have my answer."

He cupped the back of her head and kissed her slowly,

tasting every inch of her mouth until she was rubbing her pussy against his suddenly aching dick.

"I want you so much, darlin'," he whispered against her mouth.

"I want you too," she murmured.

They repeatedly kissed, their tongues tasting and teasing until Porter pulled his mouth away and pulled her shirt over her head. He cupped her breasts and dipped his head to suck at her nipples. She curled her hands into his hair and held tightly as he licked and sucked.

He licked her upper chest before sucking on her throat. She inhaled sharply and tugged his head up.

"Don't bite me, Porter."

"I won't, darlin'," he said.

She studied him for a moment before reaching into the nightstand drawer. She brought out a condom and ripped open the packaging. He helped her smooth it over his cock, groaning at the feel of her soft hands on his dick.

"Can I be on top?" she asked shyly.

"Whatever you want," he rasped.

Her smile turned into a low moan when he stroked the head of his cock against her pussy.

"Spread your pussy lips open for me," he said.

Her cheeks reddened with embarrassment, but she did what he asked. He stared at her swollen clit before rubbing his cock against it. She cried out with pleasure, her free hand digging into his shoulder as he caressed her clit repeatedly. Her embarrassment forgotten, she rocked against his dick eagerly.

He cupped her breast and pinched her nipple. She arched her back and made another harsh cry of pleasure as she climaxed. Her body shook above his, and she dug her nails into his skin. It brought a sharp twinge of pain that oddly just increased his desire. He gripped her hips and lifted her to her knees above him.

"Porter," she moaned softly, "please."

"Slide my cock into your tight pussy," he demanded.

She grasped his cock and pushed it into her warm core. He watched his dick sink into her wet warmth and controlled the urge to release his fangs.

"Ride me," he growled.

She braced her hands on his shoulders and bounced up and down on his cock. He cupped her ass, his fingers digging into the soft skin as she rode him with slow strokes.

"Faster," he moaned.

She shook her head, and he squeezed her ass warningly. She smiled at him and continued with the slow, deep strokes as she bent her head and kissed him lightly on the mouth.

"Maggie, faster," he begged.

"No," she whispered against his mouth. "Nice and slow, honey. I want to drive you crazy."

"Darlin', I'm already there," he muttered.

She laughed, and he groaned when her pussy squeezed around him. "Fuck! Don't do that!"

She leaned forward and braced her hands on the head-board before rubbing her perfect tits against his chest. He could feel her hard nipples dragging across his skin, and he groaned again and kissed her slender neck. He didn't realize his fangs were out until she stiffened and pulled back.

"Don't bite me," she said.

His wolf growled with anger at her rejection, and he tried to ignore the hurt that rippled through him. Of course, she didn't want to be bitten. Just because she liked fucking him didn't mean she wanted to be his mate.

She had slowed to a stop and was giving him a thoughtful

look. He scowled at her and said irritably, "I won't bite you. I already told you that."

"I know," she said.

Shame rushed through him at his impatience. "I'm sorry."

"It's okay," she said.

She kissed him again, running the tip of her tongue over his fangs. It sent a lightning bolt of lust through him, and he thrust roughly into her. She moaned into his mouth, and he sat up straight and anchored his arm around her waist. He held her tightly and fucked her roughly. She clung to him, making small moans that set him on fire with need. He tilted her forward and drove deep in an effort to stroke her g-spot.

He must have succeeded because she jerked against him and cried out. "Porter, wait! It feels strange and…"

He thrust again, and she made another sharp cry. "Oh! Oh my God!"

He grinned with satisfaction and fucked her with hard, deep strokes. Her pussy tightened exquisitely around his cock, and he groaned and buried his face in her neck. Her breath exploded from her lungs in harsh pants, and he barely felt the sting when she raked her nails down his back.

She made an incoherent noise of pleasure before she raked him again with her nails, and her entire body stiffened against his. She screamed his name, her hips jerking wildly against his as her pussy squeezed and released his dick in a hard rhythm. He lost the tenuous grip on his control and howled deafeningly as his climax rushed over him. His fangs lengthened, and he tore his mouth away from her neck and turned his head to sink them into his arm as his wolf snarled at him to bite Maggie.

His head shot downward to his upper arm, but his fangs sunk into fabric instead of hard flesh. He jerked, tearing easily through the material with his sharp fangs and feathers filled his mouth. He yanked his head back, coughing out feathers as more flew out of the giant rip in the pillow and floated to the bed.

Panting harshly and her body trembling wildly against his, Maggie dropped the pillow she'd pressed against his arm. She had feathers in her hair and stuck to her body, and she picked them off as he stared wide-eyed at her. He coughed again, and she giggled a little when more feathers erupted from his mouth. Her giggles turned into a full-body belly laugh, and his shock was replaced with amusement. Her entire body shaking with laughter, Maggie picked feathers out of his hair.

"You look like a chicken attacked you," she said before laughing again.

He burst into laughter and hugged her as they laughed like maniacs for nearly five minutes. When their laughter finally trickled to a stop, she leaned back and wiped the tears from her eyes before grinning at him. "I'm sorry. It seemed like a good idea at the time."

He brushed the feathers off her breasts before pressing a kiss against the tip of her nipple. "You thought me getting a mouthful of feathers was a good idea?"

"Better than hurting yourself," she said before running her fingers through his hair.

"You're pretty quick for a human," he said with a small grin.

She laughed. "Honestly, it was probably more luck than anything. I just grabbed the pillow, shoved it toward your arm and hoped for the best. Although," she eyed the feathers that covered the bed, "I guess I owe you a new pillow."

He hugged her again, and she caressed his back. He didn't wince, but she must have felt the marks because she pulled him forward and peered around his body.

"Oh, Porter! I'm so sorry."

"It's fine, darlin'."

"It isn't. You're scratched to hell." She gave him a horrified look before staring at her own hands like she couldn't believe they were responsible for the scratches on his back.

"I don't mind."

"We should put some antiseptic on the scratches," she said.

He laughed and shook his head. "They're not that deep and will heal quickly. Besides, I don't mind being marked by you."

She flushed and bit at her bottom lip. "It was, uh, a good one. I mean, a *really* good one."

He grinned at her, and she slapped him lightly on the chest. "Don't look so smug."

"I can't help it if I'm a rock star in bed," he said.

"No, I suppose you can't. It felt a little strange at first but then," she made an exploding motion with her hands, "fireworks."

"Keep talking like that, and my ego won't fit through the door," he said with another grin.

She rubbed his chest. "I'd read about g-spot orgasms, but until you have one, you have no idea how amazing they are. Where did you learn to do that?"

He shrugged and, without thinking, said, "Lots of practice, I guess."

She didn't reply, and the grin dropped from his face. Shit, what the fuck was wrong with him? Reminding Maggie that he was a goddamn man-whore was a stupid fucking move.

"I mean, I like making women – I mean you…." He started to sweat as he tried again. "I mean, I like making *you* feel good, so…."

His wolf chuffed with annoyance at his stupidity.

"Porter?" Maggie cupped his face and made him look at her. "I don't care about your past or how many women you've slept with."

He stared silently at her, and she pressed a quick kiss against his mouth. "Please don't be embarrassed or ashamed of it. I really don't care. Okay?"

"Okay," he said as gratitude washed over him. His mate really was perfect.

"Just – if you start to be, um, interested in sleeping with another woman, will you tell me? I don't mean to sound like a prude, but I don't want to have sex with you if you're having sex with someone else."

He blinked at her. "Maggie, I would never do that to you. I don't fuck around on women I'm dating. Do you think I'm that kind of guy?"

She shook her head. "No, I don't. But we're not dating, are we? We're just pretending to date. There aren't any rules set in stone about not seeing other people when you're fake dating someone, so I thought being clear about -"

She broke off as Porter, his eyes glowing and a dark beard sprouting on his face, cupped the back of her head tightly and made a low growl. "Are you fucking someone else?"

She stared in fascination at how his fangs had descended. He gave her a gentle shake. "Are you fucking another guy?"

"No, of course not," she said. "You know I'm not."

His nostrils flared, and he took her mouth in a hard and possessive kiss before growling, "You belong to me."

"Porter, I -"

"If you let anyone else touch you, if you let someone else's dick slide into that hot little pussy of yours, I'll hunt him down and kill him. Do you understand, Maggie?"

Jesus Christ – stop it! You're scaring the hell out of her!

He wanted to stop, tried to stop, but his wolf had surged forward and was firmly in control.

She's not scared, his wolf growled. *She likes it. I can smell her arousal.*

He inhaled deeply as he gripped the back of Maggie's head more tightly. His wolf was right. Maggie's arousal surrounded her in a thick coat, and he could see her pulse beating rapidly in her neck. He licked that flickering, racing beat, and she moaned.

He reached between them and cupped her pussy possessively. "Whose pussy is this, Maggie?"

"Yours," she whispered.

He rubbed her clit, making her squirm on his lap. "Louder."

"It's yours."

He pinched her clit, and she cried out before grinding her pussy against his hand. He immediately stopped rubbing her, and she clutched at his shoulders. "Please! I want to come."

"Tell me again," he demanded.

"It's your pussy!" she cried. "Yours, Porter!"

He rubbed her clit roughly. She really *was* turned on. He could see how close she was to coming already. When he stopped, she pounded on his back in frustration. He gave her a hard grin before sliding two fingers into her.

"You're mine, Maggie."

"Yes," she said. "I'm yours."

"No one fucks you but me. I'll kill any man who touches you. Do you believe me?" He thrust his fingers in and out of her, and she moaned loudly before rocking wildly against his hand.

"Yes," she whispered as he rubbed her clit. "Only you, only you, only…" her voice trailed off into a loud moan as her back arched and she came all over his hand. His wolf howled with satisfaction before retreating.

As Maggie slumped forward and rested her forehead against his chest, shame filled Porter. Jesus, what was he doing? His wolf treated Maggie like his mate even though he hadn't claimed her. He was losing control, and sooner or later, he wouldn't be able to stop from biting her. He needed to put some space between them, but as Maggie lifted her head and stared at him, he pulled her even closer. She pressed her cheek against his chest, and he stroked her warm back as her body shuddered with the after-effects of her orgasm.

"I'm sorry," he said.

"For what?" she said.

"I shouldn't have forced you to say those things."

"You didn't," she said. "It was your wolf."

He hesitated. Technically she wasn't wrong, it was his wolf who had growled out the demands, but his human side felt the same way.

She lifted her head and stared at him. "Wasn't it?"

He nodded and thought he saw a brief flicker of disappointment in her eyes before she smiled at him. "It's okay."

"It isn't," he said.

"It is," she insisted before easing off of him. His cock had hardened again, and both it and his thighs were soaked with her sweet cream. A blush crossed her face. "Oh, God. That's embarrassing."

He shook his head. "It's not."

"Says you," she mumbled before easing the condom off of him and throwing it in the waste bin next to the bed. She held out her hand. "Come get in the shower with me, and I'll hose you off."

That made him laugh, and the awkwardness between them disappeared. "It's not that big of a deal."

She gave him a smile that was somehow both shy and sexy. "Okay, but I was thinking while we're in the shower, I could practice my oral sex skills."

He immediately slid off the bed and grabbed her hand, pulling her to her feet before walking rapidly toward the bathroom.

She laughed and squeezed his hand. "So, you like that idea?"

He grinned at her as he turned on the shower. "Darlin', it's the best idea I've ever heard."

CHAPTER 14

"Arlo, are you okay?" Porter stared at the weasel shifter. It was Monday night, and he swiped a rag across the top of the bar as Arlo gave him a guilty look.

"Yeah, I'm fine, man."

"Are you sure? You've been quiet since I got here."

"I'm good," Arlo said without meeting his gaze. "Just tired tonight."

"Why don't you head home. Your shift is done in half an hour anyway."

"Nah, it's fine," Arlo said. "I wanted to finish wiping down the bottles before I head out."

He turned and studied the bottles on the three rows of shelving behind the bar before grabbing one on the bottom shelf and wiping it with a cloth.

Porter shrugged before smiling at the coyote shifter who sat at the bar staring into his glass. "Another scotch and soda?"

The coyote shifter nodded, and Porter made him another drink. He sat it in front of him and took the bill the coyote shoved at him. He rang it through the cash register and gave him his change as he was tapped on the shoulder.

He turned and smiled at the short hedgehog shifter. "Hey, Bud. I thought you left already."

"Just heading out," Bud said. He rubbed his lower back and made a soft groan. "Jesus, I spent most of the day on that damn computer, and now my back is killing me. Did your lawyer get a chance to look at the paperwork?"

Porter nodded. "He was looking at it today. I'm just waiting for his text, but I'm sure everything's fine."

"Good, good," Bud said. He glanced behind him and nodded to Arlo as the weasel shifter moved closer to them and grabbed another bottle to dust. "I know you're workin' tomorrow. How about I drop by after the bar closes, and we can sign the paperwork?"

"Sure, but I can come by in the afternoon if that's easier for you. It'll be pretty late when the bar closes," Porter said.

"I gotta drive Alice to her sister's tomorrow, and it's a good two hours outside of the city. Her sister is goin' through some kind of goddamn crisis again and wants Alice to stay with her for a few days," Bud said with a sigh. "That woman's always got something wrong with her. Anyway, I'll be gone most of the day, and I don't sleep worth shit lately anyway, so I might as well meet you after the bar closes."

"All right. Thanks, Bud. I'll bring a bank draft with me."

"Appreciate that," Bud said. "I better get goin'. It's date night for Alice and me, and if I'm gonna perform in the bedroom like a man, I need to get to my massage therapy appointment and work the kinks out."

Porter bit back his grin. "Uh, okay. Well, have a good time tonight."

"Oh, I will," Bud said. "That old girl of mine is a real firecracker in bed. Good night."

"Night, Bud," Porter said.

Porter caught Arlo's eye and grinned at him as Bud walked stiffly away. Arlo gave him a small smile in return before turning away. Porter frowned. There was definitely something going on with the weasel shifter, but he wasn't close enough with Arlo to be comfortable in pushing him to share what was wrong.

A giraffe shifter sat down next to the coyote shifter, and, pushing his concern for Arlo aside, Porter grinned at him. "What can I get you, big guy?"

ARLO SAT IN HIS CAR IN THE BAR'S PARKING LOT AND STARED at the phone in his hand. The fluorescent light from the sign affixed to the front of the bar lit his hands up in a bright green glow. He wondered idly if Porter would change the sign from "Bud's Bar" to "Porter's Bar". Probably not. Why would he? Shifters liked the bar just the way it was, and they –

Make the fucking call, idiot!

He winced at the panic in his inner voice and made the call. Nausea rolled through him, and sweat dripped down his back as the ringing stopped, and a man said, "Hello?"

"Hi, uh, Officer Bales. This is Arlo. Arlo Calden? From the bar?"

"Arlo, so good to hear from you," the hyena shifter said. "I assume you have some news for me?"

"Uh, yeah." He swallowed hard as the words stuck in his throat.

"Tell me," Vaughn said impatiently.

"Porter and Bud are meeting tomorrow night after the bar closes so that Porter can sign the paperwork and, uh, pay Bud for the bar."

"What time does the bar close?" Vaughn asked.

"Around one or so. Depends on how many people they have to kick out."

There was silence, and he checked his phone screen to see if they were disconnected. "Officer Bales? Are you still there?"

"I am," Vaughn said. "Can you meet me tomorrow?"

"Yes."

"Good. Meet me at the coffee shop at the corner of Fifth and Twentieth Street at nine tomorrow morning. Bring your key to the back entrance of the bar."

"What? Why?" Arlo asked.

"Just be there at nine. Goodbye."

"Wait!" Arlo said. "My brother – is he, I mean, will the evidence…."

He flinched when the hyena shifter laughed. "The evidence against your brother will remain mysteriously lost, little weasel. How is he, by the way? Back at home with your loving parents?"

"Yeah," Arlo mumbled. "He's at home. His lawyer got him released when they, uh, couldn't find the drugs."

"Good," Vaughn said. "He's a lucky guy."

"What are you going to do?" Arlo asked.

"Nothing you need to worry about, little weasel. See you tomorrow at nine."

"Uh, bye."

He stared at his cell phone for a moment before placing it on the seat beside him. His sweaty hands trembled, and he wiped them on the front of his shirt before staring at the bar again.

"It's fine," he whispered. "You had no choice. Nothing bad is going to happen."

"You know this is the world's biggest fucking cliché, right?" Jake grumbled as he dropped into the seat next to Vaughn. He took a sip of his coffee and stared in distaste as Vaughn bit into the donut. "I don't even fucking like donuts."

Vaughn wiped some crumbs from his chin. "Shut the fuck up, Jake. I've had enough of your goddamn attitude today."

He nudged Hank, who stared at a woman standing in line. "Roll your tongue back in your head, idiot."

Hank rolled his eyes. "Can't blame me for lookin'. Stupid bitch's ass is practically hanging out of her shorts. It's like she wants me to bend her over the goddamn counter and fuck her up the -"

"Shut up, you moron," Jake hissed as a woman sitting at the table next to them gave Hank a horrified look. A little boy of about four sat beside her, and without looking at them, she hurriedly packed up his toys and put his jacket on him.

As she picked him up and walked away, the little boy stared over his mother's shoulder at Vaughn. Vaughn bared his fangs at him. He laughed when the boy bared his tiny fangs at him before sticking out his tongue. As the mother and son left the donut shop, Vaughn took another bite of his donut and washed it down with a sip of coffee.

"Everything good for tonight?" he asked in a low voice.

Jake nodded. "Yeah. I'll meet you behind the bar at twelve-thirty. Did the weasel give you a key?"

"Yes, this morning. Remember to park a few streets away. If those assholes watching over the wolf shifter catch you, I'll slit your damn throat. Got it?"

Jake rolled his eyes. "Relax, Vaughn. I've got this."

Hank cracked his knuckles. "You sure you don't want me there, Boss?"

"No, I don't," Vaughn said, "and keep your goddamn voice down before I rip out your vocal cords."

Hank scowled at him and ate his donut in three large bites. Vaughn shook his head before staring around the donut shop. A tall man wearing a dark suit entered the store, and Vaughn frowned. "What the fuck is he doing here?"

"Is that who I think it is?" Jake studied the man as he walked toward them.

"Just keep your fucking mouth shut," Vaughn muttered as the man drew closer. "Both of you."

AS BREN WALKED TOWARD VAUGHN AND THE OTHER TWO officers, he studied their body language. All three men had stiffened the moment he saw them, and Vaughn murmured something to the other two that he couldn't quite hear. He stopped at their table and smiled at Vaughn as the hyena shifter stood.

"Hello, Officer Bales."

"Detective Matthews. It's good to see you again."

Vaughn held his hand out, and Bren shook it briefly. "You as well."

"How is your father doing?"

"He's good," Bren said.

"Good," Vaughn said. "Really glad to hear that." He had a smile on his face, but his black eyes were cold and glittering with barely contained resentment.

"I'm sure you are," Bren said. "Do you mind if I join you?"

"Not at all." Vaughn sat down as Bren sat next to Hank.

There was a moment of silence that Bren broke. "Bren

Matthews." He held his hand out to Jake, who gave it a quick shake before mumbling, "Jake Sallen."

Bren turned to Hank, who shook his hand and said, "Hank Hornsby."

"Hornsby," Bren said thoughtfully. "Your father was a cop, right?"

Hank nodded. "Yeah, for thirty years."

"He was fired after interrogating a suspect, wasn't he? The guy had a dislocated shoulder, three broken ribs, and a broken leg."

"What's your point?" Hank said sullenly as his hand tightened around his coffee cup.

Bren shrugged. "No real point. You have quite a few unnecessary force complaints on your file. Is that right?"

"Fuck you!" Hank suddenly shouted. He stood and leaned over Bren, trying to intimidate him with his size and the fangs that had suddenly descended. "You think you can take me on, human? I'll rip off your head and shit down your neck before you can even blink."

"Charming," Bren said dryly. "I can't begin to imagine where the unnecessary force complaints come from."

Hank growled loudly as dark hair sprouted on his cheeks and chin. Bren stared steadily at him, a small smile crossing his mouth as Hank bared his fangs at him.

"You'd better call off your dog, Officer Bales," Bren said mildly, "before he tries to do something he'll regret."

Hank growled again, and Vaughn snarled, "Hank! Get the fuck out of here! Go sit in the goddamn car!"

Hank glared at him, and Vaughn snapped, "Now!"

With a low growl, Hank turned to stomp away.

"Good doggie," Bren said.

Jake stood and grabbed Hank when the smaller hyena

lunged for Bren. Holding him by the neck and one arm, he pulled Hank toward the door as Bren grinned.

"He seems nice," Bren said to Vaughn as Jake dragged the snarling Hank out of the donut shop.

Vaughn shoved his half-eaten donut away. "What do you want, Detective Matthews? Sure as shit, this isn't a social call."

"As a matter of fact, I did have something I wanted to discuss with you."

"Make it quick," Vaughn said. "My break's almost over."

"I want you to leave Maggie Wallace and Porter Burke alone."

Vaughn jerked and nearly knocked over his coffee cup before he sat back and said, "Never heard of them."

"Of course, you haven't," Bren said. "Let me jog your memory. You've been stalking Maggie for weeks, and last week you shot Porter Burke and then got your little hyena buddies to beat the shit out of him."

"Says who?" Vaughn said. "You have any proof?"

Bren studied him thoughtfully before leaning forward. "You saved my father's life. I know that you wish you hadn't, and hell, I can respect that. My dad's a bastard – always has been and always will be. Still, I'm grateful to you for saving him, which is why I'm coming directly to you instead of going to the captain."

"You don't have any proof," Vaughn repeated. "You think you can sit here and threaten me without anything to back it up?"

"Threaten you?" Bren said in surprise. "This is in no way a threat. Just a suggestion that you need to cool it with your obsession with a human and your attempted murdering of a shifter."

"I don't have any idea what you're talking about, but if I did, I might suggest that you mind your own fucking business when it comes to me. You don't want to fuck with me, Detective Matthews."

"Now who's doing the threatening," Bren said with a hard grin. "Do the smart thing and walk away from the situation. The woman is with the wolf shifter, and if you keep harassing her, I will go to the captain."

"Go ahead," Vaughn said with a sneer. "The captain won't believe a word you say. Just because you're the Senator's son, don't mean shit. Why don't you do me a favour and fuck off."

Bren studied him for a moment before standing. "Good to see you again, Officer Bales."

"MAGGIE? I'M LEAVING FOR WORK. WHAT TIME ARE YOU going to Willow's?"

Porter stuck his head into the kitchen. Maggie was just stuffing her cell phone into her pocket, and at the sight of her pale face, he hurried into the room.

"Darlin'? What's wrong?"

"That – that was Detective Matthews. Ava gave him my number. He talked to Vaughn this afternoon."

"And? What did he say?" Porter asked.

Maggie rubbed at her forehead. "Vaughn denied everything. He said he didn't know who we were."

"Of course, he did," Porter said in disgust.

"Bren told him to leave us alone and that if he didn't, he'd go to the captain, but Vaughn just told him to go ahead. That he didn't have anything on him and no proof that he'd done anything wrong."

Tears leaked down her cheek, and Porter pulled her into his arms. "It'll be okay."

She sighed. "I don't know why I'm so upset. I knew it wouldn't work. I guess it's time I contact Vaughn and tell him I'm not a virgin anymore."

"No!" Porter said.

"Porter, I have to. It's the only thing that will work."

"He's not just going to take your word for it," Porter said. "You'd have to fucking prove it to him, and there's no way in hell that's happening."

He growled under his breath, and he tried to relax when Maggie rubbed his back. "I know you're right. I'm just – I don't know what to do."

"You stay here. We keep showing him that we're a couple, and eventually, he gives up," Porter replied.

"What if that doesn't work? I can't expect you to put your life on hold indefinitely," Maggie said.

"It's fine."

She laughed bitterly. "Fine? You were almost killed last week, and it's fine? Porter, I can't -"

"You can and you will," he said. "I need to get to work, okay? Are you still going to Mal and Willow's tonight?"

Maggie nodded. "Yes. Fenton said he would drive me over there."

He pressed a kiss against her mouth. "Good. I'll be late tonight. I'm meeting with Bud to sign the paperwork for the bar after it closes."

"Just be careful, all right?" Maggie said anxiously.

"I will, darlin'. Besides, Garth will be right outside the bar, and he'll follow me home. Don't worry, okay?"

She nodded, and he kissed her again. "Everything will be fine. Don't worry."

"THANKS FOR DOING THIS, HEATH. I KNOW IT'S LATE," Porter said as he tossed the lemon wedges into the trash.

Heath took a sip of his club soda. "It's fine. I asked one of the partners at the firm to look at the contract as well, just to make sure I didn't miss anything."

"You didn't have to do that," Porter said. "I trust you."

Heath shrugged. "I've been a lawyer for less than a year. Trust me, it's better to have a partner look at it as well. Anyway, he said it looked good. Did you bring the bank draft?"

"Yeah," Porter said.

Heath smiled and raised his glass, tipping it in Porter's direction. "Well, congratulations, big brother. You'll be your own boss by this time tomorrow."

Porter grinned at him. "Thanks, Heath."

He moved down the bar to the pig shifter slumped over on the bar stool. He tapped the shifter on the shoulder, and the pig shifter squealed loudly and jerked in his seat. Porter grabbed his arm before he could fall off the stool. "Hey, buddy. Bar's closed."

The pig shifter blinked owlishly at him before sniffing the air. "Closed?"

"Yeah. I've called you a cab."

"I don't need a cab," the pig shifter said as he slid from the stool. He took a few stumbling steps forward before tripping over a chair and falling to the floor. Porter hurried around the bar and helped him to his feet.

"Yeah, man, you do. C'mon, I'll help you outside."

He half-carried the pig shifter out the door. He helped the shifter into the cab as Bud pulled into the parking lot. He climbed out of his truck and slammed the door shut before glancing at the dark sedan parked in front of the bar. "Who's that?"

Porter waved at Garth, who nodded to him before studying the parking lot.

"A friend of mine," Porter said.

"Oh." Bud ran his hand through his short hair, and Porter grinned. It made Bud's spiky hair even spikier than usual.

"You okay, Bud?" he asked.

Bud nodded as he studied the glowing sign above the bar's door. "Just feeling a little sentimental, I guess."

He cleared his throat and then said, "You gonna change the name?"

He was trying to appear casual, but Porter could see small spikes starting to jut out from his chin in response to his anxiety. He shook his head. "No. It'll stay Bud's Bar."

Bud gave him a grateful look as the spikes receded. "That's real nice of you, Porter. It means a lot to me. Well, let's get in there and sign some paperwork so we can both go home."

BUD SIGNED THE PAPERWORK WITH A SHORT HARD SLASH OF the pen before sliding it across the desk to Heath. Heath tucked the papers into his briefcase. Bud opened the bottom drawer of his desk and pulled out a bottle of scotch and three glasses. "Why don't you fellas have a drink with me."

"Thanks for the offer, but I need to be at the office early tomorrow," Heath said as he stood. He shook Bud's hand before clapping Porter on the back. "Congratulations, Porter. I'll talk to you tomorrow, okay?"

"Thanks, Heath," Porter said.

As Heath left, Porter handed Bud the envelope with the

bank draft. Bud glanced inside before making it disappear into the inside pocket of his jacket.

"Thank you, Porter."

"It's me who should thank you." Porter took the glass of scotch from Bud.

They clinked glasses as Bud said, "To the bar and its new owner."

Porter swallowed the scotch as Bud tossed his back with a grimace and poured them both another glass. "I can't believe I'm retired."

Porter smiled at him. "Any retirement plans?"

"Nah. Just spending time with Alice and the kids and the grandkids. We might go to Mexico in a few months. My daughter and her husband got a timeshare there, and we ain't never had the time to visit before. You know my Alice is a lizard, and damn if that girl don't love the sun. She can soak it up all day if I give her half a chance."

He sipped at his scotch. "What plans do you have for the bar?"

Porter took a sip of scotch. "I'll do some upgrades to the interior, maybe add a few more beer selections, and I'm thinking of expanding the food menu. That's about it. Shifters love the bar the way it is – I just want to give them a few more things to love about it."

Bud nodded. "That's real good. I know it's gonna do well with you as the owner. I'll make an official announcement to the staff tomorrow. Most of them already suspect, I reckon."

"Yeah, I think so," Porter said. "Hard to keep secrets here."

"Ain't that the truth," Bud said with a soft sigh.

They finished their drinks, but Porter shook his head when Bud went to pour him another. He poured himself one and rubbed his back again before winking at Porter. "Alice really buttered my bread last night."

Porter laughed and stood. "I'd better go. Maggie will be waiting up for me."

"Never thought I'd see you dating someone seriously," Bud said before sipping his scotch. "I'm happy for ya, though."

"Thanks, I am too," Porter said. "Do you want me to wait for you?"

"Nah," Bud said. "I'll finish my drink and then pack up some of my stuff in the office before I head out."

"Are you sure?"

"Positive. Get home to your woman. See you tomorrow, Porter."

"Good night, Bud."

Porter left the office and walked across the bar. He shut off the main lights but left the lights on over the bar. He studied the gleaming surface of the bar top before grinning. It was his. He owned the bar. Tomorrow he would tell his parents the news, but he'd go home and celebrate with his mate for tonight. He decided that a long, slow, and very thorough session of eating Maggie's sweet pussy would be a fine way to celebrate.

He was reaching for the door handle when he heard the noise. He cocked his head and turned to stare down the narrow hallway. Bud's office was at the end of the hallway, just past the washrooms and before the hallway snaked to the left toward the back door. He hesitated, listening intently. It had sounded like a chair was knocked over, but he wasn't sure. He waited for a moment and reached for the handle again when there was nothing.

He jerked in surprise at the second noise that came out of the hallway. This one was louder. It sounded like a hefty book dropped on a desk. He walked down the hall toward Bud's office. The door was still closed, and he knocked lightly before opening it.

"Bud? You okay? Shit!"

Bud's chair was knocked over, and he could see the hedgehog shifter's lower body sprawled out behind the desk. He hurried across the room.

"Bud? Did you slip and – fuck! Bud!"

He knelt next to the hedgehog shifter. Blood poured from a wound in his chest, and Bud moaned softly. A gun was lying on the floor next to Bud, and without thinking, Porter reached to pick it up!

Don't touch it! His wolf growled loudly.

He snatched his hand back as his heart pounded in his chest. What the fuck was happening? Had Bud tried to kill himself?

He pressed his hands against the bloody wound in Bud's chest and leaned over him. "Bud? Open your eyes, man."

Bud's eyelids fluttered open, and he stared blearily at Porter. "Porter? Shot me… fuckin' asshole shot me."

"Who shot you?" Porter said urgently.

Bud's eyes slipped close, and Porter cursed. What the fuck was he doing? He needed to call 9 1 1 before Bud bled out all over the goddamn floor. He kept one hand pressed against the wound - not that it was doing much fucking good, blood was flowing out at an alarming rate – and fumbled for the phone in his pocket. His hands were slick with blood, and he cursed again when he just succeeded in shoving his cell phone further into his pocket.

"Hold on, Bud," he muttered. "Just hold on. Help is -"

His wolf growled a warning, and his entire body stiffened as he lifted his head and sniffed the air. He could smell the foul scent of hyena. Adrenaline rushed through him, and his

247

wolf surged forward as he jumped to his feet. Before he could turn around, there was a sharp, intense pain to the back of his skull. He pitched forward onto his knees. Bud's pale and sweaty face was the last thing he saw before the room went black.

CHAPTER 15

Bren pulled into the parking lot of Bud's Bar. There were police cars everywhere, their lights flashing and blinking in the darkness. He parked his car and showed the beat cop his badge before ducking under the yellow tape. Forensic investigators were suiting up in white coveralls, and he nodded to them. As he headed for the door of the bar, he glanced to the right where a dark-haired, barrel-chested man was glaring at two cops.

"There's no way in hell he did it!" the man shouted. "Jesus Christ, are you fucking idiots? Let me talk to your goddamn supervisor!"

"That is one angry bull shifter," a voice said.

Bren shifted his gaze to the bar. Frank stood in the doorway, and he gave Bren a tired smile. "Hey, Bren."

"Hey, Frank."

"Sorry to get you out of bed."

Bren followed him across the bar and down a narrow hallway. "It's fine. Who doesn't love a three-a.m. wake-up call?"

Frank grinned at him. "Yeah, tell me about it."

"What have we got?" Bren asked as they stepped into a small office.

"Dead hedgehog shifter," Frank said. "Forensic hasn't been through here yet, so be careful where you step."

Bren studied the body on the ground as Frank said, "This is Bud Sindle. Sixty-seven years old, white hedgehog shifter and owner of Bud's bar. He took one to the chest and one to the head. Obviously, it was the headshot that killed him. The coroner says the chest was already trying to heal itself."

"Robbery?" Bren asked.

"Nope, nothing was taken."

"List of suspects?"

Frank grinned at him. "We got the guy who did it in custody already."

Bren gave him a surprised look. "What?"

"Yep. The responding officer caught him right in the act. Said he saw the suspect shoot the victim point-blank in the head."

"Who was the responding officer?"

"Our resident hero cop and the guy who saved your father - Vaughn Bales." He frowned at the look on Bren's face. "What's wrong?"

"Why am I here?" Bren said. "If you already caught the guy, then why did you call me in?"

"That's where it gets really interesting," Frank said. "The suspect says he knows you. Asked me to call you."

"What's his name?" Bren said. He had a very bad fucking feeling in the pit of his stomach.

"Burke. Porter Burke."

"MAGGIE, WAKE UP."

Maggie blinked dazedly at Willow. "Willow? What – what are you doing here?"

She sat up in bed, and dread filled her stomach when she saw Porter's side of the bed was empty. She had waited up for Porter until two but must have fallen asleep.

"Where's Porter," she said as she stared at Willow's pale face. "Willow! Is Porter okay?"

"He's okay, honey," Willow said. "But you need to get dressed and come with me."

"Where is he?" Maggie shouted. "Where's Porter?"

"He's been arrested," Willow said.

Maggie sagged against the headboard. "What? Arrested for what?"

"Murder," Willow said. "C'mon, get dressed. We need to go."

"PORTER, DON'T SAY ANOTHER WORD," HEATH BARKED OUT as he stormed into the interrogation room.

"Heath, it's okay," Porter said. "This is -"

"If you've been questioning my client without his lawyer present, I'll have your badge. Do you understand?" Heath snapped at the tall, dark-haired man sitting across from Porter. "Leave so I can talk to my client in private."

"Heath, wait!" Porter said. "Just listen to me for a minute."

"Porter, keep your mouth shut!" Heath snarled at him. "Jesus Christ, listen to me for once in your goddamn life."

"Mr. Burke? I'm Detective Bren Matthews, and I -"

"Leave," Heath said.

"Heath!" Porter shouted. "Just sit down for a minute."

Heath scowled at him before sitting in the chair next to

Bren. "Porter, as your lawyer, I'm telling you not to say anything. As your brother, I'm telling you to shut the fuck up."

"Bren is on my side, Heath," Porter said.

"Yeah, that's what they do," Heath said. "It's called good cop, bad cop, you idiot."

Porter sighed and rubbed his forehead. The handcuffs around his wrists glinted in the fluorescent lighting. "Just listen, Heath. Bren is a friend of Ava's and Bishop's. He knows I didn't kill Bud."

Heath gave Bren a suspicious look, and the detective nodded. "It's true."

"Then why the hell is he locked up?" Heath asked.

"Because Vaughn Bales says that I killed Bud. He says he saw me shoot him in the head," Porter said.

"Fuck," Heath said. "Tell me what happened."

"Honestly, I don't know what happened," Porter said.

Heath stared at him, and Bren leaned forward. "Here's Porter's side of the story, Mr. Burke. Your brother met with Bud last night because he was purchasing the bar. They signed the paperwork, and Porter paid him with a bank draft."

"Yeah, I know. I was there," Heath said.

"Right. After you left, Porter and Bud had a couple of drinks, and then Porter said goodnight. As he was walking to the front door, he heard a noise that sounded like a chair being knocked over."

Bren glanced at the notepad in front of him. "So far, so good, Porter?"

"Yeah," Porter said.

"He then heard something that sounded like a book being dropped. Right?"

Porter nodded, and Bren scratched at the scruff on his jaw. "No doubt that was the first gunshot to the chest."

"A gunshot is a hell of a lot louder than a book being dropped," Heath said.

"Not if it has a suppressor on it," Bren said. "Porter returned to the office and -"

"Garth!" Heath said suddenly. "Garth was sitting outside of the bar. He can tell you that Porter didn't shoot him."

"We've already spoken to Mr. Donnen," Bren said. "Unfortunately, he didn't hear anything. The shooter wanted Porter to hear Bud being shot, but Mr. Donnen wouldn't have heard it. He didn't know anything had happened until the officers arrived on the scene."

"Fuck," Heath muttered again.

"Porter returned to the office and found Bud lying on the floor with a gunshot wound to his chest. He applied pressure to the wound and was attempting to call 9-1-1 when he was knocked out."

"You didn't see anything?" Heath asked.

Porter shook his head. "No, but I smelled hyena right before I was hit over the fucking head."

"Did you get pictures of his head?" Heath asked. "Proof that he was attacked?"

"Unfortunately, your brother was already healed from any injuries," Bren said.

"When I woke up," Porter said, "the gun was in my hand, and Bud was dead." He swallowed heavily as his face paled. "He's dead because of me."

"It's okay, Porter," Heath said. "Tell me the rest."

Porter cleared his throat roughly. "Vaughn was standing in the office with me and had his gun pointed at me. He told me to drop the gun and stand up. I did what he asked, and he handcuffed me. Then he called for backup and told the other officers that he saw me shoot Bud in the head."

"Are you fucking kidding me?" Heath said.

"No." Bren flipped a page in his notebook. "Officer Bales story is that he went to the bar to speak to Porter. He admitted that he pulled Porter over for a routine traffic stop last week, got a little overzealous, and broke his taillight. He says he was going to the bar to apologize to Porter over the incident."

"Garth didn't see him walking into the bar?" Heath asked. "He was parked right out front. He would have seen him."

"Officer Bales says he went in the back way."

"Why?"

"He drove in off of Larkin Street, and he says he was driving through the back parking lot to get to the front when he noticed the back door was open. He says it made him suspicious, so he parked his vehicle and went in through the back. In the hallway, he heard Bud and Porter arguing about Porter purchasing the bar and then a gunshot. He says he went into the office just in time to see Porter shoot Bud in the head. He arrested Porter and called for back-up."

"I can point out fifty holes in his story right now," Heath said. "The main one being – why would Porter kill Bud over purchasing the bar? They both signed the paperwork agreeing to the price, and Porter gave him a bank draft."

"About that," Bren said. "Did you see Porter give him the bank draft?"

Heath shook his head. "No, I left before he did." He glanced at Porter. "You gave him the draft, right?"

"I did," Porter said. "Right after you left. Bud stuck it in his pocket, only they didn't find it on him. Vaughn took it so that it would look like I killed Bud so I could have the bar without paying him for it."

"Again, that theory won't hold up in court," Heath said. "Technically, the bar isn't yours until you've paid him. So, killing him before Bud can deposit the draft is a ridiculous idea on your part. You'd never get the bar."

He studied Bren for a moment. "So, this Vaughn guy is trying to frame Porter but doing an absolutely pathetic job of it. Why?"

"Because he wants Maggie," Porter said.

"Yeah, I get that," Heath said impatiently, "but why not do a better job of it? Jesus Christ, a toddler with an overactive imagination, could think up a better way. I know hyenas are stupid, but this goes beyond stupidity."

"The problem," Bren said, "is that Porter's prints are all over the gun, and Vaughn is well-respected on the force."

"Yeah, yeah, saved the Senator, hero cop," Heath said irritably. "I remember."

"We've already spoken to a few of the staff members at Bud's. Both a waitress and the bouncer told us that they overheard Porter and Bud having a screaming match about the bar a few weeks ago."

Heath glanced at Porter, who nodded. "Yeah, it's true."

"You might want to think about firing those two," Heath muttered.

"To be fair, it was like pulling teeth to get anything out of either of them. They don't believe Porter did it," Bren said.

Heath drummed his fingers on the table. "Okay, don't worry. I'll get this fucking shitshow of a case thrown out before it even goes to court. All I need to do is prove that Vaughn is trying to frame you. That won't be all that difficult, considering how he messed this up. I'll talk to Judd and get a recorded statement from him about saving your ass from the hyenas. I'll also get a recorded statement from Maggie that details everything Vaughn has been doing to her and -"

"No," Porter said. "I want to leave Maggie out of this. She's been through enough."

"Well, that's too fucking bad," Heath said bluntly. "Because Maggie's statement that Vaughn has been stalking her and she came to you for help is what's going to get your ass out of this mess."

"Heath, I don't -"

"I don't fucking care," Heath said. "I might be younger than you, but you're going to listen to me about this, Porter. Got it? We can fight about it after you're no longer in jail for murder."

"Yeah, okay," Porter said.

"Good. I'm going to bring Marty from the firm in on this."

"What? Why?" Porter asked.

"Because I'm not a criminal defense lawyer," Heath said. "Marty is, and I want to make sure I don't screw up anything. Have they filed charges against him yet?"

Bren shook his head. "No, not yet. But I'm pretty sure the DA will. The fingerprints on the gun and Vaughn's police report will most likely be enough to convince her to file charges."

"He filed a false police report," Heath said as his eyes glowed angrily. "I'm going to nail that fucker's balls to the goddamn wall."

"I'll speak to the captain," Bren said. "I can't guarantee he'll believe me, but it'll at least put doubt in his mind about Vaughn."

"Thank you, Bren," Porter said.

"Okay, they can't hold you here without filing charges for more than seventy-two hours. Hang tight, and I'll get this cleared up before they even get the chance to file charges," Heath said.

"I have to stay in jail?" Porter said.

"Yes," Bren said.

Heath scowled. "What if Vaughn goes after him?"

"We'll make sure a guard is keeping an eye on Porter," Bren said.

"Twenty-four, seven?" Heath said. "How?"

Bren hesitated before glancing at Porter. "Suicide watch."

Porter grimaced before rubbing his forehead again. "Great."

"It's for your own safety," Heath said. He stood and walked around the table to give Porter a rough hug. "I'll talk to Mom and Dad and tell them what's happening, okay."

"Maggie as well," Porter said. "Make sure she isn't alone ever. Okay?"

Heath nodded, and Porter frowned at him. "I mean it, Heath. Ask Mal if she can stay with him and Willow until I get out of here."

"I will. Don't worry about her," Heath said.

"She's my mate," Porter said. "I'm going to worry about her."

"You've claimed her?" Heath said.

"No," Porter admitted. "But the minute I get out of here, I'm asking her to be my mate. I love her."

"Okay," Heath said before squeezing his arm. "We'll keep her safe. I promise."

Maggie stood numbly in Mara and Roland's crowded kitchen as Heath finished talking. She watched as Roland took Mara's hand and squeezed it gently. "It'll be all right, sweetie."

She gave him a trembling smile as Jessa placed a steaming mug of tea in front of her. "Drink this, Mom."

"Thank you, JJ," she said.

"Don't worry," Heath said. "I've already talked to Marty,

and he's going to help me. He's one of the best defense lawyers in the city."

"Right," Roland said. "Okay, so what can we do?"

"Nothing at the moment," Heath said. "I'll get statements from Judd and Maggie, then speak with the DA. Hopefully, it'll be enough to keep her from even filing charges against Porter. We'll get a copy of the receipt of the bank draft from Porter as proof that he at least intended to pay Bud the amount they agreed on. Vaughn's statement is flimsy and full of holes."

"Porter's prints are on the gun," Mal said. "How are you going to explain that?"

"Vaughn obviously planted it on him. Tomorrow I'll go to the hospital and get the medical records from Porter's stay in the hospital. Once the DA hears about Vaughn stalking Maggie and how he got his hyena pack to nearly kill Porter, it'll help convince her that Vaughn planted the gun. I'm also going to point out that a wolf shifter using a gun to kill a hedgehog shifter is stupid. Porter could have just shifted and torn Bud's head off. He had no need for a gun. I'm starting to think this Vaughn guy is a fucking moron."

"Are you sure there isn't something we can do to help?" Willow asked. Her slender arm was planted firmly around Mal's waist, and she kissed his upper arm before squeezing him lightly.

Maggie dropped her gaze to the floor and tuned out Heath's reply. Porter was in jail because of her. He would be charged with murder because of her. She could fix all of this. She just needed to talk to Vaughn.

"Maggie? Honey, look at me."

She looked up to see Porter's family staring at her. Willow smiled at her. "Heath asked you a question, honey."

"I'm sorry," Maggie said to Heath. "What did you say?"

"Can you go to the office with me this afternoon and give a recorded statement," Heath said.

"I – I have to work in half an hour," Maggie said.

"Can you call in and ask to miss your shift?" Heath asked patiently. "This is important, Maggie."

"I know," Maggie said. "I'm sorry, but I can't miss another shift, or I'll lose my job."

She was lying. Colin would find someone else to cover her shift, but she needed to get away from Porter's family. She needed to talk to Vaughn as soon as possible, and that wasn't going to happen unless she was alone.

"Are you sure?" Heath said. "Couldn't you just call and ask? It's essential that we get this done."

"I'm sorry," Maggie repeated. "I really can't."

"Are you kidding me?" Becky shouted. She stood up, knocking her chair over and slapping Ellet's hand away when he tried to grab her arm. "This is all your fault! Porter's in jail because of you – he nearly died because of *you* – and now you won't even help him? What is wrong with you? I wish Porter had never met you! I wish that stupid hyena had -"

"Rebecca - enough!" Roland roared.

Becky shut her mouth with a snap before baring her fangs at Maggie and growling. She snarled at her father when he took her arm and marched her out of the kitchen.

"Becky ain't wrong. It is the human's fault," Amos growled. He stood and glared at Maggie before limping out of the room.

There was a moment of silence as the others stared solemnly at Maggie. She prayed for Mara to say it wasn't her fault, but Porter's mother didn't say anything. Maggie wasn't confident she had even noticed her daughter's outburst. Mara's face was pale and worried as Jessa sat down beside her and put her arm around her shoulders. Maggie's chest tightened until she could barely breathe, and her stomach rolled with nausea.

"I'm sorry," she said in a low voice. She had to choke the words past the lump in her throat. "I – I can make my statement this evening after my shift is over. It's done by seven."

Heath ran his hand through his hair and nodded. "Yeah, okay."

"Ronin will drive you to Heath's office, and then you're coming back to our place to stay the night," Willow said.

"What?" Maggie said. "No, I – I don't need to stay with you. Porter's place is perfectly safe, and you have someone watching me, so Vaughn isn't going to…."

Mal gave her a grim look. "That isn't what we're worried about. Or rather, what Porter is worried about."

His tone was clear that they believed she would try to run away, and it was only Porter who didn't want that. Maggie blinked rapidly to stop the hot tears from spilling. Porter's family finally hated her, and she couldn't blame them for it. He was sitting in a jail cell, charged with murder, and it was entirely her fault.

"Maggie?" Willow said with a soft frown at Mal. "We want you to stay with us. Okay?"

Maggie didn't believe her, but she nodded. "Yes, that's -"

Her voice broke, and she cleared her throat loudly. "Yes, that's fine. I should get to work, though."

"Leave your car here. Fenton's out front and will drive you," Mal said.

"Yeah, sure," she said in defeat. She hesitated before approaching Mara and touching her shoulder. "Mara? I'll fix this. Porter will be home soon. I promise."

Mara didn't reply, and Maggie squeezed her shoulder lightly. "I promise, Mara."

Porter's mother looked up at her blankly before smiling

faintly. "Okay. Bye, Maggie."

"Bye," Maggie whispered. The tears were impossible to hold back now, and as the room wavered, she fled out of the kitchen. She yanked open the front door and stumbled down the porch steps toward Fenton's car. The cheetah shifter got out of the car and met her on the passenger side.

"Maggie? What's wrong?"

"N-nothing," she said. "Mal wants you to drive me to work. Can you do that?"

"Of course," Fenton said. "Are you sure you're all right?"

She nodded and swiped savagely at the tears on her cheeks. "I just want to leave, okay?"

"Okay," Fenton said. He opened the passenger door, and she climbed in, buckling the seatbelt and leaning her head against the headrest. She closed her eyes and kept them shut as Fenton drove away.

"HEY, GIRL," SIMONE SAID WHEN MAGGIE WALKED INTO THE coffee shop. "How's it going?"

"Hi," Maggie said. "Can you cover for me for five minutes? I need to make a phone call."

"Sure," Simone said. "Is everything okay? You look kind of terrible."

Maggie smiled wanly at her. "I'm fine. I'll be right back."

She headed to the back where Colin's office was and stuck her head inside. It was empty, and she shut the door and pulled out her cell phone. She silently thanked God that she hadn't gotten around to erasing Vaughn's number from her phone and quickly scrolled through her contacts. As the call connected, her stomach churned, and she held tightly to the edge of Colin's desk.

"Hello, Maggie. I had a feeling you would be calling," Vaughn's low voice washed over her, and she swallowed down the bile that had risen in her throat.

"What do you want?" she said.

Vaughn laughed. "That's a stupid question. You know what I want. The real question is – are you going to give it to me?"

"Yes," she said, "but you have to tell them the truth about what happened to Bud."

Vaughn didn't hesitate. "Of course. I'd do anything for my mate."

"Will you?" she asked. "You'll lose your job when they find out you lied."

"I don't care about my job," Vaughn said. "All I care about is you. Now, why don't you come by my place and -"

"First, you tell them the truth about Porter," Maggie said.

Vaughn barked more laughter. "That's not how this works. I love you, but you're not exactly trustworthy, are you? As soon as you're with me, I'll get the wolf shifter out of jail. The sooner you get here, the faster he's free, sweetheart."

"I'm at work," Maggie said, "and my shift isn't over until seven."

"So, quit," Vaughn said carelessly. "Once we're mated, and you're carrying my pup, you won't be working anyway."

"I'm being watched," Maggie said. "They won't even let me have my car. I can't just come over."

"Well, I guess that's your problem, isn't it?" Vaughn said.

Maggie didn't reply, and after a moment, Vaughn sighed. "Fine. I'll help you, but you'll need to be more self-sufficient once you're my mate. Do you understand?"

"Yes," Maggie said.

"Good. What time did you say your shift finished?"

"Seven."

"I'll be waiting at the back entrance for you at seven," Vaughn said.

"I told you, Vaughn, they're watching me. I can't just get in your car and -"

Vaughn snarled into the phone, and she shut her mouth as he said, "Enough, Maggie! You're a smart girl. I'm sure you'll figure out a way to escape your wolf shifter's friends. I'll be at the back entrance of the coffee shop at seven. Don't keep me waiting, or your wolf shifter will rot in prison for the rest of his life. Are we clear?"

"Yes," Maggie said.

"Good. See you soon, sweetheart."

The line went dead, and Maggie stared at her cell phone before shoving it into her pocket. She turned and made a low shriek of surprise. Simone stood in the doorway, and Maggie gave her a guilty look.

"What's going on, Maggie?" Simone said.

"Nothing," Maggie said. "I need to get to work."

She tried to ease past Simone, and the girl grabbed her arm. "Tom's up front, and there are only a few customers. Tell me what's going on. I heard you say that stupid hyena shifter's name. I thought you were dating Porter now?"

Maggie tried to yank free of Simone's grip. "It's nothing. Just forget about it."

"No," Simone said. "I'm your friend, and it sounds like you need help. Let me help you."

She hesitated before nodding. "Yeah, I need help."

She hated dragging Simone into her fucked-up life, but she would need the woman's help to distract Ronin while she left with Vaughn tonight.

"Okay," Simone said. "Tell me everything."

CHAPTER 16

"Detective? Do you have a minute?"

Bren looked up from his computer. It was just after five, and Christ, he was tired. He should have left the precinct half an hour ago. Tyler's soccer game started in ten minutes, and he would be late. He tried his best to go to all of his brother's games, especially considering their father didn't give a shit about Tyler's interests. He sat back in his chair and nodded at the officer standing next to his desk.

"What's up?"

"There's a guy here who says he has information on the dead hedgehog case. You're on that case, right?"

Bren sat forward. "Yes. Who is it?"

"Arlo something or other. He says he works at the bar. Do you want to speak to him?"

"Yes, where is he?" Bren said.

"He's in interrogation room B," the officer said.

"Thanks." Bren hurried down the hallway and opened the door to the interrogation room. A young man with short brown hair and a narrow face paced the room nervously. He stopped abruptly when he saw Bren.

"Who are you?"

"Detective Matthews." Bren held out his hand. "You are?"

"Arlo Calden," he said. "I – are you working on Bud's case?"

"I am," Bren said. "Are you thirsty? I can get you a coffee or some water."

"I'm not thirsty," Arlo said. "I just want to talk."

"Have a seat, Mr. Calden," Bren said. Arlo sat down, and Bren sat in the chair across from him. "Now, before we get started, I want to let you know that this conversation is being recorded. Are we clear on that?"

Arlo nodded. "Yeah, clear."

"Good. You work at the bar, is that right?"

"Yes," Arlo said. He gave Bren a look that was half-terror and half-guilt. "I killed Bud, not Porter. It was me who killed Bud."

Bren folded his hands on the table. "You shot Bud in the head."

Arlo shook his head. "No. But I killed him just the same. It's my fault he's dead, Detective. I should be the one in prison, not Porter."

"Why is it your fault?" Bren asked.

"Because I gave that bastard hyena, Vaughn, a key to the back door of the bar. I told him that Porter and Bud would be there. I know he shot Bud, but it might as well have been me holding the damn gun," Arlo said. "This is all my fucking fault, and I swear to God, if I had known that Vaughn was going to kill Bud, I would never have given him that key! I just – Andy needed me. My parents needed me, you know? I never thought Vaughn would do something like this. You have to believe me!"

The man's pale face darkened, and long black whiskers

sprouted from either side of his mouth. His front teeth lengthened as he made a chittering sound.

"Calm down, Arlo," Bren said. "Just calm down for a minute before you shift."

Arlo took a few deep breaths. "I'm sorry."

"It's fine," Bren said. "Why don't you start from the beginning."

"Yeah, okay," Arlo said. "I have a brother named Andrew, and he's a drug addict."

NEARLY TWENTY MINUTES LATER, ARLO WIPED A SHAKING hand across his face. "I'm sorry," he said. "I'm so sorry."

"Are you sure the guy at Vaughn's house was named Jake?" Bren asked.

Arlo nodded. "I'm sure."

"Okay, sit tight," Bren said. "I have a few phone calls to make."

He left the interrogation room and headed to the officer at the front desk.

"Hey, Bren. How are you?"

"Good. I'm looking for Vaughn Bales and Jake Sallen."

"Well, Jake's on shift now, but I guess you didn't hear the news about Vaughn."

"What news?" Bren asked.

"He sent an email to the captain and resigned effective immediately."

"What?" Bren said.

The officer nodded. "Yep. Maybe an hour ago. The captain just about lost his shit. He's tried calling Vaughn, but he's not answering his phone."

"Shit," Bren said. "Is the captain here?"

"Yeah, in his office."

"Good. Can you do me a favour?" Bren pulled out Heath's business card from his pocket. "Call this guy and ask him to meet me here at the station. Tell him it's an emergency."

The officer took the card, and Bren, excitement churning in his belly, headed toward the captain's office.

———

"Maggie, I don't think this is a good idea," Simone said with a nervous look out the front window of the coffee shop.

"You said you would help me." Maggie checked her watch before yanking on her jacket.

"I know, but this isn't the right plan."

"It's the only way to help Porter."

"Vaughn might hurt you. If he does, how do you think I'll feel knowing I helped you escape with him," Simone said.

"He won't hurt me," Maggie said with confidence she didn't feel. "He's in love with me."

"So, you're just going to marry some guy that you hate?" Simone said. "You get how screwed up that is, right?"

"Once Porter is released from jail, he'll find me," Maggie said. "He'll get the police to help him."

Simone gave her a doubtful look, and Maggie forced herself to smile. "I'll be fine, Simone. The police will know that Vaughn lied, and they'll go after him for that. I'll be safe until then, I promise."

She was lying through her teeth. She knew without a doubt that she was a dead woman. Vaughn was insane, and as soon as he found out she was no longer a virgin, he'd kill her.

Her smile faltered, and Simone gripped her hand. "Maggie, I -"

"It'll be *fine*," Maggie said. "I have to go. It's almost seven, and Vaughn will be waiting for me. Wait a few minutes and then run out to the car. Tell Ronin that Vaughn is inside the coffee shop, and I'm in trouble. Vaughn and I will be gone by the time he realizes the truth. Okay?"

"Yeah, okay," Simone said. "But I want it on the record that this is a really stupid fucking plan, and I'm mad at you."

"Noted," Maggie said. She hesitated before hugging Simone. "Thanks, honey. I'll see you soon."

"You'd better," Simone said. She kissed Maggie's cheek. "Please be careful."

"I will," Maggie said. "Goodbye, Simone."

"WHAT'S GOING ON?" HEATH STARED IN SURPRISE AT PORTER standing next to Bren. "Why are you not in a jail cell?"

"They let me go," Porter said. He had a dazed expression on his face.

"They let you go?" Heath repeated.

Bren nodded. "We had a witness come forward who said they gave Vaughn a key to the back door of the bar. He told them that he was certain that it was Vaughn who killed Bud."

"Who's the witness?" Heath asked.

Porter grimaced. "Arlo. His younger brother is in trouble for dealing drugs, and Vaughn offered to make the evidence against his brother disappear if Arlo agreed to help him."

"Was Arlo there?" Heath asked. "Did he see Vaughn kill Bud?"

"No," Bren said, "but what he told us, combined with the fact that Vaughn abruptly resigned today, was enough to get the captain to call the DA and ask her not to file charges."

"Thank God," Heath said.

"Porter is still a suspect," Bren said. "I'm about to go and talk to one of Vaughn's pack, a police officer named Jake Sallen. I have a feeling that he's the one who took the evidence against Arlo's brother. No doubt, he was also involved in killing Bud. Once I get him to confess, then we'll put out an arrest warrant for Vaughn."

"He won't betray Vaughn," Heath said. "Hyenas don't turn on their pack members."

Bren smiled. "I can convince him that Vaughn is hanging him out to dry."

"You sure about that?" Heath said.

Bren's smile grew wider. "Yes. It's just after seven, and Jake's shift isn't done until eight. He's directing traffic at an accident at the corner of Richter Street and Main. I'll drive there and -"

He paused as Heath's cell phone rang. Heath checked the number and glanced at Porter. "It's Mal."

"ARE YOU FUCKING KIDDING ME?" MAL SHOUTED.

Mal stalked back and forth in his parents' kitchen as Willow, Bishop, and the rest of his family exchanged nervous glances.

"Are you sure she went with him? Okay. Fuck!" Mal ran his hand through his short hair. "Did she have any idea where they were going? Right. No, it's not your fault, Ronin. Stay where you are for now. I'll get back to you."

He ended the call before slamming his fist on the counter.

"Mal? What's wrong?" Willow asked.

"Maggie," Mal said. "She took off with Vaughn."

"What? How?" Mara asked.

"She had her coworker run out to Ronin and pretend that

Vaughn was in the coffee shop and Maggie needed help. By the time Ronin did a sweep of the place, Maggie had fled out the back door and left with Vaughn."

"Do we know for certain that she's with Vaughn?" Bishop asked. "Maybe she just ran on her own."

Mal shook his head. "No, she's with him. The coworker admitted that Maggie had asked her to distract Ronin so she could escape with Vaughn."

"Oh my God," Mara said. "What was she thinking?"

"No doubt she believes if she gives Vaughn what he wants, then he'll take back what he said about Porter."

"She can't be that naïve," Roland said.

"She's desperate," Jessa said.

"We have a bigger problem," Willow said. "What Vaughn wants from Maggie is her virginity, and she isn't... I mean, she and Porter have...."

"Oh no," Mara said. "We have to find her. If he hurts her, Porter will go crazy. He thinks of her as his mate."

"How do you know that?" Mal said.

"A mother always knows," she said distractedly. "Do we know where Vaughn lives? Maybe you and Bishop can go to his place. Maybe he took Maggie there."

"I don't, but Heath is at the police station. I'll call him and see if he can ask Detective Matthews to give him the information. Hell, if we tell them that Vaughn kidnapped her, we might even get the support of the police."

"Doubtful," Bishop grunted. "Hero cop, remember?"

"I remember," Mal said, "but we need to try something."

———

"HEATH? WHAT'S WRONG? WHAT DID MAL SAY?" PORTER asked.

Heath stuffed his cell phone into his pocket. "Nothing."

Porter sniffed at him before shaking his head. "I know you're lying. I can smell it. Tell me."

"Maggie snuck out of the coffee shop after her shift. Her coworker lied to Ronin and told him that Vaughn was in the shop and Maggie was in trouble. Ronin did a sweep of the place before realizing that Maggie was gone," Heath said.

"Shit!" Porter said. "Okay, we need to check the bus station, the train station, and maybe the airport. Bus station first. Maggie doesn't have a lot of cash, so -"

"Porter," Heath said, "she didn't leave on her own."

"What do you mean?"

"She left with Vaughn."

Porter stared wide-eyed at him before lifting his head and howling. Bren winced, and Heath grabbed Porter's arm as his body swelled and dark hair sprouted across his cheeks.

"Porter! Stop!" Heath said sharply. "Shifting won't help her!"

"He has my mate," Porter snarled as his fangs dropped. "He has my mate!"

"I know. We'll get her back," Heath said. "Just calm down."

Porter slumped against the wall. "I should have bitten her," he said in a low voice. "I should have claimed her as my mate, but I didn't because I'm a fucking fool. If I had bitten her, Vaughn would have left her alone."

"Or he would have killed her for betraying him," Heath said. "We don't have time for your pity party, so get it the fuck together."

Porter snarled at him, and Heath gave him a grim smile. "Better. Detective Matthews, this Vaughn is dangerous and if he has Maggie...."

"We'll send units out to Vaughn's house. I doubt he's

there, but it's a start. In the meantime, I'll find Jake. He may know where Vaughn has taken Maggie," Bren said.

"I'm coming with you," Porter said.

"Not a great idea," Bren said.

Porter bared his fangs at him. "I'm coming with you. Try to stop me, and I'll rip out your fucking throat."

"Porter!" Heath snapped. "Knock it off."

Bren gave Porter a thoughtful look before grinning. "Well, when you put it that way, I'd be happy to have you tag along. Let's go."

As Porter and Bren walked away, Heath pulled out his cell phone and called Mal.

"WHERE ARE WE GOING?" MAGGIE ASKED VAUGHN. THEY had left the city, and she stared in trepidation at the dark woods that lined either side of the road.

"I've got a little place tucked away where we can finally be alone," Vaughn said with a cheerful smile. "You'll like it. It has all the comforts of home."

She swallowed heavily. "You said you would call the station and free Porter. I want to hear you make the phone call right now."

"I already did," Vaughn said. "I emailed the captain before I picked you up from work. Told him that the wolf shifter wasn't involved."

"Did you lose your job?" Maggie asked.

Vaughn laughed. "I resigned."

Maggie blinked at him as butterflies twisted and turned in her stomach. "Why would you do that? You can't, uh, support me as your mate if you don't have a job."

"Don't you worry about that, sweetheart."

She cringed away when Vaughn patted her knee, and he gave her a dark look. "Don't do that."

She forced herself to relax against the seat. "How do I know for sure that you told them the truth about Porter?"

"I guess you'll just have to trust your mate," Vaughn said. "You do trust me, don't you, Maggie?"

"No," she said defiantly.

Anger flickered across his face again before he smiled at her. "You will with time. I only want what's best for you."

"What I want is to be left alone," Maggie said.

"But that's not what's best for you," Vaughn said with maddening patience. "You need me. I know you think you're in love with that asshole wolf shifter, but once we're mated, you'll understand what real love is."

Maggie stared out the window into the darkness as Vaughn patted her knee again. "That reminds me – give me your cell phone."

"Why?" she asked.

His hand tightened painfully on her leg. "Never question me. Give me your cell phone."

He squeezed again, and she bit back her whimper of pain before handing him her cell phone. He shut it off, rolled down his window, and tossed it.

"You asshole!" she shouted.

He laughed and slapped her sharply on the thigh. "You don't need it. Besides, we don't want your friends getting ideas that they can track your cell phone to find you, now do we?"

Panic clawed at her stomach, and she took a few deep breaths.

It's okay, Maggie. They can track Vaughn's cell phone. It's okay.

"I know what you're thinking, Maggie. You think they

can track my phone," Vaughn said. "They can track it – right to my apartment." He pulled out a cell phone and waved it at her. "Tracking the burner phone, though? A little more difficult."

He tucked it back into his jacket pocket before giving her a smile that chilled her to her bones. "Don't worry. I'll get you a new cell phone when we're settled in our new home."

"I don't want to live in a cabin in the middle of nowhere," she said.

He laughed. "Oh, sweetheart. That's only temporary."

"What do you mean?"

He just smiled at her before turning off the highway right onto a gravel road that wasn't marked. "You'll see, Maggie."

CHAPTER 17

"Well, look at that, the gang's all here," Bren said as he shut off his car.

They were parked on Richter Street, and ahead of them at the intersection, Porter could see a few police cars, a fire truck, and an ambulance.

"What are you talking about?" Porter said as he climbed out of the car.

Bren slid out from behind the wheel, and he slammed his door shut before pointing behind them. Porter turned to see Mal and Bishop getting out of Bishop's truck. Ronin was already out of his car, and he joined them as they headed toward Porter and Bren.

"Mal? What are you doing here?" Porter said.

Mal hugged him roughly. "Heath told us you and Bren were going to be here. Hello, Bren."

"Mal. I'm not entirely surprised to see you and Bishop here, but I'm a little perplexed by Ronin joining us," Bren said. Ronin's usual cheerful grin was replaced with a stony grimness, and he stared briefly at Bren before turning to Porter.

"Porter, I'm sorry. This is my fault, and I'll do whatever I can to help."

"It isn't," Mal said. "Maggie deliberately tricked you, Ronin."

"Mal's right," Porter said. "You didn't know she would use her coworker as a decoy." He turned to Mal. "I'm glad you're here."

Mal clapped him on the back. "Me too."

Bren's phone rang, and he pulled it from his pocket and answered it. "Matthews."

Porter growled impatiently, and Mal squeezed his upper arm.

"Okay, thanks." Bren ended the call. "I asked one of the techs to try tracking Maggie's phone."

"Did it work?" Porter asked.

Bren shook his head. "No, not really. It pinged off a tower near the city's outskirts before the signal was lost. Vaughn probably took it from her and turned it off."

"Fuck!" Porter snarled.

"It's okay," Mal said, "We've still got that shithead hyena over there. Let's go find out where the fuck Vaughn has taken your mate."

"Whoa, hold on," Bren said as the shifters started forward. "I'll talk to Jake. The rest of you can wait here by the car."

"What? No!" Porter said. "If he doesn't tell you where Vaughn is, then I'll -"

"Beat it out of him?" Bren asked. "There are about four other officers at the scene, Porter. You go after Jake, and the only thing that will happen is your ass will be back in a jail cell for assault. Stay here, and I'll find out what we want to know."

"If you don't?" Ronin said.

Bren grinned at the bird shifter. "I can be very persuasive when I want to be."

He walked off, and Porter gave Mal an anxious look. "I love her, Mal. I should have bitten her and claimed her when I had the chance, but I didn't because I wasn't sure how she felt about me. I'm an idiot."

Mal shook his head. "No, you're not. Trust me, one of us biting our mate without asking first is enough. Besides, if you had claimed Maggie, it would have just pissed off Vaughn."

"What if we don't find her before…." Porter made a low whimper. His wolf was alternating between bouts of rage and fear for his mate, and he could barely control the urge to shift.

"We'll find her," Mal said. "We'll find her, and she'll be okay."

"Officer Sallen, it's nice to see you again," Bren said.

The hyena stared suspiciously at him. "What are you doing here?"

"We need to chat." Bren glanced at an officer who was talking to a firefighter. "Would you mind taking over for Officer Sallen?"

The officer nodded and took Jake's place in the middle of the street. Jake walked slowly toward Bren. "What do you want?"

"Let's talk over here," Bren said.

He moved down the sidewalk until they were out of earshot of the other emergency responders.

"What do you want?" Jake repeated. "I'm busy."

"I'm sure you are," Bren said. "I won't take up much of your time. I just have a couple of questions for you."

Jake grunted in reply. Bren shoved his hands into his suit

jacket. "First question – what did you do with the drugs you took from evidence?"

Jake jerked all over and took a step back before glancing around the street. "I don't know what the fuck you're talking about."

"Really?" Bren said. "So, when Arlo Calden told me that you took the drugs from evidence that his brother was arrested for, he was lying?"

"That little fucking weasel don't know shit," Jake barked. "I didn't have anything to do with that cocaine going missing."

"How'd you know it was cocaine?" Bren asked. "I didn't say it was cocaine."

Jake hesitated, and Bren laughed. "Jesus, you are one terrible cop."

"Fuck you!" Jake snarled.

Bren glanced at his watch. "Tempting, but no. Here's the thing, Officer Sallen. I have officers heading to your place right now. I'm assuming you aren't so stupid that you stashed the cocaine at your place, but hey, I'm a detective, and I like to cover all the bases."

Jake's tanned face had turned pale, and he licked his lips compulsively as Bren cocked his head. "Were you a naughty hyena and stashed the cocaine at your place? Wait, wait – let me guess – under the toilet tank lid, right?"

"I wasn't even at the precinct the night it went missing," Jake said. "Ask Vaughn. He'll tell you I was with him the whole time."

"Didn't you hear?" Bren said. "Vaughn resigned today."

Jake's mouth dropped open. "What?"

"Yes. Not even two hours ago. Sent an email to the captain and resigned. He didn't tell you?"

"I – no, he didn't," Jake said as his hands clenched into fists.

"Interesting. I have a theory I want to share with you, Jake. Do you mind if I call you Jake?"

Jake shook his head as his hands clenched and unclenched.

"Good. First – here's what I know, Jake. I know that Vaughn told Mr. Arlo Calden that he'd make the evidence against his brother disappear in exchange for information about Porter. I know you were at that meeting because Arlo has already identified you as being there. Now, since you look like you're going to vomit on your shoes, I'm confident Vaughn had you take the evidence and that it's currently at your apartment about to be found by your coworkers."

Jake stared silently at him, and Bren smiled. "Now, here's what I think, and I'm going to make it short and simple because you're stupid, and I'm on a time limit. I think you and Vaughn went to the bar, used the key that Arlo gave you, murdered Bud Sindle and then framed Porter Burke for it. Does that sound about right?"

Jake didn't reply, and Bren leaned a little closer. "Porter's already free because the two of you did a shit job at trying to frame him. Vaughn's left town because he got what he wanted – Maggie. What did you get, Jake?"

"I - I don't know what you're -"

"I'll tell you what you got. You got left behind holding stolen evidence and on the hook for murder. Vaughn's gone, but you're here. At the very least, you're going to prison for tampering with evidence. But between you and me – I'll do everything in my goddamn power to make sure you go to prison for Bud's murder. You'll be in general population, Jake. No protection."

Jake made a sound that was a cross between a whine and

a growl. Bren placed his hand on the handle of his gun and gave him a hard smile. "But hey, it's your lucky day, Jake."

"What do you mean?" Jake rasped.

"I'm willing to get the DA to cut a deal with you, ask her to charge you with manslaughter instead of murder because I know you were just following Vaughn's orders, right? If you tell me what I want to know, maybe you won't spend the rest of your life rotting in prison."

"What do you want to know?"

"Where's Vaughn?"

"I don't know," Jake said.

"Don't bullshit me," Bren said. "You have thirty seconds to tell me where Vaughn is, or I tell the DA to go after you with everything she's got."

Jake licked his lips again and studied the sidewalk for a few seconds. "Vaughn has a cabin outside of the city. He – he might be there."

"Well done, Jake," Bren said. "Exact address, please."

Jake recited the address, and Bren smiled at him. "Turn around."

Jake turned around with another low whine, and Bren handcuffed him before squeezing his shoulder. "Jake Sallen, you're under arrest for evidence tampering and the murder of Bud Sindle."

"WHAT DO YOU THINK?"

Maggie studied the cabin. It was small, just one large room with a tiny kitchenette on the left side and a small living area on the right. A loveseat sat in front of the fireplace, and an old and worn wingback chair was to the right of it. A bed was against the back wall, and she suppressed a shudder when Vaughn put his arm around her and kissed her temple.

"Do you like the bed, sweetheart? It's very comfortable, but you'll find out for yourself soon enough."

This time she did shudder, and Vaughn's grin widened before his nose wrinkled. "You fucking smell like that wolf shifter. Maybe I should punish you for letting him mark you."

Metallic tasting fear flooded her mouth, and Vaughn inhaled deeply before licking her cheek. "You taste delicious when you're afraid, Maggie."

She bit back her panicked moan and pulled away from him. "I – I have to use the bathroom."

"That door right there." He pointed to the door just past the kitchenette before rubbing the goosebumps on her arm. "Are you cold, sweetheart? I can build a fire."

She nodded even though her goosebumps were from fear. He clamped his hand down around her wrist and squeezed hard. "I love you, Maggie. I know you don't believe it, but I do." His black eyes glowed. "Tonight, I'll take you to my bed and take the sweet gift of your virginity. I'll erase that fucking wolf shifter's scent with my own, and you'll be mine forever. I won't let anyone hurt you," he brushed a strand of hair away from her trembling lips, "touch you, take you from me. Do you understand? You're mine now."

"Please," she whispered as he bent his mouth toward hers, "I need to use the washroom."

He stepped back and released her wrist. "Of course. Go and freshen up. I'll start a fire, and we'll have a nice dinner before we go to bed. We have an early start tomorrow."

"Why? Where are we going?"

He just smiled at her before pushing her gently toward the bathroom. "Go, sweetheart. We'll talk about it later."

"I'M GOING WITH YOU," PORTER SAID TO BREN.

"We all are," Mal said.

Bren shook his head. "No. I'll call the precinct, get some backup and drive out to Vaughn's cabin. If he's there with Maggie, we'll arrest him and bring Maggie back to you."

"She's my mate!" Porter snarled at him. "I'm going with you, and you can't fucking stop me."

"You owe us," Bishop said suddenly.

Bren raised his eyebrow at the grizzly shifter. "Owe you for what?"

"We let you come along when we saved Kat and Ronin at the lab."

"Technically, you didn't let me come along," Bren said, "In fact, you lied to me about Kat and Ronin. I followed you to the lab and then saved your ass."

Bishop flushed and made a low growl. "We're going, Matthews."

Bren sighed loudly, and Mal said urgently, "Bren, he's a hyena shifter and insane. You're going to need shifters to help you. What happens if he has members of his pack there with him? You'll need us."

"You're civilians. If one of you gets hurt, I'll lose my job," Bren said.

"We're not going to get hurt," Mal said patiently. "You've seen what we can do."

Bren hesitated, and Porter glared at him. "I don't care what you say. I'm going after my mate. We are wasting valuable time. The longer Vaughn is alone with Maggie, the more likely he'll hurt her. We need to get to them now."

"Fine," Bren said abruptly. "Let's go."

"You're not eating, sweetheart," Vaughn said irritably. "I made dinner. The least you can do is eat it."

"I'm not hungry," she said. She pushed her plate away as Vaughn sighed.

"Are you always going to be this stubborn?"

"I want to know where we're going tomorrow," she said.

His face lit up, and he leaned back in his chair before staring at the flickering flames in the fireplace. "We're starting our new life tomorrow."

"What do you mean?" she asked cautiously.

"We're leaving the city. By this time tomorrow night, we'll be in Europe."

She gaped at him. "What? I – I can't move to Europe."

"You can and you will."

"I don't have a passport," she said. "I can't travel internationally without one so -"

"All taken care of," Vaughn said. "Your new name is Maggie Thompson, by the way."

"What?" she said.

He stood and took the plates to the small kitchen. "I took the liberty of getting us both new ID's and passports. I'm now Vaughn Thompson, and you're my wife Maggie. I booked us flights yesterday."

"We – we can't leave," she said. "We don't have jobs or money -"

"No, *you* don't have any money," he said. "My dad was a real asshole. Did I ever tell you that while we were dating, sweetheart?"

She shook her head, and Vaughn piled the dishes in the sink before returning to the small table and sitting beside her.

He took her hands, scowling when she tried to pull away and tightened his grip.

"He was. Beat my siblings and me when we were young, beat my mother too – although just between you and me, that bitch deserved the beatings. She never figured out when to keep her mouth shut, you know?"

Maggie didn't say anything, and Vaughn rubbed his thumb across her wrist. "Anyway, I was the oldest, and my dad beat the shit out of me the most. I hated my old man and moved out when I was sixteen. I had to live on the streets for a few years, but it was still better than being around my father. I hadn't talked to him or my mother in years until two months ago when a lawyer tracked me down. Turns out, my old man is dead. Hell, my mother too. She died nearly three years ago. Official reason for death was a fall down the stairs, but I'd bet my left nut that the old man shoved her down them. Anyway, my baby brother murdered my old man – cut him up into tiny pieces and tried to use lye to dissolve his body in the bathtub. Guess he was tired of the beatings from my father."

Maggie gave him a horrified look, and Vaughn grinned chillingly at her. "He deserved it, Maggie. Trust me. So, this lawyer contacted me because it turned out my old man was sitting on a fucking fortune. Over a million bucks, and guess who he left it to? His oldest. Didn't leave nothin' for the other six kids, and they're super pissed about it. They're thinking of contesting the will – idiots."

Maggie stared blankly at him as Vaughn squeezed her hands. "They don't deserve any of the money. My father beat me more than any of them, and I like to think this is his way of saying he's sorry for what he did to me when I was a kid. I'm not letting them get a single cent of that fucking money. It's mine, Maggie."

Dark fur was thickening across his jaw, and she leaned back in her chair as his hands tightened painfully on hers. "We're going to start our new life together. Far away from my family and that fucking wolf shifter."

Maggie stared wide-eyed at him. She was in the grip of fear so deep she felt faint from it. Vaughn was going to take her to another country, and she'd never get away from him. She'd be his prisoner for the rest of her life.

She wished bitterly that she had convinced Porter to bite her. She loved him, and it suddenly didn't seem to matter to her that it was only Porter's wolf who wanted to claim her.

It's better that he didn't. Vaughn will kill you when he discovers you're not a virgin. If Porter had claimed you as his mate, your death would destroy him.

She took a shuddering breath. Her inner voice was right. She was just being selfish. Going with Vaughn was the right thing to do, even if she was about to die. Porter had done so much for her and gotten nothing for it. He would be out of jail by now and free. He could live his life and forget that he'd ever met her. He would be safe, and that's all that mattered.

Do you actually believe that Vaughn confessed to killing Bud?

The thought nagged at her, and she cleared her throat. "Did you tell your captain that Porter didn't kill Bud?"

Vaughn grinned at her. "What do you think?"

Her heart sank, and she pushed back her chair. "The deal was that I would only go with you if you got Porter out of jail."

He laughed. "Relax, sweetheart. Maybe I didn't exactly tell the captain that the wolf was innocent, but the charges won't stick. Honestly, I didn't have a lot of time to set him up, so if he gets himself a good enough lawyer, he'll go free."

He laughed again. "It was a piss-poor set-up job to tell you the truth, but since all I needed was him to be in jail long enough for you to accept my proposal, it didn't matter. Did it?"

"You're a monster," she whispered.

His grin faded and turned into a scowl. "No, I'm your mate. You need to get used to the idea, Maggie."

"You aren't my mate," she said in a low voice.

A kind of madness was stealing over her. Porter was still in jail, and if Vaughn didn't kill her, he was taking her out of the country tomorrow. If she didn't figure out a way to escape from him, they'd never find her. Her gaze drifted to the poker by the fireplace as Vaughn growled under his breath.

"You're mine. Come on. It's time for bed. Once I've taken your virginity, you'll realize you belong to me forever."

She took a deep breath and stood up before walking to the fireplace. She held out her trembling hands and stared at the flickering flames. She needed to make Vaughn angry. She needed him distracted and furious with her. If he didn't kill her immediately, she might have a chance to knock him out with the poker and escape into the woods.

"The bed, Maggie. Now," Vaughn said.

"I'm not a virgin anymore, Vaughn."

There was silence behind her, and she turned around and casually backed toward the poker that was resting against the fireplace. Vaughn stared at her, and as his face turned red, she backed up even further. The heat of the fire soaked into her legs as Vaughn stood up abruptly.

"What did you say?" he whispered.

"I'm not a virgin anymore."

"No," he said. "No, you're lying."

She made herself laugh scornfully. "I'm not lying. I've

been dating Porter for weeks. Did you think I wouldn't sleep with him? I gave my virginity to him."

"No," he said again.

"Yes," she replied almost gleefully. "Did you think he would mark me if I hadn't slept with him?" She grinned at him. "I've fucked him repeatedly, Vaughn. And you know what? It was incredible. His dick was huge. I'm so glad I waited to give it to him and not you."

She flinched and wrapped her hand around the poker when Vaughn screamed in rage and flipped the table over. He turned and punched the wall, driving his fist through the boards with a sharp crack before screaming again.

"You bitch! You goddamn whore! That was for me! It was mine!" he shouted.

He slammed his fists down on the small bookshelf against the wall. It cracked in half, and books spilled to the floor. He howled and screamed and pounded on the wall again.

"I'll kill you for this! Do you hear me, you stupid bitch? Do you -"

"Vaughn," Maggie spoke in a low voice, and the hyena shifter whirled around.

She stood directly behind him, and he blinked at the poker raised above her head. She swung it down in a whistling arc, and he screamed wild laughter and threw his arm up. The poker hit his arm with a loud heavy thud, and he shrieked in pain as Maggie grunted and swung the poker across his face. It caught him in the jaw, and he yowled with rage and pain as blood flew from his mouth. He fell to his knees and gave her a look of dazed confusion.

She raised the poker to hit him again and squealed in surprise when he grabbed her calf and yanked her off her feet. He knocked the poker out of her hand and grinned at her as blood dripped down his teeth. His fangs were out, and fur was sprouting across his face.

"You're dead," he muttered.

Maggie screamed and kicked frantically at his head with her other foot. The toe of her sneaker caught him just below the eye, and he yelped in pain. His grip on her leg loosened just a little, and she kicked him in the chest. He barked and released her calf as he grabbed at his chest. Maggie scrambled to her feet and backed away as he shook his head. Blood flew from his mouth to spray across the floor, and he glared at her.

"Stay where you are," he wheezed as Maggie backed away.

He was already trying to stand, and with a frightened cry, Maggie turned and fled out the cabin door. It was dark, and the light rain falling made the air misty and cool. She ran straight for the woods, head up and fists pumping at her sides as Vaughn barked and yipped into the night air. It sounded like he was already running after her, and ignoring the urge to look behind her, she forced herself to run faster.

"This has to be the place," Bren said as they pulled into the driveway of the small cabin. A car was parked to the side of the cabin, and the front door was wide open.

"Okay, the plan is – son of a bitch! Porter, get back here!"

Bren climbed out of the car and muttered another curse. Porter had already disappeared inside the cabin, and he wasn't surprised when the giant grizzly ran by him, followed by a grey wolf and Ronin.

They had just reached the cabin when Porter came running out.

"She's not in there!" He gave the wolf a wild look of panic. "There's blood on the floor, and her purse is on the counter, but she's not there."

The wolf barked at him as Bren joined them. Porter nodded. "You're right, okay, you're right."

He lifted his head and inhaled deeply before turning in a circle and inhaling again. A look of relief crossed his face, and he studied the woods to his left. "Her scent leads that way."

"Can you smell Vaughn?" Bren asked.

Porter nodded as he gave Mal another fleeting look of panic. "Yeah. He went after her."

He suddenly stripped and shifted to his wolf form. He barked at Mal and Bishop before running into the woods. They chased after him, and Bren and Ronin followed.

HER HEART THUDDING PAINFULLY IN HER CHEST, MAGGIE stumbled through the dark woods. She had a stitch in her side, and she had twisted her right ankle trying to climb over a fallen log. She limped quickly, turning her head from side to side and listening intently for any noises. Vaughn was in his hyena form, she had heard him barking and yipping excitedly not five minutes ago, but now there was complete silence.

She forced herself to limp faster. Maybe she could climb a tree and hide in it until dawn. She had no idea where she was going, and she was most likely moving deeper into the woods and away from help. Once it was light, she would double back to the road and hope that a car came along and found her before Vaughn stumbled onto her.

Stumbled onto you? Maggie, you idiot, he can smell you.

He's a fucking hyena, remember? You need to find a weapon and kill him. That's your only chance. He'll kill you if –

"Maag-gieee, come out, come out wherever you are."

Vaughn's voice drifted out of the dark, and she froze in terror as her heart stuttered to a stop. After a couple of beats, it started up again, and she pressed her hand against her chest and tried to breathe shallowly.

Run, Maggie! Her inner mind screamed at her. *He knows where you are! Run, you fool!*

She darted forward, screaming in terror when a hand shot out of the dark and wrapped around her wrist. It jerked her to a halt, and she beat frantically at the hand, gouging it with her nails as Vaughn made a low chuckle and stepped out of the bushes.

"You shouldn't have run, sweetheart," he crooned to her. He was half in his human form and half in his hyena form. She screamed again, and his hand, covered in wiry black hair with long, sharp nails, squeezed her wrist painfully.

"Shh, sweetheart," he said. "You've left me no choice. This is your fault for giving what belonged to me to the wolf shifter."

He grinned at her as more dark hair sprouted on his face. His fangs were long and gleamed dimly in the darkness as he shook his head. "Such a shame, Maggie."

"Vaughn, don't -"

Burning pain in her abdomen took her breath away. She stared at her stomach as warm liquid splattered over her shoe. She blinked slowly as Vaughn yanked his hand away from her stomach. Her shirt was covered in a red liquid, and she studied the ropy flesh that bulged from the rip in her t-shirt.

Were those her intestines? More blood flowed from her stomach to soak into the ground. She touched the bulging flesh as pain speared through her belly, and Vaughn laughed again. He dropped her wrist and lengthened his claws again as he raised his hand to her throat.

"Goodbye, Maggie," he said.

Darkness edged her vision, and she blinked rapidly. She needed to run, but her legs were completely numb, and the pain in her stomach was growing steadily worse. She pressed her hand against the loops of intestines slipping out of her belly, and watched as Vaughn's hand dropped toward her throat.

Before he could slice her throat open, loud howling filled the night air, and a dark shape came hurtling out of the darkness. It hit Vaughn like a freight train and threw him into the air. Vaughn shifted to his hyena form as he landed on the ground with a hard thud. Snarling loudly, he jumped to his feet and bared his teeth at the dark brown wolf standing protectively in front of Maggie. Maggie fell to her knees as the wolf barked harshly and leaped for the hyena.

HIS MATE'S SCREAM OF TERROR SENT HIS WOLF INTO A frenzy of anger. Howling madly, Porter raced through the woods toward the sound. Her scent grew stronger, and his wolf growled in fear and anger when the metallic smell of his mate's blood drifted to him. His brother and Bishop were close behind him, but he ignored his brother's barking. His mate needed him.

He dodged past a tree, the rain clinging to his fur, and howled loudly before leaping for the hyena shifter who was attacking his mate. He sent him tumbling to the ground, and he snarled with satisfaction as the hyena jumped to his feet. He barked at his brother to stay back – Vaughn was his to kill

– and leaped for the hyena. He sank his fangs deep into the hyena's shoulder, tearing him open to the bone.

Vaughn screamed and twisted away as Porter tried to sink his fangs into his throat. Porter caught him in the back instead, and he sank his fangs in and shook the hyena roughly as it dropped to the ground. He released him and blinked in surprise when Vaughn immediately shifted to his human form and rolled to his back. He held his hands up, blood pouring out from his shoulder and made a harsh, moaning cry.

"Please," he begged, "please no. Don't kill me!"

Mal was barking at him, but Porter ignored it. He stared at the frightened man on the ground and bared his teeth. Vaughn needed to die for taking his mate. Before he could rip the man's throat out, there was the sharp retort of gunfire. Porter's head jerked up, and he stared at Bren, who stood a few feet away. Bren's gun was pointed skyward, and he lowered it and pointed it at him.

"Let him go, Porter."

Porter growled at him, and Bren took a step forward. "Let him go. He's surrendered. I'll arrest him, and he'll go to prison."

Porter shifted to his human form and bared his fangs at Bren. "He deserves to die."

"Walk away, Porter," Bren advised.

"Or what? You'll shoot me?" Porter snarled.

"Porter, do what he says," Ronin said as Mal and Bishop shifted to their human forms.

"Porter," Mal said.

"He deserves to die, Mal!" Porter shouted at him. "He tried to take my mate."

"I know," Mal said, "but if you kill him now, Bren will arrest you, and you still won't be with your mate. Is that what you want?"

Porter hesitated before glancing at Vaughn. "He deserves to -"

"Porter."

Maggie's whisper made him whirl around. He realized how strong the scent of his mate's blood was for the first time, and his wolf made a low whimper of fear as he stared at Maggie. She was on her knees with her hand clamped over her stomach, and blood flowed down her legs.

"Maggie!" He forgot entirely about Vaughn and ran to his mate as she slowly tipped over. He caught her before she could land on her face and sat on the wet ground, easing her into his arms.

"Darlin', let me see."

"Hurts," she whispered. Her face was deathly pale, and her entire body was trembling. "Hurts, Porter."

"Let me see, darlin'," he said as he kissed her cold forehead. "Move your hand so I can -"

Vaughn's howl of rage drowned out Mal's sudden shout of warning. Porter instinctively covered Maggie's body with his own as the hyena leaped for them both. He flinched at the second gunshot, and the hyena flew backward as the back of his skull exploded in a spray of brains and blood. Vaughn fell to the ground, his body shifting back to his human form. His eyes stared blankly into the sky as Bren lowered his weapon.

"Well, fuck," he muttered.

"Maggie!" Porter gave her a look of panic as she slumped against him. He pulled her hand away, and a howl of fear burst from his throat as the others crowded around him. Maggie's stomach was torn open, and he could see her intestines hanging out.

"No!" he screamed as Maggie's eyes rolled up in her head. "Maggie, no!"

"Move!" Ronin tried to pull Maggie out of his arms.

"Don't touch her!" Porter screamed and tried to pull her closer.

"Mal! Bishop! Get him away from her!" Ronin shouted.

Porter struggled furiously as Mal grabbed one arm and Bishop grabbed the other.

"Stop it!" He howled at them as they dragged him away from his mate. "Maggie! Maggie!"

He sank his teeth into Bishop's forearm. The bear shifter grunted in pain but refused to release him. They pinned him to the ground, and he released Bishop, spitting out his blood as he snarled at Mal.

His brother shook him hard. "Porter! Stop! Ronin can save her. Just stop."

"What?" Porter slumped against the ground as Bishop pressed his knee into his abdomen.

"Ronin can save her," Mal repeated. "Just calm down."

"What the hell is he doing?" Bren said in a low voice.

"Let me up!" Porter struggled against Bishop's weight, and the grizzly shifter glanced at Mal. Mal nodded, and they let him sit up, keeping their hands on his shoulders as he stared past them.

Ronin had Maggie in his lap, and Porter watched in confusion as he pushed up Maggie's torn shirt and lowered his face to the wound.

"What is he doing?" Porter said as tears flowed down Ronin's cheeks.

"Is he…crying?" Bren said.

The tears flowed steadily onto the wound in Maggie's stomach, and Porter tried to break free when Maggie's eyes opened, and her entire body stiffened. She shrieked repeatedly and tried to twist away as Ronin held her tightly.

"Maggie!" Porter shouted and renewed his struggles.

"He's healing her!" Mal said. "I promise he's healing her, Porter. Just wait!"

Maggie's screams died out, and she slumped in Ronin's lap. Porter studied her pale face before dropping his gaze to the wound in her stomach.

"What the fuck?" he said.

Mal and Bishop released him, and he scrambled over to Maggie, pulling her out of Ronin's arms and into his own.

"Maggie?" He said as he touched the smooth skin of her stomach. The wound was completely healed. Nothing was left but streaks and smears of blood on her pale skin, and she gave him a dazed look of incomprehension.

"Porter? What happened?"

He pressed kisses all over her face before tucking her against his naked chest and staring at Ronin. The bird sat cross-legged in front of them, and he smiled at Maggie. "Do you feel better?"

"Yes," she said.

"What did you do to her?" Porter said.

Ronin glanced at Mal, who crouched next to Porter. "Ronin's a phoenix. He can heal with his tears."

"Of course he can cry on someone and heal them," Bren said. "That's not fucking weird at all." He nudged Vaughn's body with his foot. "Don't suppose you can heal this, huh?"

"I can't bring back the dead," Ronin said.

"Right," Bren said.

"Why would you want to?" Bishop growled at him.

"No reason," Bren said.

Mal studied him for a moment. "I guess it's not going to go over well with your father or the press when they find out you killed the shifter who saved your father's life."

Bren just shrugged. "I need to call this in."

He pulled out his cell phone and walked back toward the

cabin as Mal said, "Let's go back to the cabin for our clothes and give Porter a few minutes alone with his mate."

Ronin climbed to his feet, and Mal squeezed Porter's shoulder before the three of them followed Bren toward the cabin.

"Ronin!" Maggie called.

The bird shifter stopped and turned to stare at her.

"Thank you," she said.

"You're welcome, Maggie." He suddenly grinned at her and tipped an imaginary hat before walking away.

Porter cupped Maggie's face and kissed her with a desperate need. She returned his kiss, and when they broke apart, he whispered, "I love you. I love you, Maggie."

Tears started to slide down her cheeks, and she whispered, "I love you too."

"Thank God," he muttered before hugging her tightly. He touched her stomach again and ran his fingers over the soft skin as she pressed kisses against his throat.

"I want to claim you as my mate," Porter said.

"You or your wolf?" she said.

"Both," he said. "I can't live without you, darlin'. I denied everything I felt for you and tried to pretend it was just my wolf because I'm an idiot and because I was afraid that I would scare you away. But I can't deny it anymore. I love you. Please, be my mate."

She studied his face for a moment before touching his face. "Yes."

He grinned, and she smiled sweetly at him.

"It's forever," he said. "Wolves mate for life, Maggie. Do you understand what that means? Once I claim you, you'll be mine forever. Other shifters will know you belong to me."

"I know," she said.

He stroked her wet hair. "I just want you to understand

what you're agreeing to. I'll understand if you need to think about it or -"

"I don't," she said. "I want to spend the rest of my life with you." She tilted her head to expose her throat. "Bite me right now, Porter."

He bent his head and kissed her soft skin. "No, darlin'. Not here, not when you're covered in blood and Vaughn's scent. Can you stand?"

She nodded, and they climbed to their feet. He took her hand and kissed the grimy knuckles. "Let's go home, my mate."

"BETTER?" PORTER ASKED AS HE TOWELLED HER DRY.

Maggie nodded and dried the drops of water from Porter's chest. It was close to three in the morning, and it had taken far longer than she would have believed to give their statements to the police. Mal and Bishop had driven them back to Porter's place, and they had immediately hopped into the shower together. Porter had washed her entire body before quickly washing his own.

Now, he wrapped the towel around her and combed her wet hair before leading her out of the bathroom and to his bedroom.

"Get into bed, my mate," he said.

"Where are you going?" she asked.

He squeezed her hand. "You should eat something."

"I'm not hungry," she said. "Please, Porter. Get into bed with me."

He hesitated, and she gave him a pleading look. "Please, honey."

He climbed into bed, and she clung tightly to him. He

stroked her hip and side before kissing the top of her head. "Get some sleep, darlin'."

"No," she said.

He laughed softly. "It's late."

"I don't care. I want you to claim me right now," she said.

"Maggie, maybe you should sleep on it, and we can talk about it when you're not so exhausted."

She sat up, letting the covers drop to her waist and smiled inwardly when Porter's gaze dropped to her naked breasts. "Have you changed your mind about claiming me?"

"Of course not," he said. "I just don't want you to regret –"

"I won't. This is what I want, and a few hours' sleep isn't going to change my mind. Claim me right now, or I'm going to my apartment."

"You're not leaving. You belong to me." He growled and sat up before pushing her onto her back on the bed and hovering over her.

She smiled at him. "Then prove it."

He studied her face, and she grabbed his head and yanked his mouth to hers. She kissed him hard, pushing her tongue past his lips to stroke his tongue. He groaned into her mouth and returned her kiss, cupping her breasts and teasing her nipples until she was gasping and twisting beneath him.

She reached down and stroked his cock, squeezing firmly until he was moaning and thrusting his hips against her. She tried to urge him between her legs and made a harsh cry of disappointment when he pulled away and sat up.

"Just a minute," he rasped as he leaned over and grabbed a condom from the nightstand. He quickly rolled it on, and she spread her legs wide when he moved between them. He propped himself up on his hands above her and rubbed the head of his cock against her clit. She gasped and raised her hips, rubbing her pussy against his cock as he made a low growl.

"I need to be inside you, darlin'," he said.

"Yes," she said as she slid her arms around his waist and tugged him closer. "Please."

He pushed into her with one hard thrust, and she clung tightly to him when he started a slow slide and retreat rhythm that sent lightning bolts of pleasure through her entire body. She met each of his thrusts eagerly and urged him to move faster. He refused, and she pounded on his back in frustration. He buried his face in her throat and kissed her soft skin repeatedly as she gasped and moaned.

"You feel so good, darlin'," he whispered into her ear before sucking on the lobe.

"Oh please, Porter," she moaned. "Bite me,"

He pulled out of her, and she smacked his chest in anger. He grinned at her before hooking his hand around her waist. "Flip over."

He helped her flip to her stomach and cupped her hips before pulling her to her knees. She spread her legs eagerly and lowered her upper body to the bed as he ran his hand over her ass. She keened with pleasure when he slipped his hand between her legs and rubbed her clit. She ground her pussy against his hand, and he squeezed her ass with his other hand before pushing up against her and guiding his cock to her entrance.

He pushed in again, holding her hips to keep her in place, and Maggie squealed happily when he made three hard and rough strokes.

"Better, my mate?"

"Yes," she panted. "I need more."

He held her hips firmly and thrust in and out as she rocked back to meet him. His pelvis slapped against her ass, and he reached under her and rubbed her clit. She screamed and arched her body as she shook wildly and came hard on his cock. He tried to retreat, but her pussy squeezed him so tightly that he made a loud groan and bent over her.

His hard body pressed against her back, and he groaned again. "I love you."

She squeezed him again and gasped when she felt his fangs press against the back of her shoulder. He paused, and she whispered, "Do it, Porter. Make me yours forever," before squeezing his cock again. He howled against her skin and thrust hard and fast before sinking his fangs into her flesh.

Pain and pleasure rolled through her at once, and she arched her back as Porter growled and bit more deeply as he came deep inside of her. The bite set off another orgasm, this one so violent that she shook uncontrollably as she screamed his name. His arm around her waist kept her from collapsing against the bed. He retracted his fangs and licked the bite mark on her shoulder before lowering her to her stomach on the bed.

He pulled out of her and threw the condom in the waste bin. He curled on his side next to her as she panted and moaned lightly. He licked the bite mark until the blood stopped and rubbed her back.

"My mate," he whispered into her ear.

Feeling shaky and weak, she rolled to her side and stared blearily at him. "Porter?"

"What's wrong?" he asked as his hand tightened on her hip.

"Nothing. That just – that was amazing."

He grinned at her, and she cupped his face and kissed him lightly. "I love you, Porter."

"I love you, my mate."

CHAPTER 18

"A va, are you sure you're okay?" Willow asked worriedly.

Ava smiled at her. "I'm fine. Stop worrying about me and get dressed, for heaven's sake."

Willow glanced at Ginger. "She's pale."

"I'm not," Ava said before Ginger could reply. She picked up Willow's wedding dress and held it out to Ginger. "Help her get dressed, Ginger. I have to pee."

She hurried down the back hallway of the church and into the ladies' room. The minute the door shut behind her, she rubbed her stomach and took a few deep breaths. She winced when another cramp flowed through her belly and rubbed it again.

"C'mon, baby, just a few more hours, okay?" she whispered. "You've waited this long. You can wait a little longer. Please? For mama?"

The baby kicked her hard, and she winced again before staring at herself in the mirror. "You are not in labour, Ava. Do you hear me? You are *not* in labour."

She took a deep breath and returned to Willow and

Ginger. Mara had joined them, and she was helping Ginger button Willow's dress. Tears slid down her cheeks, and Willow reached behind her and patted her arm.

"Don't cry, Mara."

"I'm just really happy," Mara said. "You look beautiful, Willow."

"Thank you." Willow stared anxiously at Ava. "Are you okay, honey?"

"I'm fine," Ava said with a cheerful smile. "Are you ready to get married?"

"Yes," Willow said as there was a knock on the door. "Come in."

The door opened, and Roland stepped into the room. "Willow? Are you ready to…"

Mara moved toward him when his mouth trembled.

"Roland?" Willow said worriedly. "What's wrong?"

"Nothing," he said as tears slipped down his cheeks.

"Now, don't you start crying," Mara scolded gently as she wiped at the tears on his face. "If you start crying, I'll start crying again, and the wedding will be ruined."

Roland sniffed loudly before clearing his throat. "You're right, of course." He moved toward Willow and took her hand. "I'm so happy for you and Mal."

"Thank you, Roland," Willow said. Her eyes were bright with unshed tears, and she squeezed his hand tightly. "Thank you for walking me down the aisle."

"It's my honour, Willow," Roland said.

Willow hugged him, and he kissed her cheek before smiling at her. "Let's get you married to my boy."

"Yes, let's," Willow said with a soft smile.

"DO YOU, WILLOW, TAKE MALCOLM TO BE YOUR HUSBAND, in sickness and in health, in happiness and sorrow, until death do you part?"

"I do," Willow said.

"And do you, Malcolm, take Willow to be your wife, in sickness and in health, in happiness and sorrow, until death do you part?"

"I do," Mal said before grinning at Willow.

She returned his smile as the minister said, "Rings, please."

Bishop handed him the ring, and the minister cleared his throat before tapping Ava on the arm. She stared blankly at him before flushing and giving him the ring.

"Sorry," she said.

Willow smiled at her as she took the ring from the minister and slid it onto Mal's finger. He placed his ring on Willow's finger, and they squeezed hands as the minister said, "I now pronounce you husband and wife. You may kiss the bride."

Ava watched as Mal slid his arm around Willow's waist and drew her up against him. He kissed her deeply, and their friends and family cheered and clapped their hands. Willow, blushing brightly, grinned happily at Mal. He kissed the tip of her nose and, holding her hand, led her down the aisle. Ava walked toward Bishop and hooked her hand into the crook of his elbow.

He gave her a nervous look as they followed Willow and Mal down the aisle. "You okay, baby?"

"Yes," she said.

"Are you sure?"

She nodded and tried not to wince when another cramp went through her belly. She stumbled a bit, and Bishop stopped and gave her another anxious look.

"Ava?" Ginger and Porter were behind them, and Ginger pressed her hand against Ava's lower back before saying in a low voice. "Are you in labour?"

"No, of course not," Ava said quietly. "Let's go. Pictures need to be taken."

She tugged on Bishop's arm, and he followed her dutifully out of the church.

———

AVA GRIMACED AND HELD HER BELLY AS ANOTHER CRAMP rippled through her. She stood in the hallway, and the music drifted out the open door of the reception. She made herself straighten as a soft voice said behind her, "Ava? Are you okay?"

She turned and smiled at Maggie. "Yes. I'm fine. How are you?"

"Fine," Maggie said. She stared worriedly at Ava. "You don't look very good. You're very pale."

"I'm good," Ava said. "Um, congratulations. Bishop told me that you and Porter are mated now."

Maggie smiled. "We are."

"That's wonderful. I'm very – oh!"

"Ava!" Maggie grabbed her arm as she hunched and pressed her hand against her belly. "Honey, are you in labour?"

Ava took a deep breath. "No, I think it's just some cramping. I'm not…"

Maggie followed her gaze to the front of her dress.

"Oh no," Ava moaned.

Maggie's eyes widened. "Did your water just break?"

Ava nodded and gripped Maggie's arm. "Can you find Bishop?"

"Of course," Maggie said as Porter walked out of the reception and waved at them.

"Hey, gorgeous ladies, what's going on?"

"Porter, can you find Bishop?" Maggie said urgently.

"Sure," Porter said. "Is everything okay?"

He suddenly twitched as he looked at Ava. "Holy shit. Did your water break?"

Ava nodded, and Porter squeezed her hand. "I'll get B right now."

"Be subtle about it, okay?" Ava said. "I don't want Willow's and Mal's day ruined because of me."

Porter nodded and disappeared back into the reception. Maggie took Ava's hand as Ginger stepped out of the washroom and wandered down the hall toward them.

"Hey," she said. "Why aren't you in there dancing up a… Ava?"

"She's in labour," Maggie said.

Ginger grabbed Ava's other hand. "Take deep breaths, honey. How far apart are your contractions?"

"Not sure," Ava said.

"Where's Bishop?"

"Porter's getting him," Maggie said.

"Ava!" Bishop ran into the hallway with Porter close behind him. "Is it the baby?"

Ava nodded. "I'm in labour. My water just broke."

"Okay," Bishop said calmly. "We'll go to the hospital right now, and everything will be fine."

Ava's anxiety eased, and she rested her head on Bishop's broad chest as he put his arm around her waist. "I love you, Bishop."

"I love you too, Ava," he said. He bent to pick her up and then froze when he heard Willow's voice behind him.

"Hey! Did the party move out into the hallway, and no one told us?"

Ava gave Bishop a frantic look, and he rubbed her back again before turning. "Hey, Willow, hey, Mal."

"What's wrong?" Willow said.

"Nothing," Bishop said. "There's nothing wrong. Mal, why don't you take Willow back into the reception and -"

"Ava!" Willow pushed past Bishop. "Honey, what's wrong?"

"Nothing," Ava said. She gritted her teeth as another contraction hit her.

"Holy crap, you're in labour," Willow said.

"No, I'm not," Ava denied.

"You are too!" Willow nearly shouted. "You're standing in a damn puddle. Mal, Ava's in labour. We have to get her to the hospital."

"No," Ava said. "Bishop will take me to the hospital. You stay here and -"

"Like hell, I'm staying here!" Willow said. "My best friend is having a baby! Mal, how much have you had to drink? I've had too much champagne to drive. Can you drive?"

He shook his head, and she cursed lightly as Ava squeezed her arm. "Willow, I am not ruining your day. Go back and join your guests."

"Nope," Willow said. "They won't even notice we're gone. We're going to the hospital with you."

"I'll find Fenton," Ginger said. "He isn't drinking tonight, so he can drive us and Willow and Mal to the hospital. Bishop, are you okay to drive?"

Bishop nodded, but Porter said, "Maggie and I will drive B and Ava to the hospital."

"Willow," Ava said, "I'm not ruining your wedding day, dammit!"

"Ruin it?" Willow said. "This is the best wedding gift ever! Ginger, find Fenton! We need to get our girl to the hospital!"

"AVA?" WILLOW STUCK HER HEAD INTO THE HOSPITAL ROOM. "Can we come in?"

"Yes," Ava said.

She smiled at her best friend as Willow walked to the bed. Mal was right behind her, and he grinned at Bishop. "Congratulations, buddy."

"Thanks, Mal," Bishop said. He leaned down and kissed Ava before brushing his lips across the baby's head. "I'm going to call Mara and Roland."

"They're in the waiting room," Mal said. "Hell, half the wedding guests are in the waiting room."

Bishop laughed and kissed Ava again. "I'll be right back, baby."

"I'll go with you," Mal said. He leaned down and kissed Ava's cheek. "Congratulations, Ava."

"Thanks, Mal," Ava said.

Willow kissed Ava's cheek. "She's beautiful, honey. Look at all that red hair."

She sat on the side of the bed as Ava handed her the baby. She stroked the baby girl's soft cheek and kissed her forehead. "Did you decide on her name?"

Ava nodded. "Lila."

"Lila," Willow said softly. "Hello, Lila. I'm so happy to meet you, sweet one. She looks just like you, Ava."

Ava smiled tiredly. "That's what my mom said."

"Where are your folks?" Willow asked.

"They just went down to the cafeteria to grab a coffee. Not that my dad needs it, he was practically vibrating as it was."

Willow grinned at her. "I bet. Thank God Bishop was so level headed. Your parents were at the wedding, for God's sake, and I never even thought to tell them you were in labour."

"Neither did I," Ava said, "but Bishop called my mom's cell on the way to the hospital. I'm sorry I ruined your day, honey."

"Don't be silly," Willow said. "You didn't ruin anything. It was the perfect ending to our wedding."

She kissed Lila's forehead again before handing her back to Ava. "Is she a shifter?"

Ava shook her head. "No, she's human like me. I was worried that Bishop would be disappointed, but he," she paused as tears dripped down her face, "he thinks she's perfect. You should have seen his face when they put her in his arms, Will. He – the look on his face – I've never seen him so happy in my life. He's going to be an amazing dad."

Willow wiped away her tears. "You're both going to be amazing parents. I'm so happy for you, Ava. I love you."

"I love you too, Willow."

"HELLO, DARLIN'." PORTER PUT HIS ARMS AROUND MAGGIE as she stood in front of the vending machine in the hospital waiting room. He gently kissed the healed scar on the back of her shoulder.

"Hi, honey." Maggie squeezed his hands and leaned against his broad chest. "Did you see the baby yet?"

He shook his head. "No. Mom, Dad, and Grandpa are in there right now, but B said Ava is pretty tired, so I told him we'd wait until she was home from the hospital and ready for visitors. Apparently, she has red hair and looks just like Ava."

"A grizzly shifter with red hair?" Maggie said.

"She's human like Ava," Porter said.

"Really?" Maggie said.

"Yes. She had a fifty/fifty chance of being a human."

"Do you think Bishop was hoping she would be a shifter?" Maggie asked.

"Honestly, I think Bishop is already so in love with her that he hasn't given it a second thought," Porter said.

Maggie smiled at him. "I just realized that I never asked if you wanted children."

"I do," he said. "Wolf shifters like to have big families. Do you, uh, want kids?"

She nodded, and he relaxed against her. "Good, that's good."

"There's still so much we don't know about each other. Do you regret biting me?" she asked.

He stiffened again. "No, I don't. Do you regret letting me bite you?"

She turned in his arms and stared up at him. "Not in the least. I know we still have a lot to learn about each other, but I will never regret this. I love you, and I want to spend the rest of my life with you, Porter."

He kissed her lightly before resting his forehead against hers. "I love you too, my mate."

Keep reading for an excerpt of book five in the Shifters Series, "Bria and the Tiger".

BRIA AND THE TIGER EXCERPT

(THE SHIFTERS SERIES BOOK FIVE)

Bria, this is madness.

No, what was madness was trying to finish her heat cycle alone. She stood in the parking lot of the nightclub, staring up at the flashing neon lights as her cat growled restlessly.

"Why is this happening?" she whispered.

She had gone through her last heat cycle alone, and it was bad, but this – this was something so much worse. She had spent the previous day and a half alone in her apartment, masturbating furiously, and she still couldn't get rid of that ache, that deep need to have something in her. Desperation and madness had driven her out of her apartment and to the closest nightclub in search of a shifter to relieve her need.

Please, Bria, don't do this. Be strong. By tomorrow morning, your cycle will be finished and you –

Shut up! her cat hissed.

She was dangerously close to shifting. She closed her eyes and took three deep breaths before walking quickly to the entrance. Her hands shaking, she paid the cover charge as the human bouncer stared curiously at her. She was tempted to grab him and drag him into the alley behind the club. A little bolt of fear ran through her.

Stop it. Get a hold of yourself! The way you're feeling, you'll tear that human to shreds while you fuck him, and you know it. You need a shifter – preferably a powerful one.

And willing – don't forget willing.

Right.

She walked toward the long, curved bar. The music was loud, and she seemed to feel every pounding beat deep in her pelvis. It throbbed miserably. The need was now at the point of pain, and she blinked back the tears that were suddenly blinding her.

She made a startled little hiss when she ran into a warm wall of muscle. Unable to stop herself, she pressed her hands against the shifter's chest. She ran her fingers over that hard flesh separated only by the thin fabric of his shirt and purred loudly.

"Sorry, miss. You okay?" His deep voice sent lust spiraling through her lower body.

Please God, please God. Don't let me lose control.

She forced her gaze upward, staring into the tiger shifter's eyes as he cleared his throat. She realized with horror that she was moving her hips in slow circles against his pelvis. She whined low in her throat when his hands cupped her hips and stilled her incessant rhythm. He inhaled deeply, and she tore herself from his grip before she lost it completely and tried to fuck him in the middle of the damn club.

"I'm so sorry," she repeated.

"Wait." He tried to touch her arm, and she hissed at him before backing away.

"I – I' m sorry."

She slipped through the crowd toward the bar, each brush

of her body against the other shifters and humans making her cat cry out with need. She found an empty stool and ordered a beer when the bartender stopped in front of her. She sipped at her beer as the music and her pelvis pulsed and thumped, and she stared grimly at the top of the bar. She needed to look around, needed to pick out a shifter who she could approach and proposition.

What if there isn't a shifter who's interested?

There is! There has to be!

"Hello, gorgeous."

Her body tensed, and she inhaled deeply before staring at the shifter standing beside her. He was a snake shifter, and she licked her lips as her cat meowed with satisfaction.

"Can I buy you a drink?"

She shook her head. "I already have one."

He smiled at her. He was handsome enough, with his dark skin and soulful dark eyes, and she licked her lips again. She had never been with a snake shifter before, but what did that matter? He would have what she needed. Her eyes dropped to his crotch. He was wearing incredibly tight pants, and she stared at the bulge between his thighs before tearing her gaze away.

The snake shifter hissed happily. She flushed bright red as he moved a little closer. "Tiger shifter, is that right?"

"Yes," she whispered.

"I get the feeling you need something else other than a drink. Am I right?"

He was so close to her now that she could feel his breath on her face. She moaned softly. "I – yeah, I do."

"Why don't we go back to your place then, gorgeous?"

She nodded eagerly, and he winked at her. "Good."

He held his hand out, and she reached for it.

Bria, wait! You know nothing about him!

She hesitated, and there was a flash of annoyance in his suddenly yellow eyes. "What's wrong?"

"Nothing. I just – let me use the ladies' room first, and then we'll go, okay?"

He frowned at her before nodding. "Okay, sure, I guess."

"I'll be right back."

She scurried away as her cat snarled in anger. The blaring music faded to a muted hum as she entered the bathroom. She smiled weakly at the woman washing her hands before hurrying into a stall and resting her forehead on the back of the door.

Get back out there! He has what we need! Her cat yowled.

Shut up! Just shut up and let me think!

Think about what? If you don't take that snake shifter home, we'll go mad, her cat hissed.

Yes, she would. The logical part of her brain retreated against the overwhelming lust and need. She flung open the stall door and blinked in shock at the tiger shifter she had practically dry-humped earlier. He was standing in the doorway of the now-deserted ladies' room and giving her a silent, assessing look. Her cat studied his long, lean length and made a happy little purr.

Forget the snake shifter. I want him. Give him to me.

"This is the ladies' room," Bria said.

"That snake shifter is dangerous," he advised.

She hissed at him. "Get out of my way."

He sighed and glanced over his shoulder. "Listen to me, okay? That shifter makes a living by preying on cats in their heat cycle. Once your heat cycle has ended, and you're back to normal, he'll tell you that unless you pay him a whole lot of money, he'll go to the authorities and claim that you raped him."

Her mouth dropped open. "How do you know that?"

"Does it matter?" He asked. "Just trust me, okay?"

"Why should I? I don't even know you," she said.

"I've seen him do this before," he said patiently. "I know you're finding it hard to think right now, and I know your heat cycle is making you crazy, but you need to hear me. You're making a big mistake."

She hesitated as the normal part of her brain that wasn't crying out for relief rose to the surface. He nodded at the look on her face. "That's right. You can't let him anywhere near you. It's better for you if you go home."

Her cat immediately surged forward, angry and upset and demanding relief. She hissed again at the tiger shifter. "I don't care."

"You do care," he said. "Just try and think past the need for a minute, okay?"

"No!" She snarled and tried to shove past him.

She yowled loudly when he grabbed her arm and yanked her back into the ladies' room. Her claws extended, and she swiped at him, narrowly missing his face as he pushed her into the accessible stall and locked the door behind them.

"Let me go, or I'll rip you to pieces," she growled.

His fangs popped out, and his eyes glowed jade at her. She made a startled meow when he pushed her against the wall and kissed her. She froze for a moment before her cat made a yowling hiss of delight, and her pupils narrowed to slits. She returned his kiss, shoving her tongue deep into his mouth and tearing at his shirt and jeans.

He muttered a curse against her mouth and pushed her hands away before unbuttoning his jeans. She purred loudly when he freed his dick. It was long and thick and delicious-looking. He shoved her skirt up around her waist and tore off her panties before lifting her. She wrapped her legs around his waist and made another soft mew of need.

He covered her mouth with his before entering her wet pussy in one hard thrust that had her screaming with pleasure. He fucked her hard and rough, his mouth never leaving hers as her hips bucked against him and her orgasm rushed through her.

He pressed her into the wall, breathing harshly against her mouth. "Better?"

"Again!" she hissed at him.

He thrust back and forth. His cock was so hard and a perfect fit within her that she could barely breathe from the pleasure. She mewled loudly as she slid her hands under his shirt. She tore at him with her claws, and he hissed in pain but continued to plunge in and out of her.

"Oh, oh, oh…" She bit him hard on the shoulder, her teeth sinking through the fabric of his shirt and into his flesh.

He growled and slammed in and out of her. She lifted her head and dug her claws into his back as her second orgasm washed over her. She shuddered and shook against him, purring and making high-pitched sounds of happiness as he buried his face into her damp neck and licked the salt from her skin.

"Oh God," she moaned.

"Need more?" he rasped out.

She nodded. A little of the need had dissipated enough that she could feel some shame creeping in. "I'm sorry."

"Don't be," he said. He dropped his mouth onto hers again and kissed her slowly this time. She sucked eagerly at his tongue, and he cupped her breast with one large hand, squeezing it firmly as he pushed his cock deep inside of her.

He released her breast and slipped his hand between them, pressing the heel of his hand against her clit. She purred and rubbed herself frantically against his hand, her pussy squeezing his cock rhythmically as he slid in and out of her.

"Harder," she panted.

He cupped his hands around her thighs and held her tightly as he pushed in and out.

"Fuck, your pussy is amazing," he muttered into her mouth.

"Your cock is amazing," she whispered.

He smiled, and his fingers dug into her smooth thighs before he started a rough rhythm that had her gasping with pleasure.

"Oh God, please, please," she whimpered.

Her third and most powerful orgasm yet shuddered through her. She clung to the tiger shifter as fire and lightning coursed through her veins. He rubbed her thighs soothingly when she collapsed against him.

He was still hard within her, but the fiery need to be fucked had abated enough for her to think clearly. She licked her lips before whispering, "I'm sorry."

"I told you, there's no need to be sorry. Are you good for now?"

She nodded, but her cat made a disappointed hiss when he pulled out of her and set her gently on her feet. She swayed, and he steadied her before tucking his erect cock back into his jeans and buttoning them. He grimaced as he adjusted, and she felt another trickle of shame.

"I – uh, should go. Thank you," she whispered.

She needed to get the fuck out of here and back to her apartment before the next wave hit. Already the slow cycle of need was starting up in her belly, and she felt a moment of panic. What the fuck was happening to her? Her cycle was never this bad before.

She smoothed her skirt as the tiger shifter watched her carefully. She couldn't look him in the eye, and she moaned in dismay when she realized blood was blooming on his shirt.

"Oh shit, I'm so sorry,"

He barely glanced at the bite on his shoulder. "It's fine. It will heal."

"I know, but I…"

She trailed off as her eyes widened. "Turn around."

"It's fine," he said. "Don't worry about it."

"Turn around!" She grabbed him and swung him around, another moan of dismay bursting from her throat. The back of his shirt was soaked in blood, and she yanked it up, staring in horror at the long, deep scratches on his back.

"You need to go to the hospital," she said.

He actually laughed. "You know I don't. They'll heal on their own."

He turned and frowned when he saw how pale her face was. "Hey, are you okay?"

She swayed again. She felt physically sick over how terribly she had scratched him – another first for her – and he grabbed her upper arms. "Don't pass out on me."

"What is happening to me?" she whispered.

He frowned. "It's just your heat cycle."

"It's never been like this before," she said. "It's never been this bad. Already, I – I'm starting to feel…."

She closed her eyes and didn't object when he put his arm around her waist. "Come with me."

"Where are we going?"

"Back to my place."

"I – I can't." She pulled away from him.

He raised his eyebrow at her. "If you don't, you'll be right back at this club. We both know that. Do you want to risk taking someone home like that snake shifter?"

"How – how do I know you're not like him?" she said.

"I'm not," he said firmly. "I'm a good guy. I promise."

"Fuck," she pressed her fingers to her temples as her pelvis began to throb. The shifter was right. If she didn't go home with him, she'd go right back to the club. The way she was feeling, her fingers and a vibrator weren't going to do shit for her.

"Okay," she said. "Do you live close?"

"Ten-minute drive," he said.

He took her hand and led her out of the stall. Two human women stood next to the sink, staring wide-eyed and slack-jawed at them. Bria turned scarlet. She wondered how long they were standing there and listening, but the tiger shifter simply nodded to them and led Bria into the dark and loud nightclub. He walked her quickly through the crowds of people. She kept her head down and tensed when she heard the snake shifter.

"Hey! She's mine."

A hand landed on the tiger shifter's arm, and she pressed her lips together when he growled loudly. "Get your hand off me, asshole."

The snake hissed but released him, and the tiger shifter led her to the exit. She took deep breaths of the clean, fresh air as she followed him across the parking lot to his car.

ABOUT THE AUTHOR

Elizabeth Kelly was born and raised in Ontario, Canada. She moved west as a teenager and now lives in Alberta with her husband and a menagerie of pets. She firmly believes that a person can survive solely on sushi and coffee, and only her husband's mad cooking skills prevents her from proving that theory.

For more information about Elizabeth, check out her website at

www.elizabethkelly.ca

facebook.com/EKellyBooks

twitter.com/ElizabethKBooks

instagram.com/elizabethkelly_author

amazon.com/Elizabeth-Kelly/e/B00EOHZ0MS

bookbub.com/authors/elizabeth-kelly

Katarina and the Bird (Book Three)

Porter's Mate (Book Four)

Bria and the Tiger (Book Five)

Rosalie Undone (Book Six)

The Dragon's Mate (Book Seven)

Rise of the Jaguar (Book Eight)

The Draax Series

Reign (Book One)

Rule (Book Two)

Rebel (Book Three)

Harmony Falls Series

Sweet Harmony (Book One)

Perfect Harmony (Book Two)

Forbidden Harmony (Book Three)

Redeeming Harmony (Book Four)

Individual Books

The Necessary Engagement

Amelia's Touch

The Rancher's Daughter

Healing Gabriel

The Contract

A Home for Lily

Saving Charlotte

Shameless

The Fairy Tales Collection

Broken

An Unlikely Seduction

Holiday Romance

The Christmas Wife

The Christmas Rescue

The Christmas Nanny

The Christmas Boss

Sordid Games